T
Fortune
Teller's
Promise

The Fortune Teller's Promise

KELLY HEARD

bookouture

Published by Bookouture in 2019

An imprint of StoryFire Ltd.

Carmelite House
50 Victoria Embankment
London EC4Y 0DZ

www.bookouture.com

ISBN: 978-1-83888-006-4
eBook ISBN: 978-1-83888-005-7

For John & Jane

CHAPTER ONE

Now

July 1991

The Virginia that features on postcards, with its green-eyed, lazy summers and patchwork autumns, keeps a secret, and that secret is the mean Appalachian winters. High in the hills, along the land's curving backbone, the wind changes its mind every minute, finds its way to any exposed softness in a person that may have gone unnoticed.

Born on an unwelcoming February day, Adella Shaw's baby girl had been perfectly ordinary, her small body slippery and fragile. People can forget that they are animals, but a mother cannot. Dell had never recognized the animal in herself as much as the moment she beheld her animal baby, from her own animal body. The child's eyes were ordinary blue, although to Dell they were the blue of ghosts held just at bay, their expression curious and wild, as if to ask: *why have you brought me here, and what do you mean to do about it?* Cradling the baby in the mottled firelight, paralyzed by a sudden, violent love, Dell found that she had no answer.

There is some deep, inherent fault line in me, something I can't fix. If there weren't something wrong with me I would surely be crying.

Dell held the baby all night and half of the next day, the little girl's weight in her arms intoxicating as a spring breeze, a newness that illuminated everything she thought she had known.

But Dell knew also that she was poorly made for mothering. She recognized a bad mother when she saw one, a skill sharpened with years of practice. Still, she savored the hours with the child, until the church lady came the next day, bearing a clipboard and promises that there were families who wanted a baby. Mothers and fathers, people who did things on purpose. Dell was not a stranger to the kinds of choices you only get to make once. She left her child behind and walked out into the winter afternoon, promising never to come back.

Winter melted, and the spring blossomed into summer heat. On one of the countless mountainsides above the Shenandoah Valley, a parking lot opened from the road, obscured by an overgrowth of locust and kudzu. There, Dell's psychic shop occupied the second floor of a beige-painted cinder block building, upstairs from a laundromat. A wide bank of jimsonweed grew waist-high in the ditch at the roadside, with its poison white-and-violet-swirled flowers, wide as a hand, beginning to open in the waning afternoon light.

The parking lot was empty, save for her green Volvo station wagon, and a litter of bottles and fast food cartons discarded by passersby. Watching from the window at the front counter, through the curlicues of the neon sign that read THE PSYCHIC IS IN, Dell looked past the parking lot and down to the valley, where she could see her hometown, Blyth, as if it were a dog that had laid down at her feet. A tired old dog, flea-bitten with gossips, blind in one eye. A brown, naked strip cut through the forest in the distance, where a gas pipeline lay under the ground, thin as a ribbon. *The water hasn't been right since they built that thing,* Aunt Myra always said, after eminent domain kicked her off her land, when the government forced the sale of the land for the construction. *It never will be again.*

The shop walls were lined with dried flowers, a cast-iron skillet, a faded red baseball cap hanging on a nail. The psychic shop looked more like a witch's den. But, then, Dell wasn't a proper psychic.

Couldn't look at a stranger's hand and know their secrets. She read palms, or tarot cards, or stars. But those things only told her what people wanted to talk about. Take Rhonda, for instance, here every Thursday afternoon, always worrying on about a new lover, or an old one. Thursday a week ago, Dell had traced Rhonda's palm and said: "You say he loves you? Rhonda, there's never been a Libra that didn't say exactly what you wanted to hear." A Libra herself, she knew this for a fact.

But today, Rhonda was late. Dell walked away from the light, back behind the bamboo panels, to the sofa and coffee table where she sat her customers. A half-busted cuckoo clock, a lucky thrift store find, hung on the wall, though it had never kept the time reliably. She reached up to nudge the second hand.

"It's ten past four, little bird," she said. "You still in there?" She brushed dust from the clock onto her dress, a blue prairie-style frock that might have been fashionable ten years ago. At the sound of footsteps on the stairs, she tied her hair back over one shoulder, its long waves the soft brown of walnut shells. As she opened her mouth to greet Rhonda, the clock issued a guttural click, as if winding itself. The wooden bird lurched out of its house and cried out one lone chime.

The door opened with a jingle. Tearing her eyes from the cuckoo bird, Dell shook her head with relief.

"Rhonda, come on back. I'm glad you're finally here. For a minute I thought there was a ghost." From its perch on the wall behind her, the bird continued to squeak.

"Adella. It's you."

Before Dell could register her mother's voice, she was wrapped in a cool, fragrant embrace. Anita was soft but slim, with whittled cheekbones and a glossy waterfall of brown hair. In contrast to Dell's bare feet, Anita wore black leather sandals, toenails painted red. She was so pretty most people forgot to wonder if she was anyone's mother, or sister, or wife.

Anita held her tight, swaying on her feet. "I've worried about you all year. It is so good to see you."

The cuckoo clock continued to chirp its lopsided, redundant note. Dell pulled out of her mother's hug, gritting her teeth. She whirled on her heel, tore the clock off the wall, and clutched it against her chest, where, despite her efforts, it continued to sing. She felt her eyes sting. It was too soon to see Anita, but Dell knew it would have always been too soon.

"You weren't supposed to come here."

Her mother couldn't hear her, buoyed on a vibrant cloud of emotions that nearly painted the walls. She lifted a hand and fanned at her prettily watering eyes, a theatrical gesture that had never failed to set Dell's teeth on edge.

"I have ten dollars that say you guilted my cop brother into finding some way to look me up. And another ten if you forget I'm here and walk back out." Dell shoved the cuckoo bird back into its house with her fingertip.

"If you really wanted to run, you'd be more than an hour away." Anita's nose pinched in a scowl. "Dell, you need to come home. Something's happened."

"Don't bother." Her heart ticked against the whirring clock. "Whatever it is, I don't care. Nothing is gonna make me leave here."

"You don't think your father would rest easier knowing you were with family? Not here, in this... whatever you call it?" Anita took the red baseball cap from its hook on the wall.

"Anita, give that back." Dell shifted the clock to one arm and reached for the hat but Anita stepped back, holding it out of her reach.

"Would it kill you to call me Mom?"

"It might." Dell snatched the hat from her mother and held it against the clock in her left arm. The clock pattered against Dell's ribs, so that she couldn't tell whether the cuckoo bird wanted into her chest, or her own heart wanted out. Hands full, she had to nod at the door instead of pointing. "Get out."

Anita picked up her handbag, eyes narrowing. "You're a psychic now, is that it? Then I guess I didn't need to come. I guess you already know your baby's missing. Good as homeless. Right?"

The whirring clock and the red cap dropped from Dell's arms, leaving them empty. "Mom, what?"

"Maybe you can divine where she is, too."

"Wait."

Anita breezed past the bamboo panels. The falsely cheery jingle of the door rang out once more as it closed behind her.

The room dimmed in her absence. This was the Anita that Dell remembered. Pretty as sin, and just as syrupy-sweet, until the second you slighted her. Nothing had changed. Dell blinked and saw the baby's tiny hands, her wide blue eyes, a blue she could drift away in. Before she knew it, she was running to the door.

Dell tripped down the stairs and out into the parking lot. Behind the tinted windshield, Anita patted her cheeks dry with a tissue.

"Wait a minute," Dell called. "Please, Mom." As she stepped off the curb to approach the car, Anita steered toward the road, leaving Dell clasping her hands, following her mother's exit with a hopeless stare. Anita's dramatic exits were only business as usual, but the jolted, cuckoo-bird patter in Dell's chest slowed to a halt. As Anita's car turned toward the left, Dell saw the pickup truck coming from the opposite direction at full speed.

Pummeled forward, the car crunched against the side of an underpass. The double impact of the collision rang like a screeching, metallic *ker-plop*. After the noise there was quiet, the sudden absence of birdsong.

Dell's eyes swiveled between the truck and Anita's battered car, until she saw a man exit the truck and run toward the sedan. It was crinkled like foil, having collided and skidded a few yards along the concrete wall. Dell walked barefoot across the road, hung behind him as he leaned over the shattered driver's side window. The truck driver was a middle-aged man with a flannel shirt over his paunch.

"She alive?"

As Dell spoke, she saw Anita's shoulders rise and fall. Breathing. That was something. She was bleeding from a contusion on her temple, leaning forward so far, her chin pressed into her neck at an acute angle.

"Can you reach the keys?" she whispered.

The man reached in, his arm just brushing Anita's shoulder, turned the engine off. As he drew back, the top of his arm caught the jagged glass that lined the window, blood welling up underneath it.

"Oh, shit. You should sit down. Come on." Dell pointed at the guard rail by the side of the road, scanning his shirt for bloodstains, anything misaligned. "Wait here. I'm gonna call for help."

She returned with a dish towel and a cup of water, sat next to him on the railing. "Ambulance is coming. They said not to move her. I told them to hurry, but you know."

"Takes a while, out here."

"Yeah. Let me see that." Dell held out her hand, gesturing for his arm. Poured some water on the towel, let his arm rest across her knees as she dabbed at the blood. Funny how this never left her: see a hurt, want to soothe it, wrap it up. Like she had ever successfully fixed one thing. His hands were shaking bad enough he probably couldn't have done it himself, anyway.

"She came out of nowhere," the truck driver said, arms crossed, hands squeezing his biceps.

"She always does," Dell said. She watched his arm as blood seeped up again, patted it with a clean corner of the towel. Palm up, she saw that the pad of his ring finger was marked with a row of short, horizontal dashes, a sign of misfortune.

"You know her?" He looked up at the building behind them. "You're the psychic, right? Is she one of your customers?"

Dell glanced out at the wreck. "She's my mother."

"Jesus. I'm sorry."

She wrapped the towel around his arm and scooted away. "It wasn't your fault. Just bad luck."

The truck driver reminded her of her father, without the pale cheeks and empty eyes. Dad, but sober.

One of Dell's old tricks to calm herself was to look around her, find three things, and they had to be real things. Say their names, either out loud or in her head. She counted: *jimsonweed, Anita's wrinkled-up car, the valley in the distance.*

Though it was summer, a strange, cool breeze whistled through the clearing. The weather here did not follow the season's rules. The land was a keyhole between mountains, the notch in their collarbone. From here, it had once been possible to see straight into the next state on a bright day, and though the haze of a nearby factory prevented that now, the view retained a stark elegance. She had spent the last year cataloging every notch in the hills, every constellation, the family of deer that pecked around the parking lot looking for scraps. In the springtime, a black bear had come down from the woods, skinny and ragged, a mother who had given her sustenance to her cubs and gone foraging. Ravenous enough to dig through trash, risk human company. Dell knew that bone-hungry feeling, the empty that winter leaves.

An ambulance arrived, followed by a police car. As paramedics unloaded, someone approached her with a warming blanket. Dell refused it, then realized she was shivering, from shock, she thought, not at the accident but at the infernal nerve of Anita to track her down and turn up in her store.

"Do you want to ride along, or follow us to the hospital?"

Dell's response was brief.

"Do you think she'll come to in the ambulance?"

"No, ma'am."

"Go ahead. I'll catch up."

Dell turned and walked back inside the shop, leaving the crew stammering in the afternoon breeze. She turned off the lights in the den, left the cuckoo clock crying on the sofa. In her bedroom down the hall, she turned up the covers on her twin bed, pulled the shades over the windows so the mountains could not see in. She looked around her at all the treasured junk, bones, feathers donning the walls. Things she'd collected lovingly, a crow lining its nest. There was a line of poetry she'd read once that stuck in her head, now resurfacing: *These gleaming shards I have braced around the wreckage.* Yet, shards were shards, gleaming or not, and wreckage was still wreckage. Anita was right. It was time to go.

Dell stepped into her black silk flats, flipped off the sign. It was a superstitious habit to keep her red canvas bag packed and ready, hanging by the door. That she should use it to return to Blyth seemed like the final act in a mean prophecy, her feet moving ahead with or without her heart. She walked to her station wagon, threw open the door, tossed the bag onto the passenger seat. The engine started with its familiar cough and growl. She rested her head on the steering wheel and saw, between her knees, an old bloodstain on the seat cushion.

Leaving him, leaving home, being alone up here, even letting someone else be your mother. I would do it all again. Her faith that the child was safe and loved had been her salvation, her only reward for all her loneliness. Her heart raced unevenly like a busted cuckoo clock. *Bloodstain, spare change, red canvas bag.*

If every mother knows that sudden, violent love that swells as she holds a newborn, then every mother also knows the partner that comes holding its hand. Just as sudden as the love that paralyzed Dell when she held the baby girl, the familiar fear resurged to eclipse it, gray as an early dawn, mean as the February wind off the mountain. Fear that stilled her fluttering heartbeat, cutting right through the high summer haze. *If I can just find you safe and loved, it will all have been worth it. When I find you, then I'll know.*

CHAPTER TWO

Now

July 1991

Seated behind the steering wheel in her old Volvo, Dell looked up at the window of her psychic shop. She knew she couldn't return after this, not in any way that mattered. Not now that Scott and Anita knew where she was. But this place had been exactly what she needed. *Add it to the list of things Anita had to waltz in and ruin.*

Dell got out of the idling car, walked over to the expanse of jimsonweed with its faintly foul-smelling, eerie-looking flowers. She took a pocketknife from her dress and cut several stems, loading her arm with the flowers that had first welcomed her there. *Can't go visiting someone in the hospital without flowers, and these ones are just right.* With the flowers laid across the passenger seat, she rolled the windows down and drove toward home.

As Dell drove the scant hour toward Blyth, she passed under a cloud in the sky which, backlit by the sunset, took on the appearance of a crooked hand. She blinked her eyes and it was a cloud again. Though she was a careful driver, one nervous hand kept straying to her hair as she drove, pulling it over one shoulder, then the other.

At the pipeline crossing, she had to stop and wait for a small convoy of industrial trucks to go by, bearing replacement pipe segments, tools for digging and cutting.

"Shit," she swore, her right hand slapping her knee. She amended her tone and continued more softly, as if denying the anger in her initial expletive. "Today of all days, really?"

She looked back up at the sky and forced a steady, patient breath. The clouds took on various shapes. She let her vision relax, blur. In the deepest sort of static and noise, people looked so desperately for shapes in the clouds. It's the most complicated times that demand the simplest solutions. Wasn't that what had taken her to the psychic shop? A clean break.

Finally, the work vehicles passed. Foot on the gas, she resumed the winding, downhill drive. Dell drove past the fork that would have led to the cabin where her father had lived, the road forming a sharp Y where it turned away from the highway. She could still see the façade of the cabin, smell the crisp fragrance of the juniper trees with their waxy blue berries. Her stomach turned and she bit her lip, sat up to draw a deep breath.

Not there, she thought. *You don't have to go back there. Not even in your mind. Not ever.*

The highway to the hospital ran over the mountainside and meandered down a hill as it led into Blyth, passing by Dell's old high school, the First Baptist Church with its tin roof, and a neighborhood of restored Victorian houses near the library where she had once rented an apartment. Blyth was sprawled out just the same as it had always been. Dell felt the squeeze of tension between her shoulders and thought again of a tired old dog, hoping she could sneak past unseen.

As she drove, Dell played at naming three things to calm her nerves until she was murmuring the names of trees aloud in a frantic patter: *chestnut, oak, maple; juniper, ash, birch.* Juniper, again. When she had to start recycling the names of trees, she moved on to invoking the names of medicinal plants. *Lemon balm, blue skullcap*: calming tonics. The passionflower vines that bloomed at the roadside here and there, despite their violet-blue, unearthly blossoms, were soothing, brewed in a tea. She drew comfort from things that were larger and more certain than her. The earth could repeat patterns year in and year out: plants with fruit and flower, foliage that turned from green to fire-red each autumn, constellations that inched around the sky sure as clockwork. The certainties of botany and the movements of stars should have settled her troubled mind into silence.

Dell cursed out loud and fussed with her hair as she approached the hospital. Greasy-orange light from the sunset glinted off the windows of the building. The Commonwealth Memorial Hospital, all but deserted now, was the small-town type of place usually called a Band-Aid station.

Dell parked her station wagon and stood up, smoothing her dress with her hands. She collected a few of the jimsonweed blossoms, keeping most of them for herself. *Anita will wake up right away. She'll be awake and talking when I walk in there. I'm a psychic, right? I would know. There's nothing to worry about.* After all, the United States had the best doctors in the world—right? She wondered if that was true in little Blyth, Virginia. It gave some comfort to know the paramedics had not chosen to transport Anita to a larger town with a newer, shinier hospital. If they trusted the Commonwealth Memorial with her care, she couldn't have been too bad off.

Inside the sliding doors, Dell wrinkled her nose at the smell of disinfectant. Made her think of procedure, all the confident uncertainty of tinkering with things best left alone and the absolute no good that came from it. She conceded that lives were saved here, that this revulsion was illogical. Yet she was ill at ease, held her breath like she was about to dive.

The waiting room was empty save for a young woman in flannel pajama pants staring at the fuzzy television screen that hung in the corner. Dell rang the bell at the counter and waited a long two minutes until the clerk returned.

"I need to see Anita Barden."

The clerk turned to a clipboard and answered without looking up. "Family only. She's critical."

After a few seconds had passed, Dell admitted, "She's my mother."

She heard a buzz, a mechanical lock unlatching the door that opened to the patient hallway, and the woman waved her arm. "Come on back. Down the hall to your left. Room twenty-two."

Anita's room was at the end of the long, narrow corridor, through which Dell's leather-soled footsteps ticked like a clock under the blinking fluorescents. Dell opened the door and saw Anita. The bruise on her temple didn't look like an injury so much as some inner rottenness that had finally crept to her surface, like a soft spot on an apple. Like you could poke a finger right into it.

The walls were white and green at the same time, a shade that made the room smell putrid just by suggestion. A plastic tube protruded from her mouth, IVs running in each arm. Dell tiptoed forward, laid the armful of flowers on a small round table by the bed. She didn't know whether they were a curse or a charm for protection.

A doctor, bald-headed and stammering, stood at the foot of the bed, making notes on a clipboard as he spoke. "We'll let you know right away, of course, when we get her MRI results…" Dell realized that she wasn't the first person here.

"Dell." A strong pair of arms wrapped tight around her. "My God, it's good to see you."

"Hey." She lingered in her brother's hug, the warmth of familiarity sinking in before she remembered how angry she was. Behind them, Scott's girlfriend Abby, bottle-blonde as ever, sat on a craggy vinyl armchair.

"Sit," he said. "Here, take my seat. Dr. Beaton's filling us in on how Mom's doing." Something about his touch on her elbow and the tone of his voice shepherded her to the empty spot on the armchair. That was the kind of man Scott was, always offering you his seat before he even noticed you were angry with him, even if you had every goddamned reason to be. She slid miserably into the armchair next to Abby, who inched almost imperceptibly away.

Scott's girlfriend of five years, Abby, was a nurse. Dell had always gotten the sense from looking at her that she felt slighted at having to wear scrubs for forty hours a week, and made up for it by going overboard on her days off. She wore snug blue jeans that buttoned at her small waist, a geometric-patterned blouse, blue earrings that bobbed when she turned her chin, and brick-red pumps with a low, triangular heel.

Dr. Beaton cleared his throat before he continued. "The medication should keep her stable until tomorrow. If it's called for, they'll operate to relieve the pressure on her brain. Now, that sounds scary but it's routine in situations like this."

"Got it," Scott said. "When should we expect her to wake up?"

Looking over his glasses, the doctor's smile faded. "I can't say it won't happen, but we really don't know."

When Dr. Beaton left, the ticks and mechanical notes of the machinery around Anita seemed to crescendo and fill the room: a surging hum, like a sewing machine, all the varying beeps and tones of the equipment that tracked her vitals.

"They think Mom's going to be okay." Scott turned an expectant glance toward the hospital bed. He was wearing a denim jacket that smelled like Marlboros and coffee.

"Probably, Scott. He said there's a good chance," Abby added. She approached him, pulling Scott's hand into both of hers. Though her job title was nurse, Dell could never quite picture her caring for Scott, in between his long hours in uniform and the odd weekends he volunteered at the firehouse. She scowled. Abby didn't have any substance.

"Right." He cleared his throat, slipped a hand into his pocket, the set of his mouth hard and expressionless.

"So, how the hell are you? And where have you been?" Scott stood in front of the armchair and finally, slowly soaked in her stunned frown. "The accident. God, I'm so sorry. I was so excited to see you, I forgot."

"Yes, Dell." Abby touched her forearm. "You must be so shaken up. Why don't you come back to the house with us and rest?"

Dell ignored her. Abby was never genuinely friendly to her. If Scott wanted her to come, he would ask. She crossed her arms tight over her abdomen. The cold fear in her chest was threatening to spill out of her eyes, and she felt too ashamed to look at her brother.

"How'd you find me?"

"Dell, I—"

"You pulled some sort of cop strings and you looked up where I was staying. You may as well have sent Anita there yourself." She spoke over the lump in her throat, pointing an angry finger at him.

"C'mon. We hadn't seen you in a year. Mom was worried." Scott twisted his left heel on the tiled floor. Dell and Scott had the same eyes and the same straight teeth. The same smile, except Dell had always smiled too much, anxious to reassure. *There is no allure in that,* Anita had often scolded. *Don't always look like you're dying for someone to smile back at you.*

"You shouldn't have told her," Dell said. There was no use trying to stay angry with Scott. She found she was relieved to know he was still the same, still sheepishly giving in to Anita's demands.

Abby stirred, crossing and uncrossing her narrow legs. She must have been uncomfortable in her tight blue jeans. "Notice, Dell," she murmured, chewing a piece of gum, "that Scott isn't asking why you left. And no one's forcing you to stay here now. You can spare us your hostility."

"It's nice to see you, Abby." Dell did her best to look like she meant it. "It's nice to see you both."

"We're on our way out." Abby stood up and moved to the doorway; Scott lingered before he followed her, like he was on a string that would only stretch a little.

"You need a place to stay? You're welcome to our guest room," he said. "This could go on for a few days."

Dell shifted her weight in the armchair, which was as uncomfortable as it looked. "I need to be here if she wakes up."

"Well, the offer stands," Scott said. "We're having a couple friends stop by for a drink later. You're more than welcome either way." He followed Abby into the hallway, leaning around the door to finish his sentence. "You remember how to get there?"

"Yes," Dell said. "Of course I remember."

CHAPTER THREE

Now

July 1991

With Scott and Abby gone, the small noises of the hospital room filled the air. Anita was pale, the color of an undercooked pancake. Bruising purple blood settled in her eye sockets. Her neck was in a collar, her arms held down with Velcro straps to the contraption called a hospital bed. Having never stayed in a hospital, Dell could not say so with any certainty, but she looked at the bed and thought you didn't have to be a psychic to see how uncomfortable it was.

I could call the police, she thought. *And tell them what? That my mother, a lifelong histrionic, made a vague claim that a child I placed for adoption is homeless? A closed adoption means I'm not supposed to know where she is. I don't even know the name of the social worker who brought the paperwork.* No; that wasn't an option. Not to mention talking to the police would mean her brother would know everything she wanted to keep hidden. The whole point was to give her girl a fair shot at a good family. That meant no connections to Dell, her brother, Anita, anyone she knew.

Motionless, Anita looked devoid of malice, her chest softly rising and falling. Her face was blank, as if she had fallen asleep waiting for her change at a register. Her French-manicured fingernails reflected the room's single fluorescent light in little rectangles just above her cuticles.

Dell walked circles between the vinyl chair and Anita's bedside, the cold in her insides spreading as the stars came into view. She'd told herself that Anita would be awake and talking when she walked in. *Where are you? Tell me. I'm listening.* Sure, telling fortunes was mostly just reading people, spooling out what they really wanted to hear themselves say. But Dell knew that she had some kind of gift for it. Not just for seeing, but for listening, for salving whatever hurts people thought they wanted to hide. She covered her eyes with one hand, squeezing her temples. Eyes closed, she pictured the tiny baby girl, her small face. *Why can't I see you? Would I even know you if I saw you now?*

"Oh, honey. Take a seat." Dell had not heard the nurse knock at the door. She let the woman push her kindly into the chair. She was matronly, with frosted hair, wearing a nametag that read Bonnie. "This is your mama, right?"

"Yes."

"Stuff like this is hard on family. Can I get you anything?"

"Would you?" Dell looked up at her. "I need a cup of water for those flowers." She pointed at the oddly scented, purple-white-swirled flowers.

"Oh. Um, sure. How nice." Bonnie left the room, then returned with a large plastic cup full of water.

"Thanks." Dell took it from her and gently arranged the flower stems.

"Dr. Beaton said she probably won't wake up tonight," Dell said. "The thing is, I have to be here if she wakes up. I have to." She forced the fear down in her throat again, felt it cold and swelling in her chest, squeezing against her ribs.

"Doctors." Nurse Bonnie shook her head. "Listen. You want a quick lesson on what's going on here?" She waved her creased, motherly hand at the gathering of machines that stood as if conversing around Anita's bed. "This one's monitoring her heart—you can see that, here on this screen. It's steady, see? And this one's attached to her finger, and it's keeping a read on her oxygen levels. This IV?" Bonnie picked up a cord in her fingertips, then let it go. "This medicine is keeping her asleep. Out cold. If she weren't medicated, and she woke up right now, she'd be in terrible pain. When you hit your head like that, your brain knocks right to the other side of the skull and bumps. And it swells. We've got to keep everything stable till they can operate. She's gonna be unconscious like this as long as that medicine's going into her veins."

"Oh." Dell's chin rested in her folded hands, elbows on her knees. She didn't realize how her voice sounded wobbly until she was already speaking. "But she's so—perfect. Always has been. This doesn't make any sense. None of it."

The nurse laughed kindly. "Your mom's a beautiful lady, that's for sure. Your brother said you saw it happen."

"Yeah."

"You should have heard him talking before you got here. He cares about you a great deal."

"Yes," Dell agreed. "He's a Capricorn. Bossy as hell, but his heart's in the right place."

"Trust me, I understand."

Dell thought of Scott's offer to let her stay at his house. She remembered how he had always insisted, when Dad passed out high: *Dad loves you, Dell. It's not about you. Mom loves you, in her way. You've gotta remember that.* It was Scott, every time. Maybe he was the only one of them that really loved her. Talking with him, even about the weather, would be more bearable than sitting here as good as alone.

"You promise she won't wake up?"

"Oh, I'm certain of it."

"But you'll call me if anything changes?" Dell stood up, slung the bag over her shoulder.

"You're leaving?" Bonnie was shocked. "Honey, you're no trouble. I can find you some pillows if you want to stay. Might be able to find you a cup of coffee. If it was my mama, I'd want to stay."

"Her?" Dell said, nodding at Anita, still luminous in her medicated sleep. "No offense, but I have a feeling she's nothing like your mother."

CHAPTER FOUR

Before

March 1979

The daughter of a flower child and a road-tripping motorcyclist, Anita had been born Amrita in a commune that had squatted in an old Italianate mansion, as good as deserted, in the woods above Blyth. When the property was resold and the commune was packing for California, fourteen-year-old Amrita slipped away by night, making her way to the town at the foot of the hill.

Dell had never understood why her mother had stopped there in Blyth, the first town she reached. After deserting the hippies, she introduced herself as Anita and moved in with the Haneys, a Baptist family that would take in any child who needed a roof and a family. At sixteen, Anita started competing in local beauty and talent shows, singing wistful covers of three-chord folk songs. She was so beautiful, Dad used to say, that nobody noticed she was actually a half-decent singer.

At seventeen, Miss Blue Ridge Regional Beauty Champion, Anita moved out of the Haneys' overcrowded farmhouse, claiming she was going to get famous and leave town. She met Gideon Shaw, a dark-eyed construction worker, the same day. Six months later, she became pregnant with Scott; Dell was born when Scott was almost six.

Dell had grown up frightened. Of adults, mostly, the ways they hated and loved each other. Frightened of growing up into one and becoming somebody she wouldn't recognize. Dad and Mom waxed and waned on opposite poles around some dark, unseen center, like a term Dell learned in biology class: *inversely proportional relationships.* One could not thrive without depleting the other.

Anita had always been too beautiful to be married. To prove it, she left Dell's father just months before their wedding day, when Dell was fourteen and Scott a sophomore in college. The *Blyth Gazette* ran a headline in February of 1979: FORMER BEAUTY QUEEN TO WED LOCAL MAN. Mom came home to their sprawling cabin with a copy crushed between her fingers.

Their home was set back from a curving gravel road, a cabin Dad had amended, one addition and one outbuilding at a time, until it was a rambling, six-bedroom home. A crop of juniper trees punctuated the clearing in front of the house; behind it, the forest thickened into wilderness.

"Former?" Mom's honey-and-spice soprano had a sharp hook at the end of her words. "You don't stop being a pageant queen just because your title year passes." She was a storm in the house, her footsteps clicking from room to room as she packed a suitcase and left for her friend Judy's house.

Dell, only three years younger than her mother had been when she received that title, knew to stay clear when her mother felt slighted, when she paced the house in search of someone to receive her anger. She had enough to worry about that year: her new breasts, a musty astrology tome she'd bought for twenty-five cents at the library sale, and her father, Gideon, a construction worker, laid off, whose recovery from a rooftop fall was going on a year.

Dad worked part-time as a line cook at a buffet restaurant, and walked a little crooked, with metal in his left leg instead of bones. Dell thought it made him interesting. But he was not interesting when he took the pills that were prescribed for the pain. Several years passed, almost longer than Dell could remember, but he kept refilling the prescription. Dell and her brother Scott always knew Dad was high when he would sit in his chair in the kitchen, drinking from a can of Mountain Dew, immune to surprise or any other emotion.

Ruth, a shapeless gossip hub who lived next door, had come by one day, chasing after her escaped pit mix, Peewee. "What's it like for you two?" she had wondered. "Are there pills, you know, out?"

Dell drew herself up straight and stuck out her chin. "Dad is always here," she had answered, "and he never scares us or loses his temper. Scott can take care of us just fine."

She was only worried when Dad fell asleep mid-meal, or when it was difficult to wake him from naps, long, rolling snores issuing from the back of his throat, like a cough that got trapped. Obligation pulled her near, but she never knew what to do for him. She would stand at his bedside and pinch the skin of his forearm, pale with dark brown hairs, till he woke, or at least roused himself from that deep, gurgling sleep into a more lifelike rest.

But with Scott out of the house, halfway through a criminal justice degree at a state university two hours away, Dad was aimless. When a month passed and Mom had not come home, Dell heard him on the phone with her, stopped to listen on the stairs.

"She's becoming a young woman," he said. News to her. Staring in the mirror as she eavesdropped, Dell adjusted her wispy light brown hair, making a side part and combing it into a coquettish sweep, half-covering her forehead. "Dell misses you, Anita. Well, we both do. But she needs a bra. Could she come down for a weekend? Mother-daughter shopping day?"

That weekend came in March, the same time Scott was due home for spring break. Mom was living in a rented bungalow in the neighborhood that bordered the center of Blyth. Dell would never understand her mother's ability to always have money. Maybe it was magic power tied to her looks, or her social reign over the women of the First Baptist Church, a small congregation that took her word for everything, though Anita herself was not particularly Christian. She was only too beautiful not to be believed.

"Adella, sunshine!" In a close-fitting linen jumper, Mom waved from the porch as Dad dropped her off. Dell approached with hesitation, the late-afternoon sun unexpectedly warm, wearing cutoff jean shorts and a flowered blouse. Behind her, Dad waved from the sidewalk.

Mom held a hand out to stop him approaching. "I'm busy, Gideon," she said. "We'll catch up some other time." As Dad got back in his car and drove home, Dell felt a snap of cold in the evening breeze. The backpack on her shoulders held her geometry book, her reading for English class, which was Ovid's *Metamorphoses*, and the astrologer's bible. Mom gave her a loose, one-armed hug as they climbed the steps. "I'm glad you're here."

But inside, the tone changed. Sultry, grown-up-sounding music hummed from a record player, and a little dinner table was set for two, with white china, two different kinds of forks set out, and stylish, geometrically patterned cloth placemats. With her back to Dell, Mom tinkered at a bar cart in the corner. Dell heard a bottle neck clink against a glass and pour. She stood near the plush olive sofa and wondered if she was allowed to sit. Mom turned around with a brightly colored drink in her hand.

"It's called a tequila sunrise," she said. "See the colors, Dell?"

"Yes."

"I'm having a friend over for dinner, so you can enjoy this nice weather and do your homework on the porch."

"Okay." Dell was glad she had not taken her sandals off. "I'll go outside when she gets here."

"Well, darling, it'll be any minute. Here." Mom put the drink in her hand and opened the front door. "This was a practice run. You take this one—it's our secret."

Dell brushed her hair to one side, wondering if it would make her mother proud for her friend to see how her daughter could be stylish just like her. "Mom, can I go to the bathroom?"

"Yes, of course." Mom waved past the kitchen. "It's right through there. I'll leave your drink here by the door."

As Mom busied herself with a tray of appetizers, Dell walked past her to the bathroom. It smelled of perfume, though dust gathered in all the corners. She flushed and returned to the porch with her backpack, cocktail in hand.

Dell was old enough to know that alcohol was a bad idea before geometry problems. But she took just a taste of the tropical-colored beverage, which looked like candy but made the inside of her mouth twist up. When a red Lincoln pulled up to the curb, Mom was already at the door, waving her hand like a princess. A tall man with graying blond hair and a thick, neat mustache stepped out.

"Jeremiah, good evening." Mom kissed both of his cheeks like a French lady and held the door open. The man wore a pale blue jacket over a button-down shirt and slacks.

"Anita, it's great to be here." Jeremiah's hand lingered on hers and he turned over his shoulder, his eyes landing on Dell. "Well, aren't you something." He smiled as if she were a kitten. "Your little sister?"

She'd seen the man before. One of Dad's doctors after the accident. The doctor and his family went to their same church. Not often, though—only on holidays. Dell went with Dad and Scott every Sunday, or at least she had before Scott left for school; now it was only her and Dad.

"Yes," Mom answered. She sent Dell a message with her eyebrows, telling her to play along. "My little sister, Adella. She's here for the weekend. Come on, Jeremiah." Again, Mom opened the door. "Let's have a drink."

Dell sat on a wide bench, took out a pencil, and started on her geometry homework, tuning out the distractions of the soft music and adult voices from inside. She liked geometry because it reminded her of astrology. Three hundred and sixty degrees, a circle, was another way of saying *everything in the sky*: a circle, divisible into slices, each one its own twinkling house.

Within an hour, she had worked through the whole lesson, rows of proofs in tidy pencil in her textbook. She took another sip from the glass, then swirled it so the colors blended to orange, and found that it was sweeter mixed up. She turned dutifully to her next assignment, opening the paperback copy of the *Metamorphoses* across her knees. As she stumbled across the opening lines, the words turned to jelly on her lips. She frowned and placed the Ovid at her side, open to the first section. Dell wasn't as good in English, anyway, and she was distracted by the cold gooseflesh specking her legs. The gauze curtains were drawn over the windows, but she could still hear the music. Finally, she decided to attempt a head start on the next geometry lesson. But her textbook turned sultry and inscrutable, the numbers on the page refusing to combine as readily as they usually did for her.

"Yes. Goodnight." The door opened, a triangle of saffron-colored light expanding and then closing as the door swung shut. Dell looked up to see Mom's friend. The man turned from the steps and looked her way.

"What are you working on there?"

"Geometry."

"Adella, right? I'm Jeremiah."

As he drew near, the textbook under Dell's hand betrayed her distraction: curlicues and constellations traced where calculations should have been.

"Do you need some help?" He sat next to her on the bench. "Poor thing—you're freezing." He tapped her knee to prove the point, and his hand lingered there on her leg, just where the flesh started to soften into thigh. "Which question are you on?"

It seemed unkind to refuse help from someone who seemed concerned, so Dell chose a proof, indicated it with the tip of her pencil.

"Quadrilaterals and parallelograms," he hummed. He smelled sharp, like cologne, and sweet. "Math doesn't come easy to girls, does it?"

She watched as he made scratches in her book, half erased them, and wrote down the steps to solve the problem. "You've got better things on your mind at this age, don't you?"

"I guess." Eyeing his work, Dell saw that he had done a step wrong and wondered if it would wear the page away to erase a second time. She glanced at the shaded window. Could her mother hear his voice over the music? Surely she would know he was still here.

"Boys, makeup, music," Jeremiah prompted. "Who's your favorite singer?"

"Joni Mitchell, I guess." Dell hugged her upper arms against her chest. A new, odd sensation troubled her. She was aware of her arms, the portions of her legs below and above her knee, the cool, soft skin of her chest; wished she could pull a blanket over all of them, and not from the cold. She had never thought of her body in pieces before.

"Joni Mitchell?" Jeremiah laughed. "What about boys?"

"I don't know." Her mouth tasted sour from the drink and she began to wonder when Jeremiah would take her hint and leave. Dell saw her mother's shadow pass by the window, footsteps receding to another room. Her heart sank.

"Oh, I do, sweetheart." He leaned closer, one elbow on his knee, the other hand still resting on her thigh. "Got a boy myself, just a few years older than you. Not much going on upstairs, at their age." He shook his head. "Minds in the gutter, and no idea how to treat a girl. I feel for girls like you, the things you must put up with."

She sat still as a rock, looked past Jeremiah's hand on her leg. Her eye fell on the old paperback again. This time, the letters lined up, the words inviting her to read. *The Metamorphoses, by Ovid. Written 1 A.C.E. Translated by Sir Samuel Garth. Book I...*

He lifted his hand from her leg to brush the inside of her thigh. The other hand rested on her forearm, lifted to her breast. Dell remembered her father's voice: *Anita, she needs a bra.* Dell was angry, too surprised to move, although she wanted to say that she had never put up with anything from a boy. Girls in her grade either liked boys or they didn't. Having a crush was no science.

Jeremiah reached into his chest pocket and took out a business card, which read: *Jeremiah Davis McCallan III, M.D., Doctor of Family Medicine.* It had two phone numbers on it, one labeled *Home* and one *Office.* With Dell's pencil, he scratched out the number printed next to *Home*, and pressed the card against her knee. "You ever want someone to treat you like a real lady, Adella, you can call me up."

She scanned the paperback again, her eyes zipping back and forth across the first line of the epic poem as she read: *Of bodies chang'd to various forms, I sing—*

Jeremiah leaned close to her face. His large hand cupped her cheek as his lips touched hers, sour-sweet like the mixed drinks her mother had made. Having a body suddenly felt like a vulnerability, a punishment, a realization that opened a fault between where she was and where she wanted to be: somewhere, anywhere else.

Dell was no longer more startled than she was angry. She pulled violently away from him, shoved the paperback square into his lap, and whispered sharply: "I don't like you."

"Oh-ho, look at you." Jeremiah stood up laughing and leaned over her. Her paperback book fell to the ground and he kicked it aside. "You're a little slut, alright. You just don't know it yet."

"Jeremiah?" Mom's mellow voice reached around the doorframe as she stepped outside. The light splashed across them: the kind-looking doctor, the girl on the porch swing with wild eyes, her mouth squeezed shut. "What—what are you doing?"

Jeremiah looked up at her with a calm smile. "Your little sister asked me for a hand with her geometry. I think she's got it all figured out now."

"You're too sweet," Mom laughed. "Goodnight, then. Adella, you can come in now."

As Jeremiah retreated down the steps to his Lincoln, his laugh hung in the cold air along with his cologne.

CHAPTER FIVE
Before
March 1979

Dell swept her books up clumsily and ran inside, relieved at the sudden rush of warmth and light. "Mom? Mom."

Mom sat down at the table, one hand on an almost empty glass, the other supporting her forehead. "What?"

"That man. He kissed me. Mom?" Dell rubbed her arms to warm them, or to scrub them clean, almost jumping off the ground with anger. "Mom, he touched my—my leg." Her hands clutched at the soft skin right at the hem of her shorts, almost at her crotch.

Mom lifted her head, her makeup smeared, and tossed back the remainder of the glass. Dell sensed the feeling of slight on her. "I thought you were a better girl than that."

"I didn't want him to." Her protest was high-pitched with disbelief.

"No? You didn't call for me." Mom swirled the ice cubes in her cocktail glass and sipped the tinted water. "You didn't get up and come inside. I thought you knew better."

"I didn't want him to," Dell repeated, her voice dropping to a squeak.

With decisive footsteps, Mom approached Dell and took her hand in a tough grasp. "Come here."

Mom pulled Dell through the kitchen, down the hallway, into the bathroom, held her shoulders and turned her to face the mirror.

"You are a stupid little girl, Dell. You've got no business meddling with adults." Her mother pulled her hair back from her face, her fingers tangling in its brown waves. "You flirt like that, and you'll get exactly what's coming to you." Reflected in the mirror, Mom's hair was dark, rich brown, her eyes flashing mahogany.

"Do you want to end up pregnant and single?" She pulled hard on Dell's hair, jerking her chin upward.

"No."

Anita held Dell's hair out behind her head. She took a pair of scissors from a shelf behind the toilet.

"Mom," she whispered. "Stop it. I'm scared."

"Because that is what you'll be, if you mess with a man like that."

Dell saw a lock of hair fall at her feet at the same time she heard the snap of the scissors, soon followed by another. "If you play with a man like that, you'd better know exactly what you're doing. You don't know it now, but I'm trying to help you."

"Mom, I won't. I'm listening." Her legs felt unsteady. She wanted to fall down and sit on the floor, but that instinct was followed by a suspicion that it would only make Mom angrier.

She felt the sharp tug on her scalp as her mother held a lock out and snipped it. "Men don't only hurt you with their muscles," she said, her voice low, edged with something beyond anger, something soft. "Men don't only hurt you with knives or guns. You can't just let anyone…" She cleared her throat, allowed for a suggestive pause. "You can't just let any man come up and sit next to you."

Dell squeezed her lips together and stared down at the sink while Mom cut her hair short. She didn't think much of her appearance, overall, but she loved her hair. Now, parted in the middle, it hung blunt-edged, reached to her chin on the left, shorter and ragged on the right, barely covering her ear. Dell held her breath. She didn't dare to look up at her mother; she knew that if she did she would start to cry.

As easily as the weather changed, Mom's eyes softened. She smoothed Dell's hair down sweetly and tucked it behind her ears, met her eyes in the mirror. "You'll understand when you're older, honey."

"I don't think so." Dell met her mother's eyes with reproach.

"Stand up straight, baby." Anita leaned close to kiss her cheek. "Proper posture makes a lady look ten pounds thinner. Now you go and lay down on the couch. Mom will clean this hair up." She turned away, lifting her delicate chin toward the ceiling, fanning at her eyes prettily as if they stung her.

As Dell studied her mother, holding her breath, she felt her jaw set hard as steel. Whatever feelings her mother had were her own problem. Dell whispered through her clenched teeth: "It's not about you, Mom."

When Anita had retired to her bedroom, Dell took the pajamas she had packed from her overnight bag and went to the bathroom to change. She turned away from the mirror, then closed her eyes tightly when she ducked her head to pull on her t-shirt. With the house dark and quiet, she rested uneasily on the sofa bed, all her senses racing. She returned to the *Metamorphoses,* read until past midnight. *Bodies chang'd to various forms* was right. Ovid's gods were always transforming people. A mortal spited a god or claimed they could do something better than them—next thing they knew, they were a spider. Trespassers, blasphemers, unlucky hunters, were changed into animals or stones. But the metamorphoses were acts of kindness as often as they were punishments. Sometimes the gods, but more often goddesses, took pity and transformed a woman who was running: from some kind of tragedy, or from public scorn, but most often from a man. Dell curled up on her side, leaning on her elbow as she whispered the names. Daphne became a laurel tree. Io, a cow. But not all were animals. Arethusa became a stream,

Syrinx a clutch of river reeds. Dell yawned and stretched, her bare
feet extending past the end of the couch. Nobody had looked out
for her when that doctor put his hands all over her. Nobody had
turned her body into something less interesting, something that
could fly away. Not unless she counted Anita, who just wanted
to turn her into an ugly little boy.

Dell got up and returned to the bathroom, walking as quietly
as she could across the cold floor. She clicked the light switch on
and studied her face in the mirror. The white plastic wastebasket
was full of strands of chestnut brown. Her hair was jagged and
short, like when she tore too many sheets of notebook paper off
at the same time. Glaring down her reflection, Dell combed her
hair into a side part, so that one side framed her temple, the other
sloping across her brow. She pulled open the bathroom mirror and
ran a crooked finger across the various items there: a nacre-handled
hairbrush, some tampons, a bronze plastic tube of lipstick. The
lipstick twirled up blood red when she opened the cap. Dell's hand
closed around the lipstick. She put it in the pocket of her pajama
pants, closed the cabinet, and went back to the couch.

The next morning, Mom was cheery, as if nothing had happened. She took Dell to a department store, picked up three
nude-colored sports bras without her input, and thanked the
cashier as she wrapped them in tissue and put them in a bag. That
morning was brisk and sunlit, and, when Dell asked her to stop
at Buddy's Ice Cream stand, she surprised her by pulling over.

"Isn't it a little chilly for ice cream?" Her mother smiled and
opened the car door as Dell hopped out, dressed in the same
lightweight floral top and shorts she'd worn the evening before.

"Not if it's strawberry ice cream. Strawberry's my favorite."

In the shade of a neighboring office building, it still felt like
winter, and her mother's silver sedan was the only car there. Mom
ordered a strawberry ice cream cone and a seltzer water while
Dell waited at a picnic table behind the stand. She ate quietly

and wondered how her mom knew how to do everything with such allure, even drink her seltzer, her cheekbones showing when she sipped.

Dell heard a car park and leaned her head around the corner of the building. Her eyes flickered back to her mother, who was studying her fingernails. She recognized the car, a red Lincoln, and the man who got out of it. She recognized his wife and the quiet, neatly dressed boy who followed him to the counter, going out of view.

"Mom?"

"Yes, honey? What's wrong?"

Dell leaned further, scooted to the edge of the bench to take another look. Mrs. McCallan, statuesque and strawberry blonde, wore a khaki trench coat and a long, olive-colored sweater dress. Their son, who looked a few years older than her, wore soccer clothes and sneakers. Dell thought he must have been cold, though he showed no sign of it. Jeremiah McCallan ordered three ice cream cones, tasted his, then handed the others to his wife and son.

"What's wrong, Dell?" Mom repeated.

Dell dismissed her mother with one brief stare as she leapt to her feet and rounded the corner. She knew the look on Dr. McCallan's face as she marched up to him. He was scared. Standing an arm's length away, she looked from the wife, back to the husband, and pointed her finger at his chest.

"He was at my mother's house last night," she said, "and he touched my leg, and he kissed me." Mom ran to catch up with her and Dell saw that she, too, was afraid. She took Dell by both elbows and pushed her toward the car. Dell twisted her chin, looking over her shoulder, held Mrs. McCallan's cold gaze. "And he smelled bad."

The doctor's wife showed no reaction, a cool smile on her pink frosted lips. She turned to her husband and the boy, who was looking at his shoes, and calmly ordered: "Both of you get in the car."

Dr. McCallan walked to the car and let himself into the driver's seat. Dell thought she saw a hint of a grateful smile on his lips. When the boy lingered, Mrs. McCallan pulled him swiftly to his feet. She was stronger than she looked.

"Get," she hissed.

Dell watched as the boy retreated. He disobeyed, standing behind the Lincoln rather than getting in, but his eyes followed every step his mother took.

Mrs. McCallan approached Dell, still standing with her back to her mother. She leaned close to her face, extended one thin finger and tapped Dell's chest. "You are a little slut and a liar. I know everything there is to know about girls like you." She glanced at Mom and held her gaze for a long second, then returned to the girl. One hand tightened on Dell's chin. "You are going to keep your mouth shut and stay far away from my family."

"Or what," Dell said, tossing the woman's hand off her face. This was a mistake, which she realized as soon as Mrs. McCallan slapped her cheek, her fingers ice-cold.

"Or everyone finds out about those pills your father likes," she answered. "And that you tried to throw yourself at my husband."

Dell's girlish floral top felt scant, the breeze all over her skin like hands. Her whole person was in plain sight and seemed to warrant some kind of correction: from the doctor, from his wife, from her own mother.

"I didn't do anything. You don't understand," Dell cried, her hurried syllables a desperate plea to be heard. "You can't tell anyone, please. Mom?" She turned back to look at her mother, but got no answer, not even a look.

"And you can tell that to your friends at church," Mrs. McCallan answered, aiming her chilly glare at Anita. "If I ever so much as see you near my family again."

Behind the red sedan, the blond-haired boy was watching Dell. He stood up straight, his posture almost unnatural. Dell could see that he wanted to be anywhere but here. She could see how badly he wanted to run.

"I swear I didn't want him to." Their eyes met. She felt herself repeating those pleas and stammers until she was senseless. "Don't tell anyone. Please don't." She thought she saw him raise an eyebrow. A silent acknowledgment that this was bullshit, all this crooked, polished grown-up talk. She lifted her head, bit her lip hard to hold the tears in, harder again as she felt her throat tighten.

Say something. Anything, she thought. *Please.* But the boy shook his head, looked away from her.

"Mom." He lifted a hand to block the sun from his eyes. "Can we go?"

Mrs. McCallan gasped when she heard her son's voice. "I told you to get in the car. Why don't you ever listen to me? And leave your ice cream. No food in the car." She tossed Dell back against her mother, turned and walked away. Their three ice cream cones lay similarly discarded, tilting on their sides on the table where they had sat. Mrs. McCallan had done this before. Dell saw the boy's face through the tinted window in the back seat, sorry but distant, and knew that he had, as well.

Dell's heart raced for the whole, long drive as her mother took her back to Dad's. Mom said nothing until she had slowed to a stop at the bottom of the driveway.

"Get out." She spoke without turning to look at her daughter.

The boards of the porch were worn, crooked at the top of the steps like rotten teeth. Dad was seated at the kitchen table drinking a Mountain Dew.

"Home already? Dell, your hair looks nice. Is it different?"

"Nope." She dropped her backpack to one arm.

"Did you have fun with your mother?"

Dell sat the shopping bag on the table. "She got me some bras." There was no way she could tell her father about the man who had visited her mother, not unless she wanted him to spend the next three days stoned, in bed. "I don't think she liked me being there."

Dad smiled peacefully. "We've got to let her do what she wants, Strawberry. That's how we're going to get her to come back."

That was what frightened Dell about Dad, and about Mom. The way he loved her was like a fire. It needed fuel, left him in embers.

Dell took her backpack and retreated to her room, a wood-paneled corner bedroom that looked over the forest on one side, the juniper trees on the other. When she heard loud rock music coming from Scott's room, she dropped her bag on the floor and went down the hall, knocking loudly.

"Come in."

She opened the door and looked in. Scott stood up to turn off the music then approached with a hug.

"Hey there, short hair. You look like a little Mia Farrow."

"Thanks." She closed the door behind her and stood quietly.

"So what's up? How was Mom?"

Scott, at twenty, was tall and skinny, dark-haired like their mother. He and Dell had the same dark eyebrows over hazel irises, bright as pennies. He cared little for fashion, dressed in simple, straight-cut jeans and a sweater, but considered himself an expert on popular music.

"I don't know." Dell's nose started to run, her chest flushed pink. She grabbed Scott's denim jacket from the foot of his bed and put it on hastily, pulling the front of the jacket closed over her flowered blouse, tucking her chin down into the Marlboros-and-coffee smell that meant her brother was home.

"What's wrong?"

"Mom's new boyfriend." She tried to hold her voice steady but her breaths shook inside her throat and her voice dwindled to a squeak. "Some doctor. Tried to pick me up." She threw Dr. McCallan's business card at Scott's feet. "Mom blamed it on me."

Scott hugged her tight. "What happened?"

Dell coughed out a sob and continued. "And we saw them all out today and I told his wife and everything. She said I was a little slut and to stay away. Like I was the bad one. She said if she sees me again she'll tell everybody about Dad." She couldn't bring herself to speak the worst part, that the woman had threatened to tell everybody at church, and therefore everyone within the confines of their small world, that Dell was somehow, inexplicably, culpable in enticing an adult, married man.

Scott squeezed her shoulder, then bent down and picked up the card.

"McCallan? Oh, Dell." He shook his head.

Dell wiped her nose on her arm. "What?"

"Be careful around those folks."

"Why?"

"They don't like anyone to get the better of them. Remember when I took boxing lessons in middle school?" Dell nodded and remembered the blond boy in the back seat. "Their kid did too. I knocked one of his teeth loose in a match. Total risk of the game. Neither of us was upset."

"Okay."

"Well, Mrs. McCallan made a scene you wouldn't believe. Threatened legal action, even after Mom and Dad paid the dentist's bill. Not that they couldn't afford it." He tore up the business card in his hands. "They've got one son, two phone lines, and three houses. They don't like us. And they do not make empty threats. Promise you'll steer clear."

"I promise." Dell's eyes watered again. "Not even Mom was on my side. And Dad's way past caring."

"Listen to me, okay? It was not your fault." Scott rested his hands on her shoulders. "If anyone ever approaches you like that again, you raise hell. I don't care who it is."

"I did."

"Well, if you ask me, you did good. It was one of you and all of them. I just want you to look out for yourself, too." Scott leaned back and stood up straight, just like their mother always told them to, pulled a Marlboro Red from his pocket and lit it.

She sniffed again. "Okay. But what about Mom?"

Scott laughed, but he didn't sound happy. "Mom is just who she is, Dell. She loves you, in her way. You've gotta remember that."

"What, so we all just put up with her? Perfect old *Anita*?" Dell crossed her arms and screwed her mouth up tight and turned to leave the room. "Not me. Not after that."

When Dell returned to school on Monday, she wore her short hair swept to the side. Anita's lesson had backfired; she looked more grown up, not less. And just in case anyone should have guessed that her new haircut wasn't her idea, she wore her lips colored bright red and stood up as tall as she could. It was her own version of a metamorphosis, the best she could do with what she had. But Dell stopped going to church with Dad, and she spent more time alone than she should have.

She spent hours over her astrology book, read everything on the subject she could find. Anita was a Scorpio, and every book agreed, Scorpios were trouble. It felt good for something to make sense, and she wished she could have squeezed her whole world into predictable categories. The next year, when she was fifteen, this wish was granted. A large energy company, which for all practical purposes owned the state of Virginia, installed a gas pipeline that ran through four states. While the pipe was buried underground, it ran through a strip where the forest was shaved to the ground, as if in preparation for surgery, mowed down again and doused in pesticide each spring. Dell's Aunt Myra, an old granny woman who smelled like soil and chewing tobacco, had lived right in the middle of the trail where the pipe was laid down. The law said she had to move, laws that changed to make room for money and business. They weren't sure where she went, but Dad got her letters every few months.

Fifteen, angry, with invisible handprints on her thighs and her new B-cups, Dell knew the pipeline wasn't the kind of wall she wanted. But it was better than nothing, and she was glad to stay on her side of it. She had begged the world around her to reflect the schism she felt: this was her side, that was everyone else's, and she stayed damn well put.

CHAPTER SIX

Now

July 1991

Outside the Commonwealth Memorial Hospital, a row of vending machines cast their bold, commercial beams like lighthouses across the empty pavement. Dell inserted some change and ordered two cans of Mountain Dew. In the humid, velvet-dark night, they collected condensation instantly, sweating in her hand as she unlocked her car. It was past nine, the stars bright overhead, but the emptiness and quiet of the parking lot gave the illusion that the hour was late.

The highway that led through the middle of Blyth was in shadow. Everyone was already home for the night, or at whatever bar they'd stay at until last call. Before she drove to Scott's house, Dell took a detour, parked in the gravel lot outside the First Baptist Church. Though she felt a prickle of discomfort at trespassing, the parking lot was guarded from view of the road by a row of magnolias, their bitter fragrance wafting around her as she stepped out of the station wagon in the dark.

Dell made her way in the moonless night past the church, past the annex building that held offices and the church preschool, and into the graveyard, all the way to the back, near the brick wall that separated it from the roadway. Dell walked up to her father's gravestone and sat down cross-legged in the damp grass, placing the Mountain Dew cans on the ground in front of her.

The grass was carefully clipped and a bouquet of carnations, only a few days old, rested at the foot of the stone. Dell sensed Abby's handiwork. In block letters, the granite stone read:

GIDEON SHAW
MARCH 13, 1935—JULY 28, 1990
BELOVED FATHER
AND DEAR TO ANITA

Dell let out a sigh of annoyance. Anita, who had ordered the headstone, had managed to squeeze in her byline despite never marrying Gideon or, Dell thought, really loving him. She opened one of the cans of Mountain Dew and leaned the other against the gravestone. The night was dark, a new moon. Besides the occasional set of passing headlights, there was only starlight. Crickets and the chirp of frogs hummed around her. Dell tasted the soda, then took a longer sip. This was her indulgence. Where others drank or smoked, she'd taken to an occasional soda or ice cream. All that sugar, all those chemicals dulling her mind.

It had taken her a year to get here. A year of Dad being dead. She saw a meteor swish past and remembered: this weekend was the Perseids, the summer's best meteor shower. Dell could picture Dad sitting here right across from her, if she didn't focus on him too closely.

"I'm sorry I pretty much missed your funeral. You already know that. Of course you do." Now she was whispering aloud, and though she reclined in the grass, staring at the sky, she saw herself sitting up, an elbow propped on her knee, sitting across from her father.

Listen to me, Strawberry, he said, his dark eyes wrinkling merrily as he scratched his mustache. *You have nothing to be sorry for. You can't live your whole life being sorry.*

"And now I'm here to ask you a favor. What a mess." Her hands played in the grass, felt the whispering summer lullaby of the ground around her.

Anything, kid. What is it?

"I have to find this baby. Please, tell me nothing's happened to her. Please, just let me find her."

But something was wrong. Her reverie was no longer under her control.

What baby?

"You're supposed to know everything over there, Dad."

Sure, kid, sure. You do me a favor, too. Now he was different. The tilt of his head loosened. He was still high, even in death. Twice as gone.

"Anything. What do you need?"

You say hello to your mother for me. Tell her she's the most beautiful woman that ever lived. Don't worry about some baby.

Dell caught her breath. It was too soon to be back here. It was always going to be too soon. She heard an owl's coo in the distance. "Go to hell, Dad. I hope you already have."

In her daydream, she looked too close, and saw her father again: the cold body, several hours dead, his forearms crooked upward as if reaching, back arched, eyes wide open, wearing the red baseball cap. But she wasn't scared of these kinds of visions, now.

Dell stared hard at the apparition, then sat up straight in the grass. "Perseids," she whispered, "magnolias, my little black slippers, Mountain Dew."

She stood up and felt grass and dew clinging to her limbs. With calm, precise steps, she walked out of the cemetery. She had never paid much mind to mosquitoes, and tried to ignore the bites when they did find her. Overall, they were kinder to her for it. This was the trick; if she stopped to wait, to feel the sting, to feel the softness of her fear, that was where she stayed.

CHAPTER SEVEN

Now

July 1991

Dell drove two miles to the outskirts of town, to Scott's brick rancher. *This whole town is an old flea-bitten dog,* she thought. *Not a hair on it has moved since I was gone.* Dell parked on the curb and looked in the rearview mirror. In the dark, her eyes were almost black. She collected the last of her jimsonweed flowers, blossoms still wide open in the dark, and got out of the car.

The flower beds outside Scott's rancher were tidy and cheerful, blooming with geraniums, lantana, pertly bobbing ornamental grasses, and rows of bright impatiens—Abby's touch showing again. As she climbed the walkway to the front door, she admired a row of tall four o'clocks, their blossoms closed for the night, nodding in the dark. Dell knocked, regretting not calling from the hospital.

Abby opened the door, swatting away summer moths and gnats, a large glass of wine in one hand. "Flowers? Thank you. Come in," she said. "How are you holding up? Where's your bag? I'll put it in the guest room."

"Um. Thanks," Dell said. Abby seemed to be so excited to see her that she'd forgotten she was standing in the doorway.

"Oh! Come in," Abby repeated, giggling as she stepped aside. She wore a black embroidered sundress with a leather belt and beaded sandals, the outfit of a girlfriend around the house in the evening, not a wife.

Dell felt the shock of the air conditioning and struggled to adjust her eyes to the light. Wine made Abby friendly. She managed a thank you and before she knew it, Abby had taken her bag, put it away, and returned to her side.

"We're out back having a drink. Won't you join us?"

"Can I put these in a glass?" She held out the flowers.

"Oh, you're so sweet." As Abby spoke, she was leading Dell through the close, brightly lit kitchen, pouring her a generous glass of white wine without waiting for her answer. Dell took a drinking glass from the cabinet, arranged the stems, filled it with tap water.

"Thanks. Abby, I won't stay up long. I'm—"

"So tired, I'm sure," Abby interrupted. "Here, take this."

She shoved the glass of wine into Dell's hand, which she balanced awkwardly, flowers tucked into the crook of her elbow. Dell felt her damp shoes sticking to her feet, the smell of them rising to her nostrils. She looked around Scott's kitchen. She saw the familiar Formica countertops, the same green-shaded hanging lamp, in place like abandoned set pieces. Not a photograph on the refrigerator had moved.

"Come on," Abby was saying. "Let's go outside."

Abby opened the back door on to the patio and held it open. Dell stepped out, scanning the wrought-iron table, anticipating a similarly familiar scene. Fireflies blinked in the air, surrounding a citronella candle, Scott, and the last person in the world she wanted to see. The wine glass slipped from her hand and hit the ground with a sparkling crack.

CHAPTER EIGHT

Now

July 1991

Dell looked down helplessly at the broken shards around her feet.

"Oh, Abby, I'm…" She fumbled, barely holding onto the flowers, their unpleasant odor wafting around her face.

"Sit," Abby insisted, smiling still, a hint of impatience edging her words. "I'll bring you another glass and we'll just get this cleaned up." She gestured at the empty chair again and Dell waited, stammering. "You poor thing, Dell. Sit down. You haven't said a word."

Scott pulled out a chair. "Come on, take a seat."

It wasn't the first time she had lingered in a doorway, her eyes locked on his, hands full of gathered flowers. But those had been delicate blossoms, little brave flowers that grow in early spring. Not like these ones, which grew tough on scrappy shrubs by roadsides, only opening up in the dark.

Dell took her seat. She placed the jimsonweed in the middle of the table as if it were a warning.

"Hey, Scott." She sat in between Scott and Mason. "You holding up okay?"

"Sure," he scoffed, laughing. As if it were a foregone conclusion. "You?"

"Yeah. Good."

"You haven't met Mason, have you?"

"No." Dell turned her face just enough that she could see him. "I don't know him." She listened to Scott explain how they worked together, although her thoughts slipped away. *Arsinoe was turned into a stone. Asteria, a quail. Aura became a fountain.*

"Nice to meet you. Sorry about your mother." His tone was polite, meaningless. Dell looked up at him with contempt. She stifled an impulse to stand up, to knock everything off the tabletop to shatter on the ground.

"You can put those flowers inside, if you want." Scott turned the glass, looking at the various blossoms. "They're nice."

"They only bloom in the dark. That's why I brought them out."

"They're pretty," Scott said. "You ought to tell Abby what they are. She might want to plant some."

"I doubt it," Dell answered. "They're poisonous. A weed, really. Most people don't want them around." She nudged one of the stems, admired its blossom.

Inside, the phone rang. Dell heard footsteps, then the door opened.

"Honey?" Abby called. "It's for you." She stepped outside, put a glass of wine in front of Dell, then returned inside with Scott. "I'll be right back," she said. "Just finishing the dinner dishes."

The door closed behind Abby and they were alone. Dell stared straight ahead, pretended she was sitting there by herself. Picked up her wine glass and took a drink. She could feel him looking at her, and was suddenly, dreadfully aware of the bits of grass that clung to her arms and her dress. She half wished some deity would take pity on her, turn her into a clutch of river reeds or an animal.

"Dell."

"Nope." She shook her head, took a long sip of wine. "Do not talk to me."

"Did you…" Mason's fingertips drummed on the tabletop. "Did you have the—"

Her face turned, met his eyes with a cold stare. "Adopted."

So she was, still, only an inconvenient body and its functions. Dell took another drink, congratulating herself for making at least one right choice.

"Adopted—what? What about you? Are you—"

Dell's anger surged. "Some nerve you have. Does that run in your family, or what? Asking me how I'm doing? Only after you ask if I—" She sighed, reminded herself to keep her voice low. "Mason, I didn't like you the day I met you. And I don't like you now."

Whatever had passed in the middle of those two points had amounted to nothing. Dell remembered an old geometry lesson. Two points in space can only form one thing. One flat line.

Mason pushed the flowers away from them. "Those smell awful, Dell."

"Good." Ignoring him took more self-control than she anticipated. Although Dell often imagined nymphs and mortals who were changed into animals, she wished now that she were Medusa. Turn his perfectly controlled face to stone with just a look. She wished she could stand up and shout at him. Tell him how angry she was, now, even a year later. How she'd be just as angry even if a century had passed.

Dell's eyes flickered toward him. If they'd been standing, the top of her head would have reached just to the hollow between Mason's collarbones. She pushed the wine glass away from her. One night during the spring, she had finished most of a bottle of wine, lost recollection around two thirds through it. She had woken with a headache, sprawled on the velvet sofa where she did her readings, a handful of crystals scattered across her lap. It made her too susceptible to the kinds of emotions she'd rather push aside.

Finally, Scott and Abby returned. Dell leaned back in her chair, felt the woven metal pressing a crisscross shape into the skin over her shoulder blades.

"So." Abby's fingernails tapped the base of her wine glass. "Dell, you haven't brought it up, but…"

"Fine. Get it over with." Dell was tired, but her voice came out sharp. "You want to interrogate me? I was minding my own business," she said. "I didn't ask for anyone to track me down and send Anita after me."

Abby swallowed her wine and set the glass down heavily. "I seem to remember saying something about sparing us your hostility. You're the one who just turned up after going missing for a year."

"Sorry." She flashed Abby a brief, pleading look. "Listen—I'm just too tired to talk. I'm not looking for an argument here."

Not only a gossip, Abby was a persistent drunk. "So, anyway. You're a psychic?"

"Yeah. I'm renting a shop an hour down the parkway. Been there about a year."

"And you live there too?"

"Yes." Dell took a long drink from her wine.

"What's it like?" Abby continued. "Do you like it?"

Dell paused. She wanted to tell Abby and Scott and Mason that she'd learned she did not need anybody to survive. That she had learned of a secret expanse behind her heart, that it was a wilderness she could forage, a proliferation of space. She knew how to find the rhythm in the noise, name the shapes in the clouds.

She smiled in the near dark, the candlelight reverberating as she spoke. "Yeah. I do like it."

"How do you know their future? The people who come to see you?"

People came to her worried and unsure, like injured animals with out-of-joint limbs, and she guided them through their own hearts. Dell didn't like revealing any tricks.

"You know what I know?" She laughed. "Curiosity and nosiness in a Gemini are one and the same."

"You're as pleasant as you've ever been." Abby turned her sullen frown at the jimsonweed flowers. "Your mom was worried, too. I just can't imagine walking out on family like that."

"Sure thing, Abby. Walking out on family." Dell repeated Abby's words, twirled the stem of her wine glass, felt the brick of fear in her chest dislodging, tightening her throat. "You have no idea."

Scott shook his head, leaned over to kiss Abby's cheek. "Easy, Abby. She's tired."

Dell took a breath and released it slowly, trying to steady herself. But her hands shook with useless energy. Anita's voice replayed in her mind. *As good as homeless. Maybe you can divine that.* But she couldn't divine anything. She held her trembling hands under the table, out of sight, and looked to Abby with a pleading stare, shaking her head.

Under the tabletop in the dark, Mason took Dell's hand. From the corner of her eye, she saw him holding her gaze, his expression steady, unreadable. In his warm grip, the tremble in her hands slowed, her fingers twining into his.

"Abby, you're grilling a woman who just watched her mother wreck her car." Mason smiled as if he were telling a joke. "Take it easy."

Scott nodded and kissed Abby's temple. "Everyone's excited she's here, baby. We'll all talk more tomorrow."

Abby huffed a sigh. "Well, I hope it's not too awful a shock to you to have to see us again."

"I'm tired. That's all." Dell realized that she was squeezing Mason's hand and loosened her grip.

She recalled the last time they'd spoken, almost a year ago this week. Seated so close to her, she wondered if he could hear that echo as well, or if it was lost in the year's silence between them. She remembered the smell of the half-renovated farmhouse, lumber and paint, and how he had leaned his elbows on his knees in the July sun and said, *What is it gonna take to get you to stay?*

Dell hadn't lingered then. She let go of his hand and finished her wine in one careless sip.

"It's the same as it's always been," she said. "People in this town expect to know everything about a person."

"Nobody knows everything," Mason answered. This time, he looked square at her. She felt the warm breeze in her hair and turned her face so that she couldn't see his eyes, the angular line of his nose, the confident, impassive curve of his mouth that gave nothing away. It had never been safe to sit this close to him. She could almost hear him breathe, smell his soap. Dell heard children shouting from down the block and the night air suddenly felt chilly.

"I'm going to call the hospital to check on Anita," Dell said. "Probably head to sleep after."

"Phone's in the kitchen," said Scott. "There's a phone book in the—"

Dell pushed her chair back and headed for the patio door. "Goodnight, everyone."

She closed the door behind her as she heard Scott and Abby's murmured voices saying their goodnights. She heard Mason's voice, saying, "Night, Adella." She pictured him driving home to the airy white farmhouse. She wondered if the painting and the woodwork were finished. She wondered if he went home alone.

Leaning over her elbows at the kitchen counter, Dell used Scott's phone to call reception at the hospital. Anita had not woken. Her surgery was scheduled for the next afternoon. It was routine, the doctor said, an attempt at reassurance.

Predictions and nightmares, Dell often said, have exactly as much power as we give them and no more. As Dell undressed and turned back the covers, she heard Abby's voice saying, *I just can't imagine walking out on family like that.*

She had done better than Abby knew. Walked away from her family in Blyth, and then, months later, turned and walked away from her own child. Dell thought she could forgive herself for leaving Blyth. But walking down those steps into the cold, a mother leaving her baby behind her?

But Dell wasn't really a mother. A birth mother isn't a mother. She had repeated these facts to herself innumerable times over the last year. Whoever had adopted her baby was its mother, wholly and without conditions.

With a can of Mountain Dew and a glass of wine in her belly, Dell was in no shape to rest. She rolled over to the cool side of the bed, kicked the sheets off her feet, then stood up and looked out the window in the dark. A smear of white streaked across the sky, then disappeared.

To a fortune teller, a meteor shower was a blank check. In years gone by, they foretold war, a change of fortunes, an omen of new understanding. Or they were traveling, restive spirits, or they could cure illness or banish ghosts. Dell imagined the Perseids in a cloud of lucid haze above the mountainside. A mirror across the room caught her eye, her reflection in the dark almost a stranger.

From an objective standpoint, silhouetted in the dark, she thought she actually had a better figure since having the baby: the same waist, softer hips, rounder breasts. Five pounds or so had lingered, a souvenir of pregnancy. Her plain, long dresses fit easily whether she was a few pounds heavier or lighter. Dell regarded her thrift store wardrobe as her uniform in which she met each day, greeted the psychic shop and the seekers who wandered in. She needed her clothes to do her work. When she had left Blyth, every object she had acquired was a tool of sustenance, like a shovel or a spear. It was lonely, but it had one thing over her former life—it worked.

Dell sprawled across the bed and watched meteors through the lace-curtained window. She needed Anita to talk, and, failing that—should the worst happen—she would find the baby herself. Without help, out of sheer determination, like she'd done everything else this past year of her life. She would find the child, stay just long enough to look at her. To know that she was safe and loved.

But even then, Dell knew she couldn't return to the psychic shop. Now that Anita knew where to find her, and Scott, and by extension, Abby, she may as well have invited everyone from her high school class too. She could pay out the lease from her savings and move on. Plan a long backpacking trip through the hazy Blue Ridge, something she'd always wanted to do. Or find somewhere else to set up shop, somewhere really far away this time, somewhere good and gone.

CHAPTER NINE
Before
March 1990

The child of a beauty queen and a pill head, Dell had grown up embarrassed by her inherited good looks. People only wrote in ink with their lives here, and people talked before the ink dried. Dell always aimed logically and not too high, not for anything that would dwarf her capabilities or her resources. After high school, she took a secretarial course at the nearby community college, then got an accounting job at a farm equipment store. She lived quiet and simple, and took pride in considering herself a little bit dull. Most of her high school classmates had assumed she'd leave town. Dell wasn't bad-looking, and she was more than a little smart. But she surprised everybody by staying where she came from. At least, she surprised anyone who didn't know that she was afraid to leave her father alone.

One sunny Friday afternoon, Dell left her office in the back of the farm equipment store an hour early and drove into the national forest that bordered Blyth on the south and west. She parked the station wagon at the bottom of a trail and walked uphill. For late winter, it was a warm day, too pleasant to let the last couple hours of daylight pass behind a desk. She wore a lace blouse over blue jeans and sandals. On her shoulder hung a patched red bag, which she carried instead of a purse. Dell had read in a fashion magazine that women who carry large bags deter male interest, the large bags serving as some kind of symbol for an excess of emotional baggage. Suited her fine. She hadn't dated much, anyway, before deciding it wasn't worth the effort. People either loved each other too much, like Dad loved Anita, or the other way around, that is, not enough, like Anita loved Dad.

An access road to the pipeline, for use only by the energy company and its workers, cut across the trail, the thicket cropped short and jagged in its wake. There was a patch of mud on either side, which she walked through, cursing, the mud sucking around her heels as she eyed the withered and brown-gray plants sprayed with pesticides.

Back when they built it, when she was fifteen, representatives of the energy company had promised that the pipeline would escape notice once it was installed. As the years passed, it became a favorite spot for lazy hunters, who would set up in the cleared strip at sunset and take aim at white-tailed deer that came out to graze. Songbirds, though, no longer frequented the woods near the pipeline. The pesticides they used to clear the land didn't always kill the grown birds, but when they ate insects and regurgitated them to feed their young, the hatchlings died. A metallic sort of quiet, and a metallic sort of smell, seeped into the forest on either side. Only last month, a recently repaired segment of the line had loosened, after some heavy snow, and exploded, burning up a hillside of forest. Intense weather was the company's explanation for the incident, a way of saying *not our fault—the weather's fault.*

Money like that knew the trick to escaping consequences, and Dell had figured it out. They made their mistakes on a larger scale than any currency could ever touch: entire stretches of forest lost, with all the life they held. The initial transgression was enough to render apology meaningless. If there was enough left here that she could still take a walk in the woods, that was enough. Only a lingering anxiety remained, pulling her outdoors at every chance, as if to enjoy it while it lasted.

As she walked, she leaned over to pick handfuls of chickweed, a plucky, early spring flower that made a good salve for bites or burns. Nobody was supposed to pick flowers here, but with the rattle of trucks on the access road almost out of earshot, it hardly seemed to matter.

When the path neared a wide, shallow creek, Dell unbuckled her sandals and stepped into the water to rinse the mud from her feet. Melted snow from uphill, the stream rose only to her knees, but with a warning current. Moss and silt dislodged in a cloud between her toes, which were turning pinkish and blue-tipped under the cold water. Dell picked up one foot at a time, swishing her ankles to loosen the mud, holding her long hair back from her face with one hand. Something about it pleased her that way: plain and long. It was possible she took after her mother, but where Anita used cosmetics and styling to soften her features, Dell's bare face, with her sharp cheekbones and pointed chin, had a pale severity. Her eyes were warm, though, and too expressive—she knew this because they were the same as her brother's eyes, which softened his whole face whenever he smiled.

"Hey, do you need a hand?"

"No. I—" Instinct turned her to face the strange voice, swiveling on her heels on the moss-slick stream bed. "I'm fine."

Dell caught a glimpse of pale blue eyes and a ruffle of blond hair, just as she found that she was losing her balance. With a gasp, she landed on her seat in the water, the brisk current swirling around her waist. She sat with a dumb stare.

He was already stepping in after her, reaching out a hand. Dell held tight, felt his callused palm on hers as she pulled up to her feet. She saw the brown jacket and badge of a park ranger, glanced at his eyes, a jolt of blue, and looked immediately back down at her feet. She was steady, but let his hand linger on hers.

Dell heard a bark and whine, and looked up to see a tall, lanky German shepherd pawing at the water.

"Down, London," he said. "That's okay, boy." At the sound of his voice, the dog took a seat and waited, tail flipping. Dell stepped onto the dry land, twigs and brush cold under her feet. She squeezed water from the hems of her jeans, as if it would do any good. The man, taller than her, with straight, slim shoulders, stood back watching her.

"You okay?"

She nodded her head yes, looked up smiling as she sat down to put on her sandals.

"Are you lost?"

Dell shook her head no, realized she was blushing. The man sat on the ground across from her, crossed one leg over the other, scratched the dog's ears. He turned to face her with a cautious smile. "Cold water kind of knocks the breath out of you."

"Yeah, it does." She managed a breathy laugh. "Thanks."

He reached forward, extended a hand. Again, she reached for it, felt his fingers squeezing hers. "I'm Mason."

"Dell Shaw."

"You know, I'm supposed to ask you to leave," he said. "The park closes at dark." At his side, the dog sat forward, ears bristling. "Down, London," he said again, patting the animal's broad shoulders.

"Why's his name London?"

"After Jack London," he answered with a shrug. "Some of my finest teenage angst reading."

Daylight waned, the tree branches overhead cast black against the sky. It would be dark before she got back to her car. She finished buckling her sandals, then held her bag up at a tilt to drain the water out, tumbling her old astrology book, a pocketknife, and a lapful of foraged chickweed blossoms across her legs.

"What's all that?" He grinned and laughed. "What about 'take only pictures, leave only footprints'?"

"Come on. Be honest." She smiled back, tucking her book into her bag. "You don't think this is all going to be gone before our children are old enough to walk?" She felt her neck prickle with an invisible blush. "God, not ours. I mean, mine, or yours, or…" Dell studied his oddly familiar face, the straight brow, a strong nose. "I don't know why I said that," she added. "I'm never having children, anyway."

"I wouldn't jump to conclusions about that."

"Oh, yeah?" Dell laughed out loud. "That's bold."

"No, ma'am. I'm…" He stifled a laugh. "I meant about the forest. The pipeline's an eyesore. But these woods go deeper than you think. If you've never walked them on foot, it's hard to know."

"And you have?"

"Walked the whole trail. Georgia to Maine. I walked through ghost towns," he said. "Places where people lived and worked once. All grown through. Nature starts reclaiming its own, as soon as people back off."

"Yeah, well, they use different poisons now," Dell said, thinking of the photos she'd seen, slicked oil on bird feathers, the death that oozed out from around the pipeline. She tucked the chickweed back into her bag alongside the astrology book. She felt him looking at her, felt her pulse stumble as his gaze traced down her legs.

"It's going to get dark fast," Mason said. "And cold, when it does. You'll be half frozen before you get home. Walk you to your car?"

"Sure." She looked back at him, saw the pale blue spark of his eyes against the twilight. "Just in case you're wondering, my brother's a cop and he'll come looking for me if I go missing." Ever since Scott had graduated the academy and become a police officer, he'd been a constant source of unsolicited advice.

Dell got to her feet and followed Mason back to the trail. When the dog nosed at her palm, she leaned over in greeting, rubbing his ears. It couldn't have been more than two miles back to the parking lot, an easy walk downhill, despite the lowering light.

"Are you from here?" Dell asked.

"I went to the military school outside of town."

"Oh, really?"

"I guess I was supposed to be an officer or something." The way he cut himself off and picked back up, Dell sensed that he wanted to say more, but something stopped him.

"You seem pretty well at home out here," she said. "I certainly didn't hear you sneaking up on me."

"Yeah, because you were busy talking to mermaids in the creek," he said. "What were you doing out there, anyway?"

"Washing my feet." She shrugged one shoulder and pushed her hair behind one ear. "How'd you end up doing this job?"

He laughed, but the hint of a smile faded too quickly. "Only by being a major disappointment to my parents in every way." As if changing the subject, he whistled and called his dog to his side, then pulled out a flashlight, clicked it on and lit the path ahead of her. "My dad's a doctor—just try telling him he doesn't know everything. If you spend enough years listening to people yell at you, believe me, nothing sounds better than walking off into the woods alone. Why am I still talking?"

Dell walked quietly beside him, the rustle of her footsteps muddling the echo of his words. By the half-light, she eyed the crest of his cheekbones, sensing something sharp beneath his surface.

"I don't mind," Dell said. "You know, people always feel like they can talk to me. God knows why—maybe they can tell I don't care enough to judge them."

"You're off the hook," he laughed. "There is nothing else to know about me."

"Figures," she joked. "The one time I'm actually interested to hear more."

"Is that so?" The blue of his eyes suggested an expanse of space, like her voice would echo there if she shouted. "Ask me about something else, then."

"When's your birthday?"

"May fifteen," Mason answered.

"Taurus."

"Is that a good thing?"

"It can be," she replied. If he was a Taurus, he was an anchor of a person, stubborn and careful. Guarded. But then, who wasn't?

"You look familiar," he said. "What's your last name? Shaw?"

"Yes." Dell looked sidelong at him, lips pursed in an uneasy pout. There weren't a lot of good reasons someone from Blyth might have known of her family. "Why?"

"Are you Scott Shaw's sister?" As they walked down the trail, he reached in front of her to hold a bramble out of the way.

"Yeah. You know him?"

"We work together. He volunteers a weekend every so often at the firehouse."

"Don't tell him you saw me. He gets overprotective when he hears I've been out late with strangers." Dell took a step closer as they walked, her shoulder brushing against his, the dog leading ahead of them. She imagined Scott's voice scolding her in the back of her mind: *Out here, all by yourself? And this late? Jesus, Dell, it'd be days before I even knew where to look for you. Think about the rest of us for once.*

"Fair enough. Guess I'm a stranger."

"I don't know your last name, Mason." Dell smiled up at him, stumbled over a root in the path, reached out for his arm at the same moment he reached back to steady her. "I don't know anything about you."

"Okay, then." He reached for a handshake again. "Jeremiah Mason Davis McCallan. The Fourth."

"Oh." Dell pulled her hand free and took an instinctive step backward, felt a chill of memory tickle her spine. "You know, I liked Mason better."

"I've seen you before," he said.

Dell tucked her chin down and kept walking. McCallan. He was the doctor's son, with those pale blue eyes, the boy standing behind the red Lincoln. The boy who had watched as she had begged Anita and his mother and anybody else she thought might listen to her little voice as she shouted *I didn't want him to do it.* Energy sparked in her limbs, ready to sprint off into the trees. Her clothes were wet, her feet sore and damp. How fast could she run even if she tried? Would she turn into a birch, watch bark grow over her skin? *Ovid made it sound like it happened in an instant: a woman running blinks her eyes, grows leaves. That doesn't happen here. No one swoops in to protect you from anything in this world.*

"Hey, did you hear me? I feel like I've seen you before." Dell felt his hand brush her arm. She dug her heels into the ground and spun to face him, her sandals scratching in the dirt.

"Keep your hands to yourself," she hissed, felt the breath hitch in her lungs. "I don't like you."

"Whoa, what?" Mason held his hands up, as if to say he didn't mean any harm. Dell wondered if Mason saw that her lips trembled; saw that her chest rattled, her heart running wild. He gave her a brief, intent glance, then nodded his head. "Sorry. I'm sorry."

She sped up, walking several steps ahead of him, shaking her head so that her hair fell long and dark around her cheeks. The German shepherd walked next to her, his steps light and easy in the near dark. The dog's low growl slowed both of them in their tracks.

"Shh," he hummed. "What is it, London?"

London let out another growl and pulled on his harness, reaching down the path into the dark.

"Quiet." Dell touched his hand. "Look."

Ten feet ahead, a gray wolf sat blocking the path, staring down her nose at them. London was only as tall as the wolf's shoulder, and half as broad. The wolf gave a low, warning howl, an uncanny melody that curled and scratched. Its amber eyes were trained on London. Mason gathered the large dog up in his arms, took a couple steps backward.

"Go on," Mason chided, watching the animal closely. "Go home."

"She is home," Dell whispered. That wolf had never been more at home.

"She? How'd you know?"

"Look at her belly."

The wolf was thin, but she had teats that gave away that she had pups, probably somewhere nearby. Dell drew a silent breath, staring into the vivid eyes. *Were you a woman once? Who took mercy, who transformed you? Are you safe out here?* The wolf lifted an ear with the breeze as if she could hear every rustling leaf, every footstep.

London hung still in the park ranger's arms as the wolf's whin-nying growl lingered in the air. Finally, the creature walked away into the trees, the bewitching melody echoing behind her. Dell looked into the woods after her, half wishing she could follow.

Suddenly, Dell remembered that there was a man with her, someone she didn't want to be alone with. But when she turned to Mason, she saw his lips curl in a smile, his eyes following the wolf with something like reverence. Their eyes met in a silent agreement that whatever they'd just seen was too wreathed in mystery for words.

"You're cold." He took off his jacket and held it out to her.

"I'll live."

"That's right—I almost forgot." Mason wasn't a regular sort of good-looking, his nose a little too straight, his eyes deep-set, but his smile turned all his features bright as daylight. It charmed. "You don't like me."

"I should have said I don't *know* you," Dell said. One of his eyeteeth was chipped. She remembered Scott telling her about the McCallans, how he'd knocked one of the boy's teeth loose in a boxing lesson in middle school.

"Here." Mason held the jacket over her shoulders while she slipped her arms into the sleeves, olive green over wheat-colored lace. "Let's keep moving."

As they walked downhill in the near dark, she let him offer her his arm, hooked her elbow around his. They walked slowly, as if it weren't dark and cold, as if they weren't strangers.

Back in the parking lot, a camel-brown Jeep on tall, rugged wheels was parked next to her station wagon. Mason opened the door and London jumped up into the passenger seat. He leaned against the Jeep and crossed his arms, though he showed no other sign of noticing the cold.

"Guess it's getting late," he said.

"Right," Dell answered. She stood next to him and leaned back, looked at the sky. "I guess it is."

I should leave. That was the right thing to say. The last thing she wanted to do.

"I keep thinking I've seen you somewhere."

Dell looked up and checked the constellations overhead. *Orion, Taurus, Canis Major.* She found herself pulled near him, into the crosshairs of some new, brighter constellation. There was a page in the timeworn astrology book where Dell had underlined the word *disaster.* It came from Greek roots: *dis,* meaning against, and *aster,* which meant star. She liked to take a word apart, parse the meanings of its individual syllables, try to look at the secrets it held.

"I don't know, Mason." She reached up to trace his cheekbone, let her cold fingers sweep a lock of hair behind his ear. "If I had ever seen you before, I think I would remember."

Falling in love could light you on fire and leave you in ashes, leave you a shell. Dell knew that. But she saw only Mason's eyes, bright in the twilight, the deepening dark of the forest behind them. She leaned closer, felt the crest of his nose brushing against her eyelashes. His lips pressed against hers and she felt him inhale, then pull her nearer, one hand resting lightly on her back. She could drown in that feeling, tumble right down that hill and drown.

Dell stepped back, pulled her hands free. "I should go." She should have gone five minutes ago. She should have never been here. "Don't tell my brother I was here. I mean it."

"I won't," Mason answered. "Promise. You can keep the flowers this time. But don't do it again."

"If I come back tomorrow at five, will you be here to kick me out of the park again?"

All her senses blazed and lulled, and she looked up at the sky, saw the stars waver and cross in her dizziness. The worn page of her astrology book leapt to mind. *Crossed stars. Disaster.* Dell wondered if it was her fear that dared her, pushed her forward, as if she were tiptoeing around her fear and her courage, and he was only an object caught in the middle of them.

"What about next Saturday? Wanna come over for dinner?"

"Sure." Dell smiled up at him, thinking that a week and a day sounded like a long time to wait.

"There's no floor in the kitchen right now. Well, there's half a floor. I'm still putting in tile," Mason explained. "Otherwise, I'd ask you over sooner. The house is kind of a project." It was a project that he loved, she could see that.

"I'd like to see it."

Mason talked about his house the way Dell talked about stars. She loved it right then, before she'd even seen it. As she drove home that night, she looked at the sky from the window of her station wagon, the map of twinkling lights, the band of the Milky Way through its middle.

But Dell's thoughts returned to that day, to the boy who stood watching from behind the car as his mother called her a little slut and a liar. How he had looked at his shoes, stared down as if he couldn't stand the sight of her. Dell chewed on her lip, parked the car on the street outside her apartment. As she walked to the door, she hugged Mason's jacket around her against the cold, turned her chin up and took one last look at the sky before she went inside.

Years ago, her brother had made her promise to steer clear of Mason's family, a promise she now found herself ready to abandon. Was this the same temptation Ovid's hapless victims felt, before they made a choice that ended in catastrophe? The tender noise of the wolf's howl swept over the fragments in her mind. In those verses, people stumbled over their pride. Dell didn't feel anything like pride, only an unexpected tenderness for those blue eyes, a newly discovered gravity, pulling her whichever way would lead her to them again.

CHAPTER TEN

Now

July 1991

In the early morning, Dell's heart began to race before her eyes opened. As recollection of the previous day washed over her, she sat up, stretched down to touch her toes, then reached her arms up as high as she could.

In the early sunlight, she studied Scott's guest room for the first time. A whitewashed dresser held a chipped music box and a porcelain bud vase, all in a layer of dust that looked like velvet in the dusky light. On the walls of the small room hung several framed pastel works, wildflowers and seascapes, Monet crossed with beach kitsch.

These were Abby's things, not gardens or graveside flowers perfectly arranged for Scott, but her own things, from a life before she met him. Dell wondered if they had an agreement that her items would be confined to the guest room, or if it had just happened that way. She pawed through her bag, found clean underwear and a black sundress. It had a square neckline and smocking tapering to her waistline, from where its length swung in gauze waves to her calves. These peasant-style dresses had gone out of style at least five years ago. These days, fashionable clothing was angular and sleek, rather than organic and flowing. But pregnancy had taught her to dress for function. There was no sense in skintight blue jeans in weather like this.

Anita's surgery was scheduled for that afternoon. Dell decided there was a decent chance of her opening her eyes before then. If Anita had needed the surgery urgently they'd have done it already. Even Dr. Beaton could not say that she absolutely wouldn't wake up this morning. Dell tucked the blankets back and fluffed the pillows, then ventured out into the hall.

In the rest of the house, Dell recognized the Abby that was Scott's Abby: the cheerfully arranged photographs, the plaid throw pillows on the sofa. Scott's shoes were organized by the door in loving rows. Dell was walking through the den when she heard Abby's voice from the kitchen, smelled coffee and something sharply chemical. Nail polish.

"No, she wouldn't tell us a thing. Quiet, yeah." Abby spoke with energy and comfort, as if to a sister or close friend. Not someone Dell knew. "She looks… The same, I think. Yeah, she looks great. I know, a psychic."

Abby sat at the table in the kitchen. She wore blue scrubs, painting her fingernails while she talked. The battery-powered wall clock read ten till six. Abby looked almost sweet, holding the phone between her chin and shoulder as she did her nails, the phone cord tangling in her permed halo. Dell barely recognized her. She coughed loudly and shuffled her feet in the dark living room.

"Abby, good morning," she said, then feigned surprise. "I didn't realize you were on the phone."

Abby waved to acknowledge her, the nail polish brush clutched between her thumb and index finger. "I've gotta go, Mom. Love you, too."

"Sorry to interrupt," Dell said. "I'm on my way out the door."

"It's fine." Abby resumed painting her nails. "I promised your brother I'd offer you some coffee if you woke up before I left. So." She pointed at the coffee pot on the counter.

Dell nodded a thank you. She opened the cabinet over the sink, chose a bicentennial memorial mug, and filled it with coffee.

"I didn't expect you to be awake this early." Abby finished painting her pinky nail, held out both hands to assess her job. "Why would anyone, if you have the choice?"

"I got used to getting up early, these last several months." She took a seat across the table from Abby, her knees pointed outward, ready to walk away.

"Oh, yeah? Does your psychic shop serve breakfast, too?"

Dell laughed, then narrowed her eyes. Had Abby made a joke? "No. Just started waking up early. It's easier when you like your job."

"I don't mind my job." Abby yawned, turned a worried frown at her reflection in the door of the microwave. "You think I look okay?"

"Yeah. Very pretty. Why?" Dell had always thought of Abby as one of the glamorous older girls, like she was still in high school. Abby was good at makeup and styling her hair, always dressed carefully. But Dell saw Abby staring at her reflection again, lift a fingertip to touch the shadows under her eyes. She began to observe aloud. "You don't mind your job. You're probably pretty good at it. But you wanna be doing something else with your time."

"Sure," Abby chuckled. "Sitting on a beach, holding a drink."

"You want to have children, don't you?"

Abby gave her a wary frown, vulnerability softening her eyes.

"And you thought Scott was the steadiest, most predictable guy out there. And he…" Dell saw the yellow sunlight creeping over the sky, heard the morning birds singing outside. Scott was steady and predictable. Wasn't he? "He isn't sure? Really?"

"You forget you're not at work," Abby snapped.

"Yeah, well, you were kind of a pill last night, too." The satisfaction of being right, seeing it on her face, was worth Abby's anger.

"This isn't your house." Abby lit a cigarette, nicked one fingernail on the lighter. "Oh, shit."

"No," Dell agreed. "It's your house. So why are all your paintings stuck back in the guest room?"

Abby took out a Marlboro Light, pursed her lips round to hold it as she lit a match.

"You ever think about putting them somewhere more visible?" Dell gestured at the kitchen wall. "Out here, maybe?"

"I don't know." Abby exhaled smoke, sat the cigarette in the ashtray. She laid her hands on the table. Her fingernails were carnation pink, flawless except for one index finger where the color had smeared. "We never talked about it when I moved in. There wasn't anywhere else to put them."

Dell reached across the table and squeezed Abby's hands, careful to avoid her nails. "Abby, this is your house. But you haven't finished moving in yet. I don't know why—maybe you do."

"I don't know," Abby repeated. She picked up her cigarette, smoking in long, uncomfortable drags.

"I think that's the real question. But I can tell you, you're very pretty." Dell finished her coffee. "And Scott knows it too. Or he better." She stood up, picked up her bag and settled the strap over her shoulder.

"I get it, alright?" Abby was smiling, a faint blush visible under her makeup. "You're good at this game. Hey, thank you."

"Thanks for the coffee." It was good to see Abby happy. Maybe she wasn't a bad match for Scott. But sometimes people needed a hand seeing their own thoughts. Turning briefly to wave to Abby, she walked through the living room and out the front door.

Dell let herself into the station wagon and wiped condensation from the windshield with her palms. The shell-colored dawn and blue shadows reminded her again of Abby's paintings. Maybe everyone living with a partner had a few treasured things that were theirs alone, hidden away. Dell had no knowledge of the way a couple navigated that balance. She had always lived by herself. Well, mostly.

She wondered again what Mason's farmhouse looked like now, remembering the care he took with every detail. Would her belongings have found themselves stuck away in a quiet, unused guest room? For a moment Dell allowed her mind to wander. She remembered the overgrown herb garden, the chipped granite lions that guarded the drive. The pale blue of the porch ceiling was meant to keep restless spirits away, an old superstition. In any case, Dell thought, Mason was never really sold on that paint she wanted in the bedroom. As she started the engine and turned onto the street, she imagined herself a spirit, a disembodied memory, lingering near a home that was never really hers.

CHAPTER ELEVEN

Now

July 1991

As Dell drew nearer to the hospital, her hands were jumpy on the wheel, her foot too ready to hit the brakes. By the time she parked, her palms were clammy. This time, the waiting room was empty, a bleary-eyed young woman behind the reception desk.

"Morning." She spoke quietly, leaning over the counter. "My mother's here. Anita Barden."

The girl lifted her chin and beamed. "Oh, you go right on in. Bonnie was telling me all about you."

Dell raised an eyebrow. "About me?"

"Oh yeah, about the car accident, and how nice your brother is. We all know Abby." Everybody knew everybody here. "I remember when your daddy died. They brought him here, you know."

"I know," Dell murmured. She wanted to ask where else they would have taken Dad, but bit her tongue.

"Of course, by the time they got him here, there wasn't a thing anybody could do." The clerk lifted one shoulder in a casual shrug, as if chatting with a coworker. "You ever wonder if he did it on purpose?"

"I don't know," Dell answered sharply, cheeks flushed with embarrassment. "At this point, I don't see why it matters, least of all to you."

The girl's mouth flapped dumbly as she stammered. "I didn't mean anything by it. I just…"

Dell gave a loud, exaggerated sigh. "Open the door, please."

She hurried down the narrow hall to her mother's hospital room.

Anita looked the same. Why shouldn't she? Only twelve hours had passed. Watching the rise and fall of her chest, Dell felt a swell of anger. A nurse came in and busied herself while Dell stood by the window. She recorded her vital signs, switched out Anita's IV, tapped on her kneecap with a little mallet.

As Dell tried to pretend she was not watching, the nurse marked two points on Anita's head with a comb. She opened a sterile razor and began to scrape gently at her scalp. The lustrous hair came away in strands.

"What are you doing?" Dell gasped, unaware of her words until she was already speaking. "Stop that—leave her alone!"

The nurse barely looked up. "Not her whole head," she murmured, brushing strands off her gloved fingers into a wastebasket. "Just where they need to cut. Of course, if she wants to shave it all when she wakes up, so it's even, she can."

Just where they need to cut. Of course. Brain surgery. Dell could barely stand to watch as the nurse shaved Anita's head. "Do you have to? Can't you just…" She flinched, crossed her arms to stop herself from physically interfering.

"This operation could save her life." The nurse was unmoved. "She'll understand. You're not gonna get in trouble."

"Sure. Right." Dell was unable to make herself laugh. Anita would have something to say about it when she woke up. She would make a point of waking just to punish somebody for this. Her hair was just as pretty separated from her head, too: deep auburn, coffee-brown, catching the fluorescent light softly as moonbeams as it collected in the trash can.

Dell was startled when Scott walked in.

"Oh, no." He laughed, but she saw the discomfort in his eyes. "Mom's gonna come screaming back from wherever she is to let us know how she feels about that."

"Just what I was thinking," Dell agreed. Scott was in his work uniform, navy blue, the badge cast green in the hospital lighting. "You here for work?"

"Morning break." He sat down in the vinyl chair and sipped from a Styrofoam coffee cup.

"You sleep okay?"

"Yeah. Thanks."

Scott nodded and held his coffee cup close to his face. "Sorry Abby gave you so much grief last night."

"I'm fine."

"Do they have to do that?" Scott winced as the nurse worked with the razor, baring a patch of Anita's scalp.

"I already asked her not to," Dell said.

They waited, watching with quiet dread as the nurse finished her work. The sun was hot through the window, and the room smelled of strong coffee and chemicals. Without ceremony, the nurse left the room with the wastebasket, marked BIOHAZARD, in tow. Anita's slack features, calmer than they ever were in consciousness, next to her remaining auburn locks that lay hastily pushed in every direction, gave Dell the almost comical impression that Anita knew her hair was a wreck and didn't care.

"Left her hair kind of a mess, huh?" Scott tapped his hands on the arms of the chair. "It doesn't feel right to leave it like that."

"Well, I'm not touching it."

Scott and Dell glared at each other. Recalling herself as a short-haired fourteen-year-old, Dell stared at Anita's disarrayed brown mop and wondered why she didn't feel any satisfaction.

"You fix it," Dell whispered. "She likes you."

"You're a girl. You fix it."

"No!" Dell's own hair swayed as she shook her head hard, as if to settle the point that she was not in the business of styling, fixing, or otherwise interfering with her own hair, let alone somebody else's.

Scott's mouth squeezed in a frown as he gingerly lifted their mother's head from the pillow and swept her hair back under her head. With an awkward touch, he returned to sweep a lock out of her eyes. "There. At least it's not all over the place."

"Sure." Dell settled into her chair, yawning. Her arms felt cold, a breeze from the air conditioner pressing against her shoulders, and she stretched, willing her eyes to stay open.

"She's sedated, Dell." Scott sipped his coffee and fixed a suspicious stare on her. "You could have slept in."

"Maybe there's a chance."

"Why are you so desperate to talk to her?"

Dell squeezed her lips to one side. "She's, uh. She's my mother. What do you expect?"

Her brother laughed, a hand clapping against his knee. "Not buying it. If there's something going on, you're welcome to tell me. Are you using drugs? You need some sort of help?"

"Nothing like that." Dell stood up straight, then slouched back against the wall. She remembered Anita scolding her. *Sit up straight. Proper posture makes a lady look ten pounds thinner.*

"Someone who disappears overnight like that is running away from something," he announced, as if it were some hard-won wisdom.

"You think it takes a cop to know that?" Dell smiled gently at his officiousness and he sighed.

"After Dad's funeral, you..." Scott finished his coffee, tossed the cup at the trash can. "You evaporated."

"I don't have anyone, like you have Abby. I needed a change." Dell was tired of answering questions.

"You needed a change so badly, without any warning, you drove off in the middle of the day and never came back?"

"Yeah, that's pretty much how it happened," she deadpanned. "And I'm not here to fix anything. Just need to talk to Anita."

Scott stretched his legs out, marking her with his stubborn stare. Dell knew that apologizing would only fuel his self-righteousness, only make it worse.

"So, tell me about Abby."

"You too?" Scott groaned. "I'll propose when I'm ready, okay?"

Dell held a hand up. "I swear, that's not what I meant. You happy?"

"Oh, that matters to you?"

"Yeah, it does." She leaned over and slapped his arm. "Of course it does. I like Abby."

"That's new." Scott's laugh was hollow. "You sure you're my sister, not some lookalike who walked down out of the forest? Who are you?"

"I like Abby," Dell repeated. "She's got a sweet side. I said, are you happy?"

He laughed as if it were plain. "Better than that. We work. Do you remember when Mom and Dad were happy?"

Dell's gaze skipped over Anita's slack body, the click and hum of the monitors around her, then quickly away. "Not really. Maybe I was too little."

"It's not the end-all thing. Being happy. Look, when I got my badge I spent the first six months on the Friday-night beat, bringing in every dumb kid who lit a couch on fire in a field or drank too much and rolled his ATV in a ditch. Abby was always here, too. Pretty soon, we just figured it out."

"Uh-huh."

"Why are you grilling me?"

"I'm not, Scott. I'm talking with you." Dell saw him glancing at his watch. "She has great taste in artwork."

"Artwork? Thought you were going to say men."

"That too, dummy." Dell smiled. "She's got all these paintings in the guest room. They're…" She didn't like them, not really. It was their simplicity of intent that struck her. Abby had chosen those paintings for herself, and what she picked was peaceful and girlish. Endearing, a girl's handwritten vows of love in the margins of a school notebook.

"Oh, that stuff." Scott shrugged his shoulders. "Look, I've gotta go. You're welcome to the guest room tonight if you need it."

"Thanks," she answered.

"It's good to have you back," he said, halfway out the door. "Feels like things are back to normal."

"Go ahead, Scott," Dell said with a wave of her hand. "Maybe I'll see you later." As the door clicked shut, she wished for a moment that he were right. *Back to normal,* she thought. *But what would that even look like?*

CHAPTER TWELVE

Now

July 1991

After Scott left, Dell sat watching her mother until the sun rose high, spilling in through the window, and she had to move out of its path. She imagined what Anita, who knew how to weaponize the most inane of details, would have to say about her ruined hair. Either she would conceal it, or she would show it off to anyone who would look, praising God for the gift of her life and for never burdening her with undue vanity. *Or something like that*, Dell thought. If she lived through the next couple days.

She heard footsteps, voices in the hallway.

"Ma'am, it's family only."

"I am," a different voice answered in an insistent squeal. "I'm just as close as family."

The door swung open and a stocky, well-dressed woman walked in, trailed by a frowning nurse. This was Judy, one of Anita's devotees from the First Baptist. She was blonde, wearing a chartreuse twinset and khaki shorts, with a look on her face that Dell disliked on instinct. A sort of self-propelled engine of righteous drama. Under one arm, Judy carried a gift bag and a paper-wrapped parcel.

"Please, ma'am, I don't want to call security."

The woman began to squeak again.

"Let her stay," Dell said. "I don't mind."

The nurse gratefully turned and left the room.

Judy fawned and kept right on squeaking, giving Dell a wide smile. "You must be Anita's girl."

"She's my mother, yes."

Judy bustled past Dell, oblivious to her contemptuous stare. "I've brought her some magazines, a change of clothes from her apartment." She deposited the package and gift bag at the foot of Anita's bed, which Dell found ridiculous. "Surely they can't ask a woman like her to wear a hospital gown the whole time she's here."

"Yeah, I'm sure that'll mean a lot to her in this state." Dell moved the gifts from the bed to the end table by the sofa.

"You're as pretty as she is, almost. You're Adella, aren't you? The psychic?" Judy stepped closer and touched Dell's wrist. "I remember when you were just a little girl."

"Anita told you I'm a psychic?"

"Yes, honey." Judy walked the narrow perimeter of Anita's bed, clucking and shaking her head. "I see her at church every Sunday, and we meet on Wednesdays for tea. We share a great deal."

"Oh, yeah?"

"You look really well, dear. Especially for a woman who had a baby hardly six months ago." Judy raised an eyebrow, as if she thought this information could shock or disarm.

"She promised not to tell anyone that." Dell couldn't even summon a pretense of surprise. Of course Anita had to bend facts to suit her theater. She watched Judy hovering over Anita's prone limbs. Maybe Anita had told Judy something she hadn't told Dell.

"Oh, I don't count. I don't run my mouth," Judy insisted. "Anita and I are like sisters."

"What exactly did she tell you? About me, the baby?"

Judy's eyes shone, fairly dripping with feeling. "Oh, Anita always wanted to be a grandmother. She was so, so happy when you became a mother."

Dell snorted a laugh. "I'm not a mother. I'm a birth mother. That's different." Sure, Anita had wanted to be a grandmother. So badly that when Dell asked her to help her care for the baby, she'd flatly turned her down.

"Oh?" Judy's eyelashes fluttered, her full cheeks quivering. "Anita said you took the baby and moved away."

Dell bent over laughing, holding her stomach. She felt her eyes water, sat up and stretched her shoulders to take a deep breath. "Oh, Judy. I needed a laugh. You shouldn't trust a word she says."

"What are you talking about?"

"That child was adopted. The day after she was born. You're telling me you don't know anything about that?"

"Nothing," Judy stammered.

The monitors beeped and hummed steadily as they spoke, as if Anita were lying there, taunting Dell. *Maybe you can divine that.*

"Well, who are her friends? Who else does she talk to?"

"I'm her friend," Judy said. She looked with some uncertainty between Anita and Dell, not sure who she believed. "You know, she still talks to the Haneys now and then. But I'm telling you, she'd never lie to me."

"Sure," Dell said. "Sure, she wouldn't. I'll tell her you brought the clothes and stuff if she ever wakes up." She squeezed her eyes shut and inhaled, opened them to find Judy watching her with something like concern. "She's got to, right?"

"There's a lot of good people praying for her, honey."

"Thanks, Judy. And thank you for talking with me."

Judy murmured something unintelligible and walked quickly back toward the lobby, her heels squeaking against the tile. Dell sat in the armchair, felt slighted by the ceaseless ticks and beeps from the hospital machinery.

Dr. Beaton walked in, flanked by two nurses rolling a stretcher. "We're scheduled to start in an hour. Let's get her into pre-op. Ma'am, do you need some more time?"

"No, thank you," Dell said. She walked toward the doorway and hesitated, remembering Anita as she used to sit in her favorite stool at the sports bar. Her mother used to tell her, *You will grow up to be so pretty, even prettier than me,* and although Anita did not know it, that was very likely the truest way she had to say she loved you. Anita could hold up a finger and tell you when the room was buzzing with talk about her, and she would do so like a weather vane, one hand on her Long Island iced tea, the glass smudged with her lip gloss. *If people are gonna talk,* she would purr, *you may as well stand up straight.*

"Dr. Beaton?" Dell paused in the doorway, stood up tall as she looked back at Anita.

"Ma'am?"

"Remember that's my mother. You take good care of her today."

CHAPTER THIRTEEN

Before

April 1990

That Saturday, early spring rustled with tender greens and yellows. The tail end of winter was full of false starts: a few days of warm weather that brought sprouts up, then days of more cold. The breeze coming in at the open windows was warm and damp and the smell of new growth in the forest filled the car. Near the pipeline, part of the road to Dad's house had turned to mud, where the absence of flora let the dirt wash downhill as the snow melted. The Volvo's tires lagged and whined before they pushed through the mud with a jolt.

On any ordinary spring day, the car would have stuck. This was just good luck. Dell had an extra pair of boots on the back seat exactly for patches like this, where she had to get out and push to get the car moving.

When Dell parked outside the cabin, she saw that Scott's pickup truck was already there.

"Hey, there." Her brother waved from a rocker on the front porch as she opened the car door and got out. "How are you?"

Dell straightened her blouse, tucked into tight jeans, and leaned over to take her bag from the passenger seat. "Good." She smiled in greeting, shaking her head to toss her braided hair over her shoulder. "I can't stay long. Got somewhere to be today."

"That so?" Scott eyed her outfit as she climbed the steps to the porch. "You look nice."

"Thanks." She ruffled his hair as she walked past to peer inside through the screen door.

"Where's Dad? He okay?"

These weekly meals with Dad, one or both of them dropping by on the pretense of a meal, were an informal tradition they'd struck up after too many nervous phone calls. *When did you last hear from him?* Today, Dell was cooking. Her bag was filled with rosemary-flecked homemade rolls, sliced roasted chicken, and a bundle of mustard greens tied together with string.

"Yeah, he's fine." Scott answered in a whisper. "Today he's fine."

Dell nodded and took a seat on the porch swing. The jeans pinched her stomach when she sat down. She hadn't worn them since high school. Hugging all the curves of her hips, they were less comfortable than her dresses, but when she had worn them the week before, she'd liked how Mason's eyes had followed her.

"There she is!" The screen door creaked open and swung shut behind Dad as he walked outside. "Not a second too soon. We're starving."

Dell jumped to her feet and gave her father a hug. Her heart turned a familiar leap, relieved to see him sober. He smelled like flannel and tobacco.

"How're you doing, Dad?" She leaned against the doorframe, studying his complexion, measuring the clarity in his eyes.

"Good, kid." He patted her shoulder. "Something's different. You look nice."

"Thanks, I guess."

"How's your mother?"

Dell shrugged her shoulders. She hadn't seen Anita since Christmas.

"She's fine," Scott said. "She's doing well, Dad."

Dell let the screen door fall shut with a whistle behind her. The house had not changed since they were children, filled with the furniture Dad and Anita had bought when they built the place in 1962. The handmade table in the kitchen used to leave splinters in Dell's hands, but it had worn smooth over years of use. A deer's head was mounted on the wall, which she always studied with a mix of fascination and pity. While Scott and Dad talked outside, she turned on the oven to warm up the rolls, put a slice of butter in the cast iron pan that lived on the stovetop. She hummed while she cooked, tuneless, cheerful. Today, everything was fine.

There in the cabinet over the stove were the yellow, floral-printed dinner plates that she'd used as a child. She filled the plates, topped Dad's extra high with chicken and bread. Next to Scott's plate and her own, glasses of ice water; for Dad, she took a can of Mountain Dew from the several dozen in the fridge, which held almost nothing else. The table was set, the damp breeze off the mountainside billowing the plaid curtains over the open windows. It needed something else. Something for a fine day.

"Is lunch ready?" Scott asked as she stepped outside.

"Almost." Dell walked down the stairs and into the overgrown garden. In the tall grass near the trees, the secretive little blossoms of springtime showed their pale faces: Jacob's ladder, seashell-colored liverwort, nodding bluebells. She plucked a handful of each, carried them back toward the house. A centerpiece.

Dad and Scott were already at the table setting into their food.

"Started without you," Scott said. "You're a better cook than Abby. Been a while since I've seen real food."

"I don't mind." Dell filled a glass with tap water and arranged the flowers in the center of the table.

"Leave those flowers and eat, kid." Dad grinned, his teeth yellow behind his beard, and took another bite of his roll. Dad's good days had always been a special occasion. Rain in a drought. Dell watched him with the same compulsion as someone putting out every cup and bowl they could find to catch the fleeting shower. "Anything new? How's life?"

"I'm fine. How've you been?" She sat back in her chair and stabbed at the greens with her fork, realized she'd forgotten to add any salt. She never forgot to add salt when she was cooking, but today wasn't a regular day.

"Your smile hasn't changed, Strawberry." Dad looked up from his plate, watched her eat. Her fork hovered over the plate. "You grew up at some point, but when you laugh, I still see that five-year-old in dusty jelly sandals."

"Should I thank you?"

"What you should do is think about having your own kids." Dad pointed his fork at her. "I miss little feet running around this place."

"Oh, I..." Dell laughed again, uneasy. "Why don't you ask Scott, Dad? He's the one who has a girlfriend."

Dell saw that her braid had fallen into her greens. She squeezed her napkin around it, trying to wring the liquid off. Drippings from the greens seeped onto her shirt, smelling of butter and garlic. She looked up to see her brother glaring at her.

"Kids? Not me," Scott said, raising his hands. "Hey, is that all you're gonna eat, Dell?" He never missed a beat.

"Unlike you, I'm still single," Dell answered. "I don't want to lose my figure. How's Abby?"

"Excuse me for a minute." Dad pushed his chair back, stood up, walked down the hallway. He passed the bathroom, walked into his bedroom. The door pulled shut behind him. Dell and Scott fell silent, looking across the wide table at each other. She glanced anxiously after him, half stood up.

"Sit." Scott reached across the table, let his hand rest on her arm. "Look, I asked him again about getting clean today."

"And?"

"What do you think?" He gestured down the hallway, lowered his voice. "Dell, you've got to be ready for the worst." She watched in disbelief as he ate a bite of chicken, looked down at her food growing cold.

"I thought we were having a nice time, though. Why'd he have to—"

"It's not about you," Scott said. "It's not because of you. Doesn't mean he don't love you."

"How do you know?"

"Jesus, Dell." Scott's whisper whittled to a hiss. "I don't. It's what I tell myself, okay?"

Dell stood up and pushed in her chair, began washing the dishes. Scott stood up to help her, drying the dishes as she washed them.

"Abby's fine," he continued. "She planted a nice garden in the front yard. The house is better with her there."

"Sounds like you two made a good trade. She plants your garden, you let her live in your house?" Dell handed Scott a plate.

"Sure," he laughed. "I even take her out to dinner sometimes."

"Kind of you," Dell laughed. "Four years in? I bet you marry her." He ignored her, took the last glass from her hand, wiped it dry.

Dad walked back into the kitchen, stretching his arms over his head. "Kids, that was a fine meal. Think I'm gonna take a few hours and lay down."

Scott slapped Dad's shoulder. "I'm gonna stay for a while, if you don't mind. Mow the lawn for you, or something."

Dell picked up her bag, training her eyes away from Dad as he hugged her. "Take care, Strawberry."

"Love you, Dad."

Dad turned back down the hall before she was out the door. The breeze stilled, then pulled back, the curtains concave in the window frames.

"Come on," Scott repeated, shepherding her toward the door. "Something had you in a fine mood when you came over here. That something have a name?"

"No." She paused, standing by the kitchen table.

"You sure?"

"Definitely." Dell could only imagine what Scott would say if she told him. *Sure, he has a name. The one boy you told me to stay away from. Remember? They don't like us and they do not make empty threats.*

"Well, whatever it was, you go and have a good day. This place is never gonna change."

"Okay, Scott. You have a good day, too." Dell took the wildflowers, stems dripping, from the glass on the tabletop. She opened the screen door, then turned back. "Don't stay too long."

"I'm just gonna keep an eye on him for an hour or so." Scott pulled out a chair and sat down. Dell knew he would be here more than an hour, that he would stay till Dad got out of bed, or sobered up, or till Scott had to go to work. "Go," he repeated, his smile forced, shooing her with a wave. "Take those flowers and get out of here."

CHAPTER FOURTEEN

Before

April 1990

When Dell drove back toward Blyth, she gunned the pedal, splattering mud as the car skidded through the washed-out patch of the road. She rolled down all the windows and turned on the radio, scanning till it landed on a Joan Baez song. Dell returned to her apartment, a studio on the third floor of the blue Victorian house that was converted for rentals.

She set aside a handful of her flowers and shaped them into a bundle to dry, which she laid in an empty wine rack, de facto converted into a drying rack for flowers and collected plants. She was not above an occasional drink. If her approach tended toward the ascetic, it wasn't from an abundance of discipline, but more that she liked to see how much she could do with how little. To do without a habit for alcohol was a type of self-sufficiency she hadn't seen much of growing up, and it felt to her like a kind of frontiersmanship, not needing a drink every day.

Dell gingerly bundled the rest of the flowers into her bag. She threw open her closet, picked out a blue top with flowers embroidered in white around the collar, changing in front of her mirror. The table beside her bed was stacked with uneven piles of books. *Medicinal Plants of Appalachia.* Jane Austen, Edith Wharton. Ovid's *Metamorphoses.*

She pushed the paperbacks aside and picked up her favorite old astrology book, bookmarked to the page about disasters. But when she rehearsed those familiar, lyrical lines to herself, all she could think of was the stars that night, how bright the constellations over Mason's shoulder were, how she had wanted to fall into his kiss, see how far she could go. She thumbed through the pages, found the profile for Taurus. *The Taurus sun cultivates their independence, so as not to rely on anyone else when life throws them a curveball. Reliable. Practical. Efficient. An eye for beauty.* She tilted the book and it fell open to Libra, her own sign, which she reread although she knew it by heart. *Charming, with a strong sense of justice. Avoids emotional challenges. Romantic above all else. Tell me something I don't know.*

When the doorbell buzzed, Dell picked up the jacket he had put around her shoulders the night they'd met. She descended the first flight of stairs two steps at a time, paused at the landing of the second, and walked down at a casual pace.

She opened the door to a cold breeze. Mason was waiting, one hand on the porch railing, studying the sky.

"Adella, hey." He turned to face her. There was the rush of seeing someone who'd so often occupied her thoughts, whose face she still hadn't memorized. The sand-colored hair that swept across his eyes. He wore a white shirt, sleeves rolled to his elbows, a smudge of dust at the shoulder.

"I brought your jacket." She took a step nearer to him.

"Keep it," he said. "You might need it. Look at those clouds."

A pale gray cloud front was spilling over the mountains past the edge of town. More cold weather; maybe snow. The Jeep, he promised, was fine in any kind of weather. Mason opened the door, helped her in. Dell smiled down at him from the worn seat. The blue jeans were a good choice.

North of Blyth, away from the pipeline, Oracle Avenue was a sharp left off of Main Street, a road that narrowed the farther it got from town. The driveway was a wide, graveled semicircle. Two chipped concrete lions, speckled with moss, sat at the head of a walkway. Mason parked the car, came around to open her door, but she had already jumped down.

"This is your house? Are you serious?" The shadowy Victorian farmhouse stood at the edge of a long meadow, weathered white paint casting it almost the same shade as the gray sky behind it. She saw wide windows, a long, covered porch that wrapped around two sides of the house, wood carved in a lacelike pattern around the roof.

"Yeah, well. It's not so impressive once you get inside. I told you, it's a project."

"That's okay." She followed him past the lions, up the footpath, bordered with overgrown firethorn bushes clustered with bright berries, and reaching arms of thorns.

"The trick is to see it as a whole," Mason said, holding aside a branch of thorns that stuck out from the hedge. "Not the pieces. Think you can do that?"

Dell nodded her head yes. *Taurus. An eye for beauty.*

As they climbed the steps of the porch, she looked up, saw that the porch ceiling was painted a pale, delicate blue.

"I know," he said, following her eyes. "Interesting color choice. It's a superstitious thing."

"Haint blue." She waited by the door. "It keeps the spirits away."

"That's what my granddad said."

"So you promise me you don't have any ghosts in here?"

As Mason unlocked the door, she heard the dog's welcoming bark. "Only a big, hairy one named London," Mason said. "I promise. Come on in."

Dell hesitated, glancing up at the whispering pale blue, wondering if she were the ghost it was meant to keep away.

Inside, the house was chilly. The foyer opened on the right into a wide living room with aged hardwood flooring and a brick fireplace. In the otherwise bare area, a leather sofa and a low coffee table faced the fireplace. Mason put an armful of kindling branches and a couple of logs into the fireplace. Dell watched, letting London sniff her hands. "I'll give you the tour in a minute," he said. "Just getting a head start on the cold."

"How long have you lived here?"

"My granddad left me the house when he died a couple years ago. But no one's lived here since the 1970s. That was when I knew he had it in for me. Pain in the ass, old mess like this." He smiled at her, held a match under the kindling. The fire lit with ease.

"Did you know him well?"

"Yeah." Mason squished an old newspaper page into a ball, pushed it under a log, his fingers dodging the flames with expert quickness. "I stayed with him after I left my parents' house."

"They kicked you out? Why?"

"It was mutual," he answered, filling the pause with a short, measured exhale. "You always this nosy?"

"Oh, I'm…"

"Sorry. It's not something I talk about much." Mason turned away from the fire and stood up abruptly, brushing his knees off. "Did you want to see the rest of the house, or not?"

Dell looked at London and silently asked: *Did I say something wrong?* When the dog trotted after Mason, she got up and followed.

She took his outstretched hand, callused, smudged with ash from the fireplace. They walked through the dining room, where he held her arm and warned her to avoid a rotten patch in the floor. A dusty cabinet stood in the corner, still filled with dishes, a bird's nest in one compartment. They continued into the high-ceilinged kitchen, where she saw the tile he had spent the last week installing. Across the counter, vintage black-and-white tiles, a breakfast nook bordered by wide windows and a Dutch door.

"You can see the garden he and my grandma planted out here."
Mason unhinged the top half of the door. Overgrown perennial
herbs, rosemary as tall as her shoulder, lavender, a pair of peach
trees. There was more she couldn't make out, overgrown now
with weeds.

"This is beautiful."

"It's held up pretty well, considering nobody's taken care of it in
ages. I know how to fix the house, but I'm no good with plants."

"It just needs some love."

"That something you can help me with?"

"Oh, sure. I'm really good with plants."

That wasn't what he meant. She blushed, standing with her hands
on the doorframe next to him. The kitchen smelled of smoke from
the fire and the sharp fragrance of the herb garden. She wasn't sure
she believed him when he said there were no spirits here.

CHAPTER FIFTEEN

Before

April 1990

Dell followed Mason up the stairs to the second floor, where he showed her its empty bedrooms, white sheets thrown over old bed frames. The sunroom, on the corner of the house, with two walls of windows, took her breath away.

"It needs a good clean." The windows were dusty, cobwebs in the corners, an animal nest and a cracked window. "But if you can picture it."

"I can picture it." Dell pulled the borrowed jacket snug around her neck. "Flowers, leafy plants. Something that smells really good—jasmine, maybe. A turntable in that corner. A wicker seat with linen cushions." She pointed to a spot on the floor near the window and sat, smiling.

"I was hiking the Appalachians when my grandfather got sick. Cancer." Mason sat next to her. "I came back home to find he'd died a month before. He used to tell me he was afraid this house would always be empty."

Dell leaned against his shoulder, draped her arm over his back. Her hand trailed over his upper arm, the muscles tense.

"Then there are ghosts here, in a way," she said. "Happy ones. They're glad to have you here."

"I like you, Dell." Mason laughed. She felt the set of his shoulders ease under her touch. "It sure does get quiet, though." He rose to his feet and helped her up, holding both her hands. "How about dinner?"

The stairs creaking under their feet sounded welcoming. She followed him back into the kitchen, sat on a tall stool at the counter and watched while he cooked. Scrambled eggs and pancakes. He knew exactly where everything was, assembled each dish in order with practiced ease, paused between flipping pancakes to fill a bowl of dog food and set it by the door with a shake. The kitchen was sparsely stocked, everything in neat rows. He worked with the type of organized habit that only developed in solitude. Dell watched as he stacked two plates with food, nodded at the doorway to the living room.

"Let's eat in there, where it's warm."

She lingered behind him, remembered the flowers in her bag. An empty drinking glass sat by the sink, which she filled with tap water. As she walked through the doorway to the living room, she arranged the delicate stems and blossoms in the glass, stopping an arm's length away from Mason.

"I brought you these." She looked up from the flowers.

"Thank you."

The air was heavy. Dell sat on the sofa across from the fire and placed the flowers in between their plates. She hadn't eaten since picking at her lunch.

"What are they?"

"They're…" Staring into his eyes, the names of the flowers which she knew so well disappeared from her mind. She cut through the stack of pancakes with her fork, a clink against the plate. "They're spring ephemerals. Flowers that bloom up early, while it's still cold like this. They disappear before the weather gets warm. Like they were never there."

"I see."

They ate quietly, watching the fire like some might watch a television. She pictured the house as she ate, its silent, cold bedrooms, those windows that let the drafts in. Then, she realized, she had not seen that one of them looked inhabited.

"You did say you live here, right? Which room is yours?"

"When I was little, whenever family visited my grandparents here, all the kids slept in the loft on the third floor. I set up a room up there. Sort of." Mason paused over his plate. "All the second-floor bedrooms still feel like the adults' rooms. Stupid, right?" He sat his plate on the ground, called his dog over, nodded permission to finish the food.

"Oh, can I see it?"

"Yeah, if you want."

London trotted beside Mason as he walked up the stairs. Dell trailed a few steps behind, looking at the walls, the paler squares in the paint where pictures had hung. Up another flight of steps, this one dusty and less stable.

"Watch that stair." He held her hand as she climbed two steps at once. The loft spanned the width of the house, whitewashed floorboards, white walls, shadowed with dust. In one corner, a door to a small bathroom stood open. A flannel dog bed sat to the right of the door. On the far wall, a large, round window looked out over the meadow, the mountains rising behind it. By the fireplace, she saw a single armchair and a camping cot, next to a bottle of water and a paperback.

"Sorry," Mason said. "It's freezing in here." He turned away from her and sat in front of the fireplace, again stacking kindling, a log. Methodical. Dell stood by the doorway watching him. London gave a happy-sounding sigh, stretched out in the dog bed by the door to relax, guarding. It was a campsite. A man and his dog. Some part of him was still a kid who'd walked off into the woods, tired of getting yelled at.

Dell sat in the armchair and watched as he built the fire. The room was dotted with remnants of children's weekends here. A dusty tin can telephone, still connected by twine, sat in the windowsill. Tiny toy cars. A small shoe strewn with cobwebs and dust rested in one corner. *There are spirits here,* she realized. *We can join them. We can be safe here, too. With your dog guarding the door.* When Mason stood up, she scooted over. He sat down beside her.

"This room felt like home," he said, picking up her hand, tracing over her fingers. "At some point, I guess I should choose one of the rooms on the second floor."

"Oh, I don't think so."

"You don't?"

Laughing, she reached her arms around his shoulders, leaning her chin against his neck, wrapped her hands over his eyes, felt the edges of his cheekbones under her fingers. "Listen. I can see it perfectly. Pretend I can see the future."

"And you need to cover my eyes for this?"

"Yes. Focus. This would be our room. A little rug by the door. A bookshelf and a desk over there, by the small window. And the walls are blue."

"Blue?"

"Yeah." She turned his face toward her, let her lips meet his. "I think it needs to be blue. Now you picture it. Name three things you can see."

"I can't."

She pulled her hands free, embarrassed. "You don't see it."

"No, I do."

Dell eased her shoulders away from him, pictured her feet walking to the doorway.

"I can picture it," Mason repeated. His hand traced over her cheek, the slope of her neck, touched the full curve of her lower lip. "But I don't see things in pieces. There's no three things. Only you."

Dell had dated before. She had been with four men, none of whom she'd intended to marry. But this was something different. When it came to bodies, to how bodies were together, men always either left her out or left her cold and bored. It drew a hard line between her thoughts and her body, one leaving the other in the dust. An inversely proportional relationship. Dell believed that if she ever did fall hard for anyone, it would burn her right into ashes, like Dad loving Anita, a ghost alive. But here, with Mason, she didn't find herself distracted, didn't find that she needed to talk herself into it, as his hands sketched over her shoulder blades, as the neckline of her top slipped aside. Dell let her hands trace his hipbones, tug at the button of his jeans.

She found that she was more of one piece, not less, as Mason pulled her up, as they stumbled to the bed. And as he counted her features with his hands, he saw her whole, not in pieces. Dell was assembled, put together by Mason's company. Maybe love didn't have to burn you up. Mason wasn't here for just her body. He wanted to see her face, her smile, her gasp, her exhausted smirk. Then, he wanted to hold her as sleep crept over them, her legs tangled with his. He snored softly, with his chin tossed back, and Dell knew she could trust him.

She woke to breakfast, pancakes and eggs again, pushing hair and sleep from her eyes.

"This okay? Sorry." Mason's smile didn't look the least bit sorry, in jeans and a threadbare t-shirt that gave away every move he made. "It's the only thing I know how to cook."

Dell sat up in bed, holding the covers against her chest. "It's perfect," she said. "Get over here. I'm starved."

CHAPTER SIXTEEN

Before

July 1990

Spring came late that year, so summer felt early. All of a sudden, the days were long, blazing hot. The farmhouse was breezy, comfortable, with oversized windows and fans placed throughout the house for drying paint and sawdust. When Mason had inherited the farmhouse and decided to fix it up, he had started projects all over the house: a new screened-in porch, kitchen walls with repurposed tile, refinishing old hardwood, all of it taking shape piecemeal, so that every room was in various stages of deconstruction. He had a talent for seeing components of a whole that did not exist yet, of seeing things through.

By July, the loft bedroom was dusted, the windows trimmed with white curtains. A tall, wrought-iron bed frame, spread with an old quilt, had replaced the cot. Even though they spent their free days cleaning and restoring the house, Mason left the deserted toys where they sat lining the floor, left the vine creeping in through the cracked window, as if he didn't really want it any different.

But he had no such nostalgia for the living room, the old bedrooms on the second floor; all scrubbed, refinished, repainted. In the mid-morning light that poured through the windows of the second-floor bedroom, Dell pressed a length of painter's tape to the bottom eight inches of the window frame.

"All done?" Mason asked from across the room. He sat on the foot of the stepladder, a paintbrush resting between his hands. Yellow smudged his hands and t-shirt. London wandered into the room, sniffed at the smell of paint in the air, cocked his head.

"Just about," she answered. "It's coming together fast."

"You're telling me." Mason tilted his head and laughed. "I was set on painting all the bedrooms white. Cool, simple. You say 'this room should be yellow,' next thing I know I'm standing here with a brush." He lifted the brush to a bare spot on the wall, then pointed it at her. "You're casting some kind of spell on me."

Dell crossed the room and took the brush, let her leg brush his shoulder as she painted. "There's a spell, alright. But I didn't cast anything." Mason turned to face her, pressed his cheek against her thigh. "It's the stars over your shoulder," she said. "It's how your eyes are so blue in the sunlight and gray at night." She leaned down to kiss him, felt his breath quicken. She could never get close enough to him, his voice, his smell. Her hands draped around his shoulders, let the paintbrush fall to the drop cloth under their feet.

But those stars that had looped her in had spelled out a warning, too. Caught her and him both in their laces, some constellation she'd never seen before. She stared into Mason's eyes and then traced a fingertip across his eyebrow, down his cheekbone, resting her hand on his neck. Those stars hadn't taken into account the warmth in his eyes, his hair ruffled from sleep, how it felt to watch their repairs on the farmhouse coming together under their hands. This was what she wanted: the two of them, out here like two kids run away into the mountains. Maybe the haint blue of the porch was here to guard her, not to keep other spirits out. Outside, there was another world to think about, where Dell had an apartment she barely visited, where she was going to visit her father for lunch today, where Mason had to be at work in an hour.

"We ought to get upstairs." Dell bent down, fussed with the taped border below the window. "You need to get to work soon. And I'm going to meet my dad for lunch; I need to get dressed."

"Sure. Let's go."

As she stood up, her stomach turned. *There's something else.* An odd feeling in between her belly button and her spine gave Dell an unshakeable sense that someone else was in the room. She braced a hand on the wall, squinted through the stars that crowded her vision. It was just her, Mason, and London. The dog whined, nosed at her hands and stomach.

"Dell."

She let herself lean into his arms, sat on his knee.

"I feel funny."

"You okay, baby?"

"Yeah. Paint fumes, probably." She stood up, holding Mason's hands to pull him with her. "Let's go upstairs. Big day."

"Yeah?"

"You have to work." She leaned against his shoulders, touched his chest. "I have to go by my dad's house. Then swing by my apartment to pick up a change of clothes."

"Oh, you want me to go with you?"

She shook her chin. "Not this time."

"Why not?"

"One day soon."

Too good a chance you'll mention me or him to your folks. Too good a chance your father or mother tells you how they know him. I'll deal with that when I have to. Not now.

As Dell followed Mason up the stairs, he looked over his shoulder, raised an eyebrow. "You know, there's plenty of room for your clothes here."

"You think so?"

"You kidding?" As they walked into the loft, he swung an arm to indicate all the empty space around them. "Bring everything you've got."

The yellow sunlight fell rich and warm on the walls. But in the bathroom, the shadows lingered. Dell turned on the shower, flipped the light switch on. She heard a sibilant whistle that might have been the rush of the old shower, might not. The light flickered out, the small hiss of a dead bulb.

"Light's out," she called. Pushed open the doorway to let in some sunlight, stepped under the shower in the near dark.

"That switch is tricky," he called back. "I need to redo the wiring. Bedroom light's on that fuse, too, does the same thing."

Following her into the bathroom, London growled gently. "It's okay. I'll be right out, boy," Dell said. "Go on."

Dell showered quickly, using Mason's soap and shampoo. Spent a moment scratching dried paint off her fingernails. Out of the shower, she draped herself in a towel, walked out into the light of the bedroom. In the top right drawer of the old dresser, she found a clean floral print dress, dropped the towel and slipped it over her head. She heard Mason's whistle as she wiggled into the material.

"Hush," she laughed. "This thing's tighter than it ought to be. You think I've gained any weight?"

"Trick question," he said. "You've never been more beautiful than you are right this minute."

"You're, what, twenty-nine?" She picked up her hairbrush from the dresser. "Why are you still single?"

"I'm not," Mason protested. "I am clean off the market. I'm yours."

"You know what I mean." Dell watched him closely. "Never met anyone who got along with your parents?"

Mason laughed out loud. "That's a high bar. My folks are..."

"They're what?"

"I told you, I didn't always get along with them."

"Right." Dell leaned over, swept her hair over her shoulder. "I remember."

Distance flickered across Mason's face. His eyes were stern, as if he were reprimanding somebody else, not his younger self. "I was wrong, holding it against them for so long. Going off on an eight-month hiking trip. I came back and my granddad was gone."

"Holding what against them?" she asked.

"Doesn't matter," he said. "Maybe my dad was kind of a hard-ass. He'd hit you if you came in five minutes past curfew." He paused as if deciding against giving any further examples. Dell sat at the foot of the bed, re-evaluating Mason's quiet manner. She understood that there was a great deal he chose not to share with her.

"You were just a kid." She wanted to hold every part of him that had ever been hurt.

He frowned at her. "The truth is, I was a bad kid."

"You were never a bad kid." Dell remembered Mason sharing her gaze from behind his father's red car. Volunteering himself for his mother's anger to pull the spotlight off her. She leaned forward on her elbows and kissed him, wished she could absorb the tension in his eyes.

"Listen." He pushed his hair out of his eyes and turned a guarded stare on her. "Whatever problems my family had, they were my fault, and they're in the past. I don't even remember much of anything before I was eighteen. Maybe there's still broken parts in here—I don't know."

"There's nothing wrong with you." Dell scooted closer to him, wishing she could forget her teenage years, too. "Whatever made you who you are—that doesn't matter to me."

He pulled her close, both of his arms tight around her, so she couldn't tell if he wanted to protect her or devour her.

"Do you think you could come to dinner with my folks sometime? They'll love you," he said. "Who wouldn't?"

"I'm not so sure that's true." Dell bit her lip. Mason hadn't met her family. She hadn't pushed the issue.

"I know it is," he answered. "What is that?"

"What's what?" She pulled herself back into the present and looked at him with caution.

"That sad look you get sometimes. You've got a sort of melancholy streak."

Dell held his stare with an apologetic smile. If she had a melancholy streak, she came by it honestly. "Do you love me anyway?"

"Yes. God, yes." The warmth of his smile made her feel hopeful that, somehow, those memories, those crossed stars, would just forget she was here. That they wouldn't be able to breach the pale blue that guarded the porch of this house.

"Maybe I'll go to the hardware store later and pick up some more paint while you're gone."

She batted her eyelashes, inched closer to him. "Promise you'll get the blue."

"I still think white would look better than... what's that blue you wanted? Juniper Berry whatever?"

Dell leaned close and held both of his hands. "Juniper Berry Mist." The blue paint chip was still laying on the floor. She picked it up, held it against the wall. "Picture this space in blue. With the light coming in it'll look coppery and warm like the mountain does at sunset. It'll be warm in the winter and cool in the summer."

Mason ran his hand down her thigh. "I'll tell you what it is," he said. "Blue's your color. It suits you and you know it."

Her cheeks flushed pink. She tugged the brush through her hair. "Hey, if you do go out, can you get me some ice cream? Strawberry?"

"Anything you want." Mason sat up in bed and scratched at the stubble on his jaw. "You know I don't like keeping this a secret. It's weird, going to work with Scott. Feels like you're hedging your bets."

"Mason, no." She met his eyes and held his hands. "Please. I love you. Trust me. I just need some time."

"Of course I trust you." He sat up and swung his legs to the floor. "As long as you know I'm all in."

"Me, too," Dell whispered. But as she looked down at her fingers twined in his, she felt again the unsettling notion that they were not alone in the room, that something echoed her from the shadows, or nearer. She leaned close for another kiss. "I promise."

CHAPTER SEVENTEEN
Before
July 1990

Dell straightened her dress as she walked to the bathroom. The old water-stained mirror faced an open closet that held a pull-down staircase into the attic, breathing a stale, strangely cold breeze into the bathroom. She reached for the light switch before she remembered that it had burned out. As she leaned over to braid her hair, she became aware of a pale face over her shoulder, barely an arm's reach behind her. Dark, empty eyes, leaning close, then closer, too fast for her to react, as if in a dream that held her still, the ashen lips whispering something urgent and silent.

Name three things, she thought, panicked. But she saw only dark.

Dell gasped. She flung an arm backward, touched only cold air as she stumbled toward the door, knees almost buckling. *Bed frame, Mason, windows. Sunlight.* She breathed in fast.

"What? What is it?" He crossed the room in three long steps.

Eyes round, she clutched his arm, pointed at the door. "Tell me there's nobody in there."

Mason walked through the bathroom, even pulled down the ladder and looked up into the attic. Dell rubbed her arms. She peered into the mirror and saw only dark.

"Nobody's there." He held her close against him, and she felt her heart pattering, like a bird stuck in her chest, trying to beat its way into his instead, get somewhere safe and quiet. "What happened?"

"A face," she stammered, looking into his eyes for steadiness. "I thought I saw a face in the mirror."

Mason led her back into the bedroom and looked into her eyes. "You feel okay?"

She gave a hurried nod, nonchalant. "I think so. It was the light, or something."

"What did it look like?"

Dell kept moving in order to hide the shaking in her arms. "Just a face."

It wasn't just a face. It was her father's face. She had sometimes had these waking dreams before, the imagination filing a thought in the wrong category. Told herself they were meaningless. Yet she shivered when she glanced back at the door.

"I'll probably go by the office after I see Dad. I'll come back around dinner time." Dell leaned over to kiss him.

"I should be back by seven. See you then?"

"See you then."

Dell walked down two flights of stairs to the first floor, where the living room and foyer were crowded with tools, planks of untreated wood, buckets of paint and whitewash. As she drove up into the backwoods to her father's house, she felt ashamed. Mason was straightforward and honest. His intentions were as simply formed as he was, simple in the way that only very well-made things are.

As if it were yesterday, not twelve years ago, she remembered the sour taste of a tequila sunrise, Dr. McCallan's mustache brushing against her cheek. Could she stomach that man, and his icy wife, as parents-in-law? And what would Mason say, if he knew she was the one puzzle piece in his life that didn't fit? Maybe his parents had forgotten her. As Dell drove, she blinked her eyes and waved a hand in front of her face as if at a swarm of gnats, batting away the words that still echoed: *You are a little slut and a liar.* She thought of the McCallans' marriage. How happy could they have been? If she was going to get married, she wanted to get it right on the first go. She had never even considered leaving Blyth, and she wasn't interested in becoming a divorcee.

The road curved steeply and climbed around a cluster of fir trees. They were junipers, their fragrant branches sprinkled with waxy blue berries. Dell thought of Juniper Berry Mist and Mason's earnest kindness. If she wanted him, she had to risk it. No other way. No matter how much she wanted to hide away in the farmhouse for the rest of their days.

Dad knew more than his share about risk and loss. If Dell caught him when he wasn't stoned, he might even be able to share some wisdom. As she approached the cabin, Dell practiced her questions silently: *Dad, how do you know somebody's worth taking a risk on? Even if it could upset your whole life?* She shook her head; that wasn't it. She already knew Mason was worth it. She started over, felt a smile spread across her face as she rehearsed what she would say. *Dad, there's someone I want you to meet.*

Dell parked her car in the washed-out gravel driveway and walked to the door. As usual, the cabin looked a little over-loved. In the garden, echinacea blossomed with purple petals over old, dead blooms. The overgrown lavender was fragrant with so many flower stalks the stems were shaded and puny.

"Hey, Dad." The door was always unlocked. That was not unusual. It was odd for Dad to leave it open, though. Dell pulled the screen door shut behind her. "It's me. You ready for lunch?"

She placed her bag on the counter and took a pan from the cabinet, went to the sink to fill it with water, and saw that the water had been left running, whispering a hissing sound into the quiet that sent her eyes darting after every shadow.

"Hey, Dad," she called again. "Answer if you can hear me."

When Dell remembered the face appearing in the mirror, she darted out of the kitchen, taking a hurried look through each room. The living room was empty, a threadbare flannel blanket half unfolded on the leather sofa that faced the wide front window. The den, two steps down through the doorway, smelling of stale cigarettes and lined with family photos in cheap frames, was empty. She returned to the kitchen, past the staircase that led to the upstairs bedrooms, into Dad's room. Violet curtains hung on the windows, just as Anita had left them when she walked out twelve years earlier.

"Dad? Where are you?"

Dell had always known that too many of the pills Dad took could stop your breathing. She found his body in bed with shoes on.

CHAPTER EIGHTEEN

Now

July 1991

Dell had never cared for hospitals. She caught herself holding her breath as she left Anita's room. It was possible her uneasiness wasn't a dislike of medicine itself, so much as an irrational fear of getting all her hair hacked off and her face slapped and finding everything else in her life rearranged afterward. Dell wasn't sure, but she didn't scrutinize her feelings too closely. She wanted to leave the artificially cold and dry air, go back outside into the damp hug of the summer humidity. Instead, she detoured back to the main desk to face the nosy clerk again.

"Can I help you?"

"Where's maternity?"

The girl's eyes asked for an explanation; Dell offered none. Finally, she answered: "Third floor. Get off the elevator and turn left."

"Thanks."

Blyth was a small town. It should have been easy to find out who had been involved in an adoption, especially a recent one. At any number of points, an adopted child should have left a paper trail. Medical exams, birth certificates, adoption certificates. Anything. If Anita refused to wake up, Dell would clear it up herself.

The elevator door was stainless steel, covered in fingerprints. On the third floor, Dell turned left, approached another reception desk. When she saw the group of women, most of them pregnant, some with boyfriends or husbands, she thought for a moment that she was in line. The receptionist stood up from her desk and walked around the counter.

"Is everyone here for the ten o'clock tour?"

There was a chorus of murmured "yes, thank you"s.

"Great. Let's get started. Please follow me."

Behind the desk, an almond-colored file cabinet was labeled "Patient Records". Dell stood with her back to the counter and pretended to be waiting.

"Ma'am?" The receptionist called to her. "This way, please."

There were nine women, in addition to her, and five of them had a man with them. Of those five, three were wearing rings. Dell joined the group and followed the receptionist down a wide hallway. When the tour leader paused, the rest of the group shuffled to a stop behind her.

"Well, ladies and gentlemen, first things first, right? When it's time, and you drive here, in the middle of the night, or whatever time of day it is, no need to worry about where you park. You can pull up outside emergency and walk on in if you need to. We promise not to ticket for the first hour." There was a round of nervous laughter. "Remember, now, third floor, and turn left. Otherwise you'll end up in orthopedics, and that won't do you any good."

The tour guide continued, offering friendly tips on what laboring mothers should bring with them (a pre-packed bag, its contents carefully planned out), what they were allowed to eat (nothing, once they were in active labor, and no water except for ice chips), what food their husbands could expect to find at the cafeteria. One time, Dell had asked Aunt Myra, *How will I know when I'm really in labor?* She had known nothing then, about birth or labor.

Myra had just laughed kindly: *You'll know, girl.* And, indeed, when the time came, Dell knew it. But she hadn't planned for it to be inconvenient. She expected that it would come on slowly and give her plenty of time to react. But then her waters had broken in the middle of the night and she had gone right back to sleep. It wasn't like this. There had been no one watching, no one to remind her when she needed to leave, no one to make sure she had packed a hospital bag with slippers and a change of clothes for the happy drive home. Dell studied the women and men who had come in pairs. They held hands, exchanging whispers and laughs. She had never had that. She had been alone.

The nurse clapped her hands twice and everyone followed her further into the building, away from the windows.

"If anyone has questions, please don't hesitate to speak up."

Someone did. "Are we going to see a birth room?"

"Oh, we sure are."

The tour guide pushed open a door, beaming as the group walked in ahead of her. Her practiced smile betrayed an affinity for the pregnant bodies that filed past her. Dell hung at the back of the group, slipped through the doorway. Her first impression of the room was its smell, an unnaturally citrusy disinfectant scent.

On the far side of the room, a window looked over the parking lot, half covered with an acrylic knit curtain. In the center of the room was a bed, like the hospital bed Anita slept in, with jointed thin-cushioned segments, almost like a beetle, stirrups at its foot. A drawer pulled out of the end of the bed to display an array of metal tools: forceps, a blade, other things Dell didn't know the names of.

The tour leader fluffed a pillow on the bed as she enumerated all the modern comforts of the room. "Here, your own temperature control. When you're in labor, you might want it a bit on the cooler side. Dad, bring a jacket!" Again, everyone laughed. "We have the most up-to-date paging system."

"What's that?" One of the women in the tour group pointed at a machine next to the bed.

"This is relatively new to us. It's an electronic fetal monitoring system." The nurse held up a wide elastic belt. "I'll show you how it works." She stepped closer and strapped the Velcro belt around the woman's bump. "You wear it tight. Tighter—like that. It keeps a read on the baby's vitals so we know everything's going okay."

"You wear it the whole time?"

"Yes," the nurse said. "The whole time. If the baby's heartbeat drops, or even if it's irregular, we know right away. This thing has saved some lives, mamas."

Dell hadn't been afraid for her baby's heartbeat. Myra had listened to it now and then with a handheld little thing she couldn't remember the name of. The guilt that swept over her was heavy and sour. What could have gone wrong that she hadn't even thought about?

She remembered when her labor had veered past inconvenient, when it took her over. The contractions were close together and strong, so that she felt them all over her body. Aunt Myra had walked her around the cabin in circles, since sitting still only increased her focus on the pain. When she was too hot or too weak, Myra and Rosie, her daughter, had fed her handfuls of fruit, small sips of water, even bites of dried meat. What had it felt like? Standing there in the hospital room, Dell traced her hands over her abdomen. She couldn't remember.

"We have such a streamlined, comfortable birth process here," the nurse said. "You can receive an epidural at any point that you choose, so long as you are less than six centimeters dilated. And even after that," she said, "I'll be with you. You'll never be alone. And you can adjust the temperature as you choose. Before you're in active labor, you can walk up and down the halls, even outside if you want."

Dell remembered almost none of that day. How could anyone measure and manage something as amorphous and immeasurable as an ocean? No wonder they needed all this machinery, all this process. Even Dell's recollections were blurry: birth defied those, too. She knew that she had been in pain, and that it had ended. Didn't want to remember another damn thing about it. Her chest felt tight and she squeezed her hands against a shadow of fear. Glanced around the room and counted: *scalpel, monitoring belt, stirrups.* Maybe she was glad she hadn't come here.

"Any other questions?"

Dell raised her hand. "Which way is the exit?"

"Down the hallway and to the right."

The nurse clapped her hands again. "For anyone who's interested, we'll take a walking tour to the cafeteria and the gift shop. If you'd like to pre-register to have your baby here, the forms are at my desk."

Dell walked back down the hallway, quiet now that the tour group and the guide were elsewhere. She kneeled behind the desk, crouching below the counter. The file cabinet was unlocked. One drawer for maternity, one for neonatal. Sliding the second drawer open, she found a long row of dark green files, beginning with the current month, stretching back nearly two years, one folder per month.

Good. That was good. The date was one thing she knew. If the baby had even been here for a checkup, for… anything else. Dell felt her heart race as her fingertips skipped over the files. *1991. February. February 19. Pisces.*

There was nothing. She checked the week before and after, just in case there had been a mistake. Any baby girls in the hospital that whole month had been born right here.

"Can I help you?" A nurse stood at the side of the desk.

"I'm with social work. Checking on a patient."

"Okay." She slid into the desk past Dell, took a seat in the reception chair. "Let me know if you need anything."

"No," Dell said. "I'm all through here. Thanks."

Dell headed back toward the elevator. All the worry she'd spent on where to deliver had been wasted. If anything, the women on the tour today were less mixed up than her. One thing was for certain: if she'd had the baby here at the hospital, she wouldn't be trying to track it down today. Dell pictured walls closing in, considered each of her options and saw them all as dead ends. *But where could a baby disappear to? What could Anita have meant?* The Haneys, Judy had said. Anita still spent time with them.

Dell took a wrong turn and, instead of the elevator, found herself facing a windowed wall into a nursery. Rows of plastic cots lined the wall, tiny babies swaddled in pink or blue. She saw the smallness of their hands, the wrinkled, peach-like faces. She stood at the glass window and looked into the room, the row of tiny heads, tiny features. Wondered if each one's birth had wreaked the kind of havoc on their mothers that her tiny child had on her. And if, like her, the rest of the parents had looked at their soft limbs and found their babies were perfect, that they loved them so much they could barely move. No, she didn't wonder. She already knew. *Of course they had.*

Dell turned away and crossed back to the elevator, back to the first floor, through the sliding doors into the warm arms of the summer air. *Even losing him,* she thought. *Even losing him, and giving you up. You had his eyes. You held my finger in your little hand. If you are happy and safe and loved, it will all have been worth it. When I find you, then I'll see it all clearly.*

CHAPTER NINETEEN

Now

July 1991

As Dell drove away from the hospital, she slowed to a halt at a stoplight, picturing the tiny faces in the nursery. She remembered her own baby's tiny face, as wide as her hand; remembered the impossibly soft hair, blonde gossamer as fine as spiderwebs crowning her small head. Dell didn't notice when the light turned green until the car behind her honked.

She knew better than to linger in memories and thoughts where there was no action to be taken. *If she stopped to let the mosquitoes bite, she knew she would get stuck.* As long as she had a destination, she could manage her fear. She followed Main Street west out of Blyth, and the road soon narrowed to one lane.

Her foot was heavy on the pedal as she thought of Anita's surgery. Make a minor mistake operating on a leg or an arm, and it stood to reason that things could be corrected, the error perhaps never even discovered. Despite the doctor's confidence, it didn't take a doctor to know that surgery on a brain is never without risks, and that disaster required only a small mishap by way of invitation. Where the mountains rose in the distance Dell saw the long, narrow bare patch where the pipeline lay, scraggly brown cutting through the green.

The Haney family home was a long, low house, built in the 1950s, guarded from the road by a row of chestnut trees. Back when Dell was in school, the Haneys had a mob of children, and she never knew who was adopted and who was not. They drew no distinction among themselves. Though Anita had remained on chilly, though civil, terms with them, Dell and Scott had made friends with a few of the Haney children, and by extension, the whole gaggle. You couldn't help but get to know at least one or two; after all, they made up half the Sunday school class.

As she walked up the path to the front door, it felt eerie to see the big gray house so silent, without a single kid playing in the yard. But the same old tire swing still hung from a chestnut tree. She wondered if they had grandchildren now.

When Dell rang the doorbell, she heard the high-pitched bark of a small dog. Carla Haney answered the door, one yapping and squirming dog in her arm.

"Hi, Mrs. Haney. I'm sorry to bother you. I'm Adella—"

"Dell Shaw, look at you!" Carla's soft brown hair had faded to gray. Tendrils escaped around her ears, the rest of the length twisted into a low bun. She wore blue jeans and a knit camisole, her upper arms wide and soft and comforting.

"I didn't know if you'd remember me." Dell stood in the doorway and looked to her left at a bright rhododendron bush, its pink-clad branches reaching toward the door. "I came with something to ask you. Do you have a minute or two?"

"Come in, dearie. Al and I were just preparing lunch. Will you join us?"

"I wouldn't trouble you."

Carla led her inside and closed the door, then set down the wiry-haired, squirming dog. "It's no trouble. The house is quiet now, with the kids all grown. And we enjoy it," she laughed softly, "the peace and quiet. But some company is always nice."

Carla gestured to the blue chenille sofa and Dell sat down. When she set the little dog loose, it bounced up onto the cushion next to her, panting with excitement. Dell clicked her tongue and patted the small, curly head.

"Al," Carla called into the kitchen, "we have a visitor. Would you please set an extra place at the table?"

Dell knew she didn't have time for a meal, but she realized that she was hungry, that she had skipped breakfast that morning and dinner the day before.

Carla walked into the kitchen, disappearing from sight, and returned with a glass of ice and a can of Sprite.

"Do you remember how you loved this stuff when you were little?" She poured the soda over the ice a little at a time, letting it fizz and recede. "Whenever you and Scott were here for a birthday party, you asked for a Sprite."

Dell had forgotten how she loved the syrupy stuff, how Mr. and Mrs. Haney used to call her Little Sprite. She had forgotten how people here drank sodas like they were water. One thing she'd been glad to get away from when she'd left was that nobody hassled her about what she chose to eat.

"With all the children running around, you somehow had more love to go around, even for other people's kids." Dell sipped the Sprite. "Thank you."

"Children are God's greatest gift," Carla answered with a warm, unwavering smile. "Our ability to provide was limited, but our love was not."

"You took in so many."

"We raised thirteen. Six I bore, but we loved them all the same. We'd have taken in more if we'd had the energy and time."

The living room had the feeling of a room where little happened, where the magazines on the coffee table always stayed in the same place. A large wooden cross hung on the wall above the fireplace.

"You know…" Dell petted the little dog, puzzling over what to say next. "It's not entirely unrelated, what brings me here today."

Al Haney leaned around the doorway from the kitchen. "Well hello, Little Sprite, all grown up."

"Nice to see you, Mr. H."

"Lunch is served, ladies. Come on into the kitchen when you're ready."

"We don't use the dining room anymore, not when it's just us," Carla explained. She stood up and clapped her hands; the dog leapt to her side, bouncing nervously. "Feels lonely, just me and Al at that big table."

Dell followed her into the kitchen, with its familiar yellow wallpaper and whitewashed cabinets. Over the sink, a little window faced back into the woods, a hummingbird feeder stuck onto the glass with a suction cup hanger.

A small, round table rested in the corner nook, boxed in by the counter on one side, tall rows of bookshelves on the other lined with dusty sets of encyclopedias. Carla slid the table out so that Dell could squeeze into the middle seat. She moved the table back into place, set Dell's glass at her elbow, then sat next to her.

"Do you have enough room, Dell? I'd put me or Al back there but neither of us would fit!"

"I'm fine. Thanks."

Mr. Haney carried over a plate of tuna sandwiches with sliced cucumbers.

"Lord, we thank you for this meal. We ask that you continue to bless us and our family with good health, and we thank you as well for bringing this pleasant and unexpected visitor to our table. May she find whatever she seeks. Amen."

"Amen," Mrs. Haney and Dell echoed.

As they ate, Dell wondered, impatient, how long she should wait to ask. Carla ate half of a sandwich, handed a bit of crust down to the dog. "There now, Buckley. You run along. That's all you get."

"The happiest little dog," Al said. "He gets all the attention we used to share among thirteen kids."

"He looks very happy," Dell agreed.

"Dell," said Mr. Haney, "we think of your father often."

She braced herself for some manner of proselytizing. Nobody could bring up Dad's death without talking about how he had died. It wasn't a loss, to most of the gossips in this town. It was a lesson.

"He was unfailingly kind," Carla agreed, "just good-natured, every day of his life. We still feel his absence at church."

"But his presence, too," said Al. "When somebody dies in the Lord, they don't leave us altogether."

Dell sat her sandwich on her plate. She wasn't hungry. "My dad had his own share of problems."

"So does everyone," Mr. Haney said. "You ever notice that you never see me drinking?"

"No. Why?" She had not noticed.

"It's not ancient history, either," Carla added, her age-spotted hand dangling over her husband's. "Alvin hasn't touched a drop since, oh, Dell, you would have been about nine."

"You could do that, for your family." Dell felt her mouth tighten in a false smile. "But my dad couldn't bother to do the same for us." The words slipped out before she knew it and she covered her mouth, fiddled with her napkin, ashamed. "I didn't mean anything by that. It's fine."

"Of course it isn't fine. Sprite, you're not wrong to be angry." Al let out a peaceful sigh. "But sometimes, making room for grief can free up some space for gratefulness as well."

"Gratefulness?" Dell laughed, almost snorting Sprite out her nose. What did she have to be grateful for?

Carla graciously chose that moment to interrupt. "You know, our new pastor says addiction isn't about what you're taking. It's about being lonely."

"Sure, it is." Dell's chuckle was cold. "If that's true, why wasn't it enough me and Scott tried to take care of him? Scott would always tell me it wasn't about us, but…" Dell nudged the cucumber with her fork.

"Yes. But try telling a child that," Carla said. Her tone was matter-of-fact, not scolding, nor pious. Dell recognized the absence of pity, sat up a little straighter. "Your brother grew up too fast. Poor boy. You both did, but him more so." Carla cleared her throat as if announcing that it was time to change the subject. "God rest your father's soul."

Dell hadn't given any thought to God in years, but she found herself repeating Mrs. Haney's blessing with a shrug. "God rest his soul. I guess."

"Alvin, I think our guest has come here with a purpose," Carla said. "Dell, what were you asking me just before we walked in here?"

"Uh. Right." She squeezed in a bite of food and swallowed as fast as she could. "You and Mr. Haney have worked closely with the adoption agencies in town, I'm guessing?"

"Such as there are," said Carla. "Many of the children that came to us had nobody looking after them."

Dell chose her words with care. "A cousin of mine, a—a distant cousin, had a child near about six months ago." They murmured excitedly as she continued. "She placed the baby for adoption. She was…" Dell faltered and looked at the encyclopedias behind her, trailing off. "Overwhelmed, I guess. Now, she's become terribly concerned, for some reason, for the child's well-being. She just wants some reassurance the baby's in a safe home."

"A mother never stops being a mother," Carla nodded. "What a tough path to walk, that is."

"She is fairly sure that the baby was placed somewhere near here," Dell said. "So, I wanted to ask you, if you know of any new babies, any that are about that age. Six months."

Carla and Al looked at each other, unsure.

"If she only could see the baby, even from a distance, it would be all she needed to set her mind at ease." Dell began to feel the table was very close, that she wanted both to keep talking and to run out of the room.

"Oh, the poor girl," Carla repeated. "What a sacrifice that is. Al, isn't there a very young one at the church daycare?"

Al finished his food and set his napkin on the plate. "Lucy, our youngest girl—Lucy's a babysitter at the church daycare. Their littlest one there is about six months, but I don't know who the parents are, or even whether it's a boy or girl. Carla, do you remember?"

"I don't, dear. Dell, more Sprite?"

"No, thank you." She felt her head aching already. Too much sugar and not enough water.

"That's where I would look," said Carla. "Oh, and you remember Miss Myra, who moved into your father's house?"

"Yes."

Al nodded. They had been married for decades, and it showed in how they picked up and finished each other's sentences, giving each other a break to chew. "Myra's two daughters live with her there. Each of them has children. Lively bunch."

"Where there's a gang of kids, it's easy for one to join the mix, unnoticed," Carla said. "We should know!"

Al laughed. "We once absorbed a kid wandering around the grocery store. Didn't realize he wasn't ours till we got all the way to the car."

Carla smiled as her eyes misted over. "Ah, I miss 'em. Those days."

Al patted her hand. "Dell, if I were in your cousin's shoes, I'd take a look at the church. And maybe even pay Miss Myra a visit."

Dell nodded, chose to take a bite instead of answering. What would Myra know? Nothing. Holed up there in her cabin, barely any contact with anyone besides her daughters. What Dell needed was to find out who had adopted the child, find where she had gone after the social worker took her away from the cabin. Just the thought of the old place gave her a shudder.

"Aren't children a wonderful thing?" Carla smiled. "Dell, I do hope you have your own one day."

"And I hope your cousin finds the news she's looking for," Al added.

The table rocked gently as Carla crossed her knees. Dell sat both elbows on the table in front of her, glancing to her left and right. Everywhere she went, there were people who knew her better than she knew herself. She wanted fresh air, a cold glass of water. It had been almost a full day since she'd spent a waking moment alone. Even the chairs and the table gated her in, stuck there in the corner as if she were propped in place, being read.

"Excuse me." Dell stood up with a clatter and inched behind Mrs. Haney's chair, her shoulder blades and hips grazing the dusty bookshelf. "Excuse me, I'm really sorry, I just can't—"

"You okay, honey? You barely ate."

"I just can't stay," Dell said. "Yes, thank you. Thank you so much."

She hurried out the door and stood in the walkway, the sun beating down hot, closed her eyes and felt its still, heavy energy. Inside the station wagon it was warmer still. Dell opened all the windows and drove back toward Blyth. Why had she lied? She could surely have told them in confidence. And no doubt the story about her unnamed cousin had landed transparent. Girl leaves town, comes back asking after her cousin's missing child? *And you're not a girl, not at twenty-seven years old. A girl could be forgiven for this kind of mess.* It wasn't even a good lie. She wasn't up to form.

And that's one thing, Dell thought, *so long as you only harm yourself.* But she could not bear the thought of the baby girl unsafe, as good as homeless. She only needed to see her face, and then she would disappear back to her psychic shop, or better yet, somewhere even further.

There were few things as soothing as fleeing the scene, to rip up roots and leave, to make her surroundings a canvas for the interior kind of chaos. Dell wouldn't need to worry if the baby were in the church daycare program. It would mean people knew her. It meant a dozen sets of open arms, including Mrs. Haney's, so sweet in her empty nest, should she happen across a baby that needed a home. Dell drove to where the road split into two lanes and took a right back toward the middle of Blyth.

Passing the graveyard, she nodded a silent hello to her father. Just ahead on the right, she pulled to the side of the road outside the church. The daycare center was in the annex, across from the reception room, which only saw use during funerals and weddings. As Dell parked and got out of the car, she saw a group of young children and two attendants in the playground outside the building. She headed toward the graveyard, trying not to stare too obviously.

One young woman, tall and stocky, officious, helped a line of children down a small plastic slide, her hand gently resting on one small back, guiding each next child up the steps, then the next. To their right, Dell saw Lucy Haney, round-faced and blonde. She led a toddler by the hand and balanced a small bundle on one hip. Propriety forgotten, Dell walked straight toward them, stopped with her hands on the chain link fence and smiled.

"Hi, there," Dell waved, her voice brimming with false cheer. "Hey, do you girls know how I could get back to the highway from here?"

Lucy, holding the baby in her arm, stayed back. The other woman patted a child's shoulder, asking her to wait, and turned to face her.

"If you go back to your left, then go three—no, four stoplights, make a right..."

The babe-in-arms was in a yellow onesie, one chubby, pale arm waving. Dell couldn't see its face. She remembered the feeling of holding someone so small, so soft. Would she even recognize her own child? Would her body not have told her, given her some signal, if she had walked so close to her?

The little voice wailed and fussed. "Hush, Bobby." Lucy patted the little cheek and bounced the baby. "Sweet little boy. There you are."

"Ma'am, did you need to go east or west?"

Sweet little boy. "Um. Yes. Thanks for your help."

Dell rushed back to the car, let herself in, and let her forehead fall against the wheel.

"What have I done?" she whispered, clutching her hands to her temples. "How am I gonna fix this? Where are you?"

She looked over to the graveyard, then ducked her head again, ashamed to think that her father could see her here, even in death. The closest thing Dell had to a plan was to make sure the baby was safe, then leave town again. But if she couldn't find her, she knew no hideaway could offer any comfort: not her psychic shop, nor any corner of the map. She thought that her heart could turn to ice right there, despite the summer heat.

Can't freeze up like this. It won't do. These were some of Myra's first words to her. *You never fixed anything by not taking care of yourself.* In the whirlwind of the last eighteen hours, Dell had missed dinner, and then breakfast, and barely managed lunch. Blyth was home to one nice restaurant, two sports bars, and one dive bar. Bessie's, a sports bar, was the closest, so that was where she decided to go next.

Bessie's sat in the corner of an old strip mall, in which almost every other storefront was empty, the naked backs of cardboard displays leaning against dusty glass. Inside, the restaurant was smoky and yellow-lit, filled with the bowling alley smell of old carpet and stale beer. Dell looked at a clock on the wall and saw that it was close to four in the afternoon.

"What can I get for you?" The bartender was a pretty girl in a raglan t-shirt and tight blue jeans, her hair in two girlish, long braids.

"Ice water, please, and a menu. And can I use your phone? Oh, and a phone book?" Dell sat in an empty barstool, threw her bag down on the stool next to her.

The bartender made a tight smile, letting Dell know she was annoyed. She carried the phone over, dropped a phone book next to it. Dell looked up the phone number for the hospital, the yellow pages gray and dirty at the edges, and dialed.

"Commonwealth Memorial. How can I direct your call?"

"It's about a patient." Dell sipped her ice water. "My mother, Anita Barden. She's in surgery. Will you call me back at this number if there are any updates in the next half hour?"

"She'll be in recovery until at least 6 p.m., ma'am."

"Regardless, if you do have any news at all, please call me here." She read off the phone number for the diner, thanked the receptionist again, and hung up.

Dell set the receiver back on the other side of the counter.

"You need anything else?" the girl asked.

Food was the smart choice. But when she heard Myra's raspy old echo again, *You never fixed anything by not taking care of yourself,* she only wanted to drown it out. Didn't Aunt Myra always carry a coffee mug half-full of whiskey with her?

"Whiskey, please."

"What kind?" came the impatient answer.

Dell looked at the rows of bottles, unfamiliar labels behind the counter. She pointed at the closest one. "That one."

The bartender sighed, a pert hip thrust to the right in exasperation. "How do you take it?"

"God in heaven. I don't know!" Dell rolled her eyes. "In a glass, okay?" She sensed other people in the bar noticing her, raising their eyebrows, and she sat up straight and proud.

A drop of liquor splashed onto the counter as the bartender set the glass down with a smack. Dell took a gulp and coughed, eyes watering as the whiskey burned down her throat. This kind of old diner had a gritty comfort. She looked around as her senses whirled, counted: *television screens, jukebox, the vending machine lined with packs of cigarettes.* Finally, she felt a wash of numbness, the alcohol hitting her senses. All the gravity of the room was sweetly thrown off. Maybe she would finish her drink and order a meal. Maybe another drink.

A dog approached her, toenails clicking on the tiled floor, a familiar, friendly squeal of greeting. London whined, the lanky German shepherd nosing at her hand in greeting. "Hi, old boy," she whispered, scratching the soft, wiry-furred ears. "What are you doing here?" The dog grinned up at her. Dell blinked. *This can't be right. I've fainted. I'm dreaming. Oh, please, let this be a dream.*

Then she saw Mason, seated four chairs down from her. He wore a gray t-shirt, one that made his eyes look bright. Blond hair, parted on the left, out of place as always. He lifted an eyebrow at her whiskey, almost half-empty now. "Bad day?"

Dell sat up with a glare. "If it wasn't before, it is now." London rested his chin on her knee and she stroked the soft fur between his ears, her mood softening as she looked into the dog's dark eyes. "Nothing is going right. I couldn't sleep. Can't eat anything. And now—" She waved a swatting hand in Mason's direction. "You again."

"Guess that makes two of us." Mason stood up, picked up his beer, leaned an elbow on the back of the stool next to hers. "Mind if I sit?"

"Not here," she snapped, indicating her bag on the seat. But she couldn't help glancing over his familiar features. The tentative smile that made her wish again that she could turn his face into stone. Those eyes, just like his baby's. She pointed to the empty stool on the other side of her bag. "Right there. You can sit there."

CHAPTER TWENTY
Before
July 1990

After Dell found her father's body, she dialed 911. When she found the phone still in her hand with nobody on the other line, she couldn't remember what she had said. Dell walked a circle through the house, stifling an impulse to tidy up, though she did not know why.

Finally, she returned to Dad's bedroom. On the dresser Dell saw a photograph of the four of them—Anita, Dad, Scott, and her, just five or six years old, framed in dusty, gold-colored plastic. Her eyes returned to her father's body. She felt some need to do something for him, and her thoughts ran in frantic, incomplete scribbles, trying to think of what it was. Couldn't just let him lay here this way.

Standing at the bedside, she looked down at his ashen face, the flannel- and denim-clad limbs awkwardly bent, so that he looked almost as though he were reaching upward, still as stone. Dell felt her lungs burning before she realized how fast she was breathing. She leaned over and pulled the faded red baseball cap from his head, then ran in frantic, stumbling steps up the stairs, down the hallway into Scott's old bedroom, sank to her knees at the foot of the bed, clutching the baseball cap between her hands.

She heard sirens and tires on gravel, two or three cars from the sound of it. Then, there were footsteps on the porch outside, walking in the door, which she had left unlatched.

"Where's the body?" a man's voice called.

"Are you kidding me?"

When Dell heard her brother's voice from downstairs, she lifted her head from her knees.

"Get your head out of your ass, Brown," he said. "My father's already dead. My little sister's here somewhere. Find her first."

Hearing a set of boots on the stairs, Dell peered out of the open doorway.

"Scott, I'm here."

With long, hurried steps, he walked into his childhood bedroom and kneeled to look into her face.

"Dell. Hey." Scott squeezed her shoulder. "I'm so sorry you had to see that."

She looked up at her brother and nodded. "I'm fine. What should we do now?"

Scott stood up and pulled her to a shaky stand. "You need to go home. There's going to be a medical examiner, detectives here."

Dell knew she needed to do something. Tried to remember what it was. "I feel like I need to be here. There's—"

"Uh-uh. No." He hugged her tight and against his shoulders she felt that her breaths were fast and unsteady, although they felt far away. It was someone else's heart in there, like a trapped bird flapping its useless wings.

"Why'd they let you come? Not a conflict of interest?"

"I insisted," Scott said. "I knew you'd be here. I always have to explain this to you, don't I?"

Dell stood up tall, almost as tall as her brother, and tried to exude calm. "I'll go home. I'll be okay."

"Oh, no you don't." Scott led her toward the stairs. "I know you. You fall apart after the fact. I don't want you alone when that happens. Can you go to Mom's?"

Dell scoffed. "Absolutely not. You okay?"

"Yes," he said. "Obviously. I'm fine. Everything's in order."

"Oh, yeah?"

Scott tugged at the top button on his jacket. "Dad's leaving the house to Aunt Myra. You remember her? He's got it all in his will. Wants to be cremated. He said he didn't want to be under the ground. People are gonna talk…" He pressed his hands against his eyes, exhaled hard. "Can't promise people won't know what happened, but it won't come from any of our friends."

"Scott, stop it," Dell whispered. Her voice came out in a squeaky whisper, betrayed her. "You're the one who shouldn't be here."

"You're gonna need to keep your head up. It's not gonna be the same."

"Hold on." Over her brother's protests, she walked downstairs, picked up the phone and dialed the number for Scott's house.

"Hello?"

"Abby, it's Dell Shaw."

"Scott's not here."

"I called for you."

"Oh? Um…" This was the kind of phone call that meant something is wrong. Dell and Abby would never have called each other just to talk.

"We're at my dad's house. He's—" She looked down at the red hat in her hand. It looked ten feet away, and her fingers and knuckles seemed distorted. "You need to come and be here for Scott. You need to take him home. Can you do that?"

"Yeah," she answered. "Right away." There was a click, followed by the dial tone in her ear.

Dell dragged her feet back up the stairs, sat next to Scott on his bed.

"You shouldn't have come," she said.

"And what? Let some cops you don't know drag you out of here, yelling?" He tilted his head back, a humorless laugh squeezed tight in his throat.

"Abby's coming to pick you up." Dell leaned over to hug him. "You gonna be okay till then?"

"Yep. Go ahead." Scott pointed at the door, and she could tell he was close to tears. "Now, Dell. I'll call you later."

CHAPTER TWENTY-ONE
Before
July 1990

Dell thought one of the police officers said "I'm sorry" as she walked past them, through the kitchen, outside into the yard. Under the low-hanging, shaggy arms of the juniper trees, the soil was damp from the last rain. She got into her car, wondering how long Dad had been there like that. It couldn't have been more than a few hours. There was no smell. She saw Dad's nosy neighbor Ruth peering through the wire fence. She rolled down the window of the station wagon.

"Hey, Ruth," she hollered. Caught snooping, Ruth's head swiveled, looking for the source of her voice. "He's dead. It's exactly like you said it would happen, all those times."

Ruth's mouth dropped open.

"You have a fine day," Dell yelled, her voice shrill. She started the engine and drove.

Took a wrong turn out of the driveway. She drove that way for four miles, anyway, until the road got too steep, turned around, drove in the opposite direction. Her apartment had been empty for weeks. She drove past the farm supply store. They would hear what had happened soon enough. Half an hour later found her at Mason's house.

Dell hurried up the walkway, mindless of the brambles of the firethorn hedges catching at her sleeves. She knocked at the door, waited and knocked again. London barked, but he did not answer.

"Mason? Hello? Anybody?" Her breath caught in her throat and she turned around, staring out at the road. Then she remembered, seeing that his car was gone. He was at work. She tried the door, found it locked, and walked around to the back of the house. The screened porch off the kitchen was open, the back door unlocked. London trotted to greet her, whining in confusion, sniffing the hat she held in her hand. She gathered an armful of cleaning supplies: a bucket of soap and water, an armful of dishcloths, a broom and dustpan, a bottle of blue glass cleaner, and climbed the stairs to the second floor.

Even in the bright sunroom, the shadows in the corners spooked her. Each creak of the floor seemed to whisper that she was not alone in the room. Dell put her father's hat on and turned on a box fan. She stood on a stepladder and cleaned each window, top to bottom, working from east to west, with a light, fastidious touch. Her hair matted with sweat.

As the sun crept lower, the dust and the smell of the glass cleaner began to make her dizzy, which didn't bother her, as it dulled her senses a little. Head tilted with concern, London stood guard in the doorway. When the windows sparkled, Dell wiped the walls with soapy water, then the floor, balancing on hands and knees as blood rushed to her head. When she had polished the room from top to bottom, she started over.

The evening had turned ripe and blush orange when Dell heard a key turn in the door. London jumped to his feet and ran down the hallway, clicking toes down the stairs.

"Adella? You here?"

"Yeah," she shouted back. "Upstairs."

Mason appeared in the doorway, London tugging on his sleeve, whining. He patted the dog's ears, studying the scene. "I see, boy," he said. "What's going on?"

"You weren't home, so I came in the back." Speaking out loud for the first time in hours, Dell realized she was out of breath. "Mason, do you remember how I said we could put a turntable over there, and a wicker bench right here?" She laughed and sat down in the middle of the floor, felt the breeze from the fan. But she seemed to go on laughing, stifled it in her throat, sat still, hugging her knees.

Mason sat down next to her, puzzling over her like a book in an unknown language. His hand brushed hers and she pulled back, too warm to be touched. "New hat?"

Dell leaned forward, head over her knees, and pulled it off. Her dress was coated with dust and sweat. "Oh, right. I took it from my dad."

"You went by his place before work, right?"

"Yes. He's..." Her head felt light, but her voice sounded calm. "He's dead, actually. I took his hat before I left. I didn't go to work. I just came here." Dell knew that she wasn't in her right head, but she was fine with being off kilter. She rose to her feet and took a rag to a spot of dust in the corner, leaning with the other hand against the wall.

"What happened? You found him?"

She sighed, held a hand out as if to say *let me be.* "Look at this room. I've been working all day."

"And it looks great," Mason answered. "I'm gonna ask you to stop working, okay? Let's go downstairs."

Dell complied, limbs buzzing with soreness as she nodded her head yes. There was a satisfaction in her exhaustion. It slowed her racing mind, the visions she couldn't stop. As she walked down the stairs next to him, she felt weightless, walking through water.

In the kitchen, Mason offered her a glass of water, which she ignored, walking to the back door. "I don't want to be inside," she said. "I just want some fresh air. I can't sit still."

"You don't have to sit still." Mason gestured toward the field behind the farmhouse, a rolling expanse of nodding grass and Queen Anne's lace. "Let's go for a walk."

She held his hand as they walked back through the meadow. In the sunset, a translucent half-moon lit the sky, reflecting silver in the pond. Mason brushed vines and tall grasses away from a weathered wooden bench, clearing space for them to sit down. Dell sat close to him, felt the quiet and still around them. She looked at Mason as if she'd been tricked. There was nothing to clean here, no distraction. London sighed and planted his slobbery chin on Dell's foot.

"What happened?" Mason picked up a rock from the ground and tossed it skipping over the water. Dell pulled a fist-sized rock from the dirt, pitched it overhand into the pond.

"I walked in and he was in bed. Like he'd fallen asleep. Don't know what happened." This was the first outright lie she'd ever told him. It didn't make any sense to be angry at Mason, but as the lie hung in the air, she wanted to get to her feet and walk right away from him.

"I'm so sorry." Mason chewed on his lip, let out a tense sigh. "I shouldn't have kept you so long this morning. It's my fault you weren't there."

"It's not like that." Dell shook her head again, disappointed with him for getting it wrong. "He'd been having... health problems for a while." She launched another rock into the pond, splashing their knees with muddy water. "Oh, I can't sit still. Why'd we even come out here?"

"I thought you wanted to come outside."

Dell's eyebrows pinched together and she scooted away from him. She didn't know what she wanted Mason to say. She didn't want him to be *so sorry*, that was for sure. Right then, she wasn't even a little sorry Dad was gone. After years of missing him while he was alive, his death left an aftertaste of selfish relief. Mason was there with her, but not there at the same time. It wasn't an unfamiliar sensation.

"What do you need?" he asked. "Just tell me."

"I'm sorry." She held his hand, though she felt as if she had to reach to get it. "This isn't your fault."

Dell closed her eyes, remembered pacing Dad's house, wondering what she needed to do. Suddenly, she remembered.

"I didn't even think to put a blanket over him." She picked up another rock and hurled it at the water, muttering out a string of swear words. London flinched at the noise.

If Dell had a star in the sky for every time Dad had made her angry, she could have disappeared into her own galaxy. All those years of being powerless, all those times she had stopped and said *But I thought we were having a good time.* All the times Ruth had stared, or kids at school had whispered. Every time Scott had insisted that it didn't mean he didn't love her. She felt a quiet wall of anger sealing her off; imagined herself turned into a tree or a rock, instead of a person.

It was better that Dad was gone. To be gone was all he had really wanted. Away from her and everything else. Dell felt Mason's arm around her shoulders, pulling her back into her body. Tears held stubborn in her eyes. She squeezed his hand tight, too tight, as if he were a riverbank and she were pulling herself to shore. But she refused to cry. That water was too deep, its current too swift.

"I love you." With his free hand, he traced her fingers, wrapped around his. "You know that?"

"I love you, too," Dell said. But she spoke with her eyes out toward the hills, far away. They weren't the same. She knew she had lied to him by omission this whole time, but an actual dishonesty felt different. "Let's go in. I just want to take a shower and go to sleep."

"I got that ice cream you wanted. Strawberry, right?"

"Oh, I can't," she remembered, looking down at her filthy dress. "My dress was tight this morning. I need to watch what I'm eating."

Dell trailed behind him through the narrow meadow path. They walked through the overgrown garden, weeds sprouting between the stones that formed a path leading up to the screened porch. There was a vine-covered concrete birdbath, a garden bed overgrown with daffodils, a bed where someone had once planted spearmint and let it go. Spearmint is a conqueror and will choke out anything growing adjacent. She recognized some stunted zinnia stems in its midst.

Dell shook the stems so that the air was steeped with their fragrance. "Spearmint energizes your mind," she hummed. "Lavender is calming." For a moment, she felt at ease there, her hands full of mint and blue lavender, rattling off their healing properties as if her knowledge itself was a charm of protection.

"You ever gonna help me fix up this garden?" Mason paused and turned to face her.

"I don't know." Their eyes met briefly, hers filled with uncertainty, before she turned away. "I think I like it better overgrown."

CHAPTER TWENTY-TWO
Before
July 1990

With Dad dead, the hours took on strange and unpredictable shapes. Some felt weeks long; some passed Dell by altogether. She didn't know how to tell Mason that she wasn't just sad, she was sick. Dell had never lost anyone close to her before, but she was not aware of grief manifesting as a metallic taste in her mouth, no matter how much water she drank. She was lightheaded in sudden spells that left her hanging onto countertops and doorframes.

London followed her every footstep, always resting his head in her lap. The dog had taken to her right away, but this was a new level of devotion. Dell was glad of London's company. She looked in mirrors for a face in the dark, troubled by a lingering sense that she was not alone, that there was someone else in the room. One thing she knew for sure was that it wasn't her father's spirit. By the time he'd died he was just his habits.

All the next week, Dell would sleep ten, eleven hours a night. She dragged herself to work during the day. Mason seemed to sense that scolding her to look after herself would have only made her mad. So, instead, he left comfort in Dell's way: glasses of water throughout the house, a carton of blackberries set in the kitchen, a loaf of fresh bread in the sunroom. Before he left for work in the mornings, he would fill a glass with dandelions from the yard and leave them on the bathroom sink.

The night before her father's funeral, Dell insisted on cooking. She didn't want to sit still. Mason sat behind the counter, London at his feet. Dell tossed the dog a scrap.

"My dad's service is tomorrow."

"I know. I'll be there."

"You will?" She should have known this. Whenever a member of the First Baptist died, everyone else in the congregation seemed to turn up, even if they didn't know the deceased very well. Even if they did.

"I'm going with my folks. Unless you'd rather go together."

"No, thanks." Slicing a cucumber for salad, she paused to eat a slice. In different circumstances, Dell knew she would have been more disturbed to hear that she had to be in a building with his mother and father the following day, but that moment found her more worried with the cucumbers, which tasted inexplicably like soap. "I'd rather our first official date wasn't my father's funeral. No offense."

"None taken."

Dell sat a plate in front of him. "You haven't met my mother. She's... Actually, try to stay out of her way." She sat at the stool next to him and poked at her food.

"You don't think she'll like me?"

"Oh, it's not that." She laughed to herself, not happily. "It won't take more than a couple hours, anyway. I'm going right back to work after."

"Baby." He sat his fork down and turned to face her. "You've got to slow down at some point. It's okay if you don't know how to feel about it."

But Mason wouldn't have said that, Dell thought, if he knew how she did feel. Angry. Some days, she was so angry at Dad she was glad he was dead. When she heard his voice saying *Hey,*

Strawberry, she felt the hair on her arms raise with a chill of anger. She'd wanted one thing from him. Wanted to ask him one thing. The first time in years she'd gone over there looking for actual fatherly advice was the day she found his body.

"I know." She smiled at Mason across the distance. "I will. When I'm ready."

Even doused in vinegar, the cucumber still tasted like soap. She regarded her food with an adversarial, nauseous stare.

"I'm not hungry." She rested her head on his shoulder.

"Again? Hey, is this because you said your dress was tight last week?"

"No." Dell leaned over to drape her arms around him. "I just want to look at you and pretend everything is okay."

"Of course everything is okay. What are you talking about?"

Later, upstairs, she held him almost desperately, let her fingernails scratch into his shoulders.

"Promise me this room is gonna be blue," she breathed. "Promise you love me. Never leave me."

And each time, Mason promised. But Dell lay awake watching as he slept, staring down every shadow that stole across the floor.

Although Dell had never lost a family member before, she had a feeling that some people were like linchpins in others' lives. Whatever their flaws, they supported the weight of what lay in place around them. Pull those pieces out, and what would happen next?

CHAPTER TWENTY-THREE

Before

July 1990

In the morning, Mason left early to meet with his family. Dell took her time getting ready. She chose a dark green dress in a tiny floral print, fitted waist and a full skirt. More appropriate for a picnic. Maybe because Anita's hair was always carefully styled, Dell had grown up with an aversion to any hairdo that betrayed effort. She left her hair alone just as she always did; why should it have been any different for Dad's funeral? He'd been gone for years. Besides, the summer heat imparted its own untamed volume, styling her hair for her. She swept its heavy, untidy waves into a low ponytail and left it at that.

Dell took a final look at her face in the mirror. She double-checked to see that the space behind her was blank and ghostly-dark. She walked down the two flights of stairs, swept her feet against each other to get the sawdust off, and stepped into the black silk flats she'd left at the door, crusted with grass seed from walks in the meadow.

That last hour passed more quickly than the others. When she looked up at the cherry wood clock in the living room, she saw that it was time to go.

*

Outside the church, there was hardly a parking spot, and the sun was high overhead, warmer than when she'd left. Dell rested one hand on the station wagon while she put on her sunglasses, patted the sweat from her forehead, and walked in.

She heard the deep, rich voice of the pastor making its way through the Lord's Prayer, felt the hush and fidget of a room full of people trying to keep quiet all at once.

"He restoreth my soul. He leadeth me in the paths of righteousness for His name's sake."

Dell checked the clock on the wall. She was only ten minutes late, but there were no seats left. She stood on her toes and looked toward the front of the church, saw the back of Anita's head, her hair in a flawless French braid.

"Yea, though I walk through the valley of the shadow of death, I will fear no evil: for thou art with me; thy rod and thy staff..."

Dell felt sweat beading between her breasts and along her hairline. Though she still knew the prayer by heart, she was losing track of the pastor's voice. There was a table prepared, someone's head anointed. She squeezed into the narrow edge of a pew next to an old man with a gray beard. "Sorry," she whispered.

"Surely, goodness and mercy shall follow me all the days of my life, and I will dwell in the house of the Lord forever."

When the pastor invited everybody to meet in the reception room, Dell finally realized she had missed the funeral. A hymn began and she sat in place as the pews emptied, sliding her knees to one side to let people edge around her.

Dell dabbed a film of perspiration from her brow again and then again. She thought she would sit here until Mason or Scott walked past and found her, but when she lifted her chin, the church had emptied and she was alone.

In the stifling warm, she walked up to the front of the church. Her father's body rested in a simple coffin, flanked by blown-up photographs that were several years old, all but one of them with Anita. He wore a suit Dell had never seen before, probably on loan from whatever funeral home Anita had used. Dell wanted to touch his hand, but the coffin was only open to his elbows.

This was the face, pale, almost a stranger, that had appeared to her in the mirror. She knew this body wasn't her father, that it couldn't hear her, but she found herself resting a hand on the rim of the wooden box, whispering an apology. Not for how he had left. Dell realized that Dad had not really wanted to be alive, maybe not for many years now.

"Were you trying to tell me something?" she whispered. But she already knew the answer. He was not. Maybe that was what that ghostly face was telling her. That he had always been gone. It had appeared at the precise moment she'd wanted to hear his voice, to talk to her dad. To hear him say *go ahead, Strawberry, be brave.*

She looked at him, felt her anger temper, only a little. *Didn't want to be buried, huh? Guess you can't have everything you want.* Anita must have known she and Scott wouldn't want to plan the day. Saw a power void and stepped in. If anyone else had made the call, if it had been by mistake, Dell wouldn't have cared. But for it to have been her mother's choice, an aesthetic choice over a dead man's wishes for his own body? This was theatrical Anita bullshit, as usual.

The reception room was down a hallway and a half-flight of stairs. At the front of the long, low room, a table was set up with more photographs of Dad: with Anita, at an overlook on the parkway; with baby Scott in the hospital; outside the old cabin. The room was crowded, faces of people vaguely familiar, but nobody Dell knew well. Friends of Dad's from when he was younger, when he still worked and left the house sometimes. Mason stood with his mother and father at a table nearby. She nodded a prayer at the ceiling, begging for them not to have seen her. The room was too warm.

Dell scanned the room until she saw her brother with Abby and Anita sitting around one of the flimsy folding tables covered with a white tablecloth. Anita was conservatively dressed in a charcoal-gray, slim-fitting dress. Abby's dour, pretty face looked perfectly appropriate, for once. She wore a black crepe dress, cinched at her waistline, black pantyhose, despite the summer heat, and soft black suede heels.

"Where were you?" Scott whispered.

"There's Dell," Anita announced, broadly introducing her to anyone who was listening. "She just walked in." She glanced over her from head to toe. "Darling, did you get dressed in a hurry?"

"I was here," Dell answered. "You started early, didn't you?"

"We started when the church was full. How was I to know you were still coming?" Anita's lips curled into a gentle, forgiving smile. "I can overlook that, Dell. I'm just glad to see you. How long has it been? Since Christmas?" When Anita stepped close to embrace her, Dell was aware of the film of sweat on her arms and chest.

"Why is Dad sitting up there in a box?" Dell shimmied her arms and pushed Anita back. "You know that's not what he wanted. Scott? You knew it, too."

"Please." Scott's face was drawn tight. "Not now."

Sitting next to her mother and Abby, Dell wished she had put on makeup. Women were rarely given the leeway to be simply disheveled. There was always a value judgment, always some embarrassing cause assigned to someone's choice not to curl her hair or accessorize or put on some goddamned eyeshadow. Maybe Abby and Anita were on to something. Maybe they had come with armor, an invisible mask of compliance, that she had not.

"Funerals are for the living." Anita sighed and turned her elegant jawline, surveying the room. "Would you deny us the comfort of seeing his face one last time?" She sipped a glass of lemonade. "She got to see him. I suppose she's forgotten the rest of us didn't."

"Saw him? I walked in and found his dead body. Like that was a privilege," Dell snapped. Scott made eye contact with her and shook his head.

"It's insult enough, leaving a perfectly decent house to a stranger," Anita continued. "Goodness knows, your father could spare a bit of generosity when it came to his service."

"Mom," Scott said. "I know you're upset, but Aunt Myra is his sister. Not a stranger."

"She's a stranger to us, isn't she?"

Under Anita's glare, Scott straightened his tie and looked away.

"Excuse me," Dell said. "I'm feeling a little warm."

As she rose to her feet and walked away, she heard Anita continue. "Poor girl. Dell's never downplayed her aches and pains."

"I'm fine," she shouted back.

Anita's power to throw those barbs, to stick a knife in her gears, was unrivaled. Accused of exaggerating her perfectly genuine discomfort, Dell felt compelled to disown it, found herself challenged to seek out any tell that she was feeling less than perfect. As she slipped between chairs, Mason caught her eye, seated between his mother and father at a nearby table. He raised an eyebrow. *Are you okay?* Dell looked the other way and kept walking. She poured a cup of ice water and surveyed the classic funeral offerings that lined the table: pitchers of punch and lemonade, coffee, trays of cold-cut sandwiches on sweet rolls, store-bought cookies, fruit and vegetable platters. Funerals around here meant food. Too much food. Pies after cakes after casseroles. Dell's stomach churned and she was nauseous and faint, salivating.

The bathrooms were down a long hallway, lit with fluorescent lights. The door to the women's room fell shut with a loud, wooden clap. Dell examined her face in the mirror, leaned over the sink.

Behind her, she heard a toilet flush; a plastic stall door unlocked and swung open.

"You okay there, girl?" A large, kind-looking woman with long gray hair hovered behind her. She had sharp-looking cheekbones, from which her full cheeks hung slack.

Dell leaned over the sink. "I feel like I'm full of ghosts. Been half sick all week."

"Expecting?"

"No," she laughed. "No way."

"You're Gideon's girl?"

"Yeah."

The woman ran cold tap water onto a paper towel and held it to Dell's clammy neck. "That help a little?"

Dell nodded. "And you are?"

"I'm your Aunt Myra."

Myra was tall and large. Dell did not know her exact age, but she was at least five years Dad's senior. Her eyes were hawk-like, sharp in the soft expanse of her wrinkled face. She wore a black shirt tucked into black jeans and work boots that were caked with mud. Holding her hair in place was a toothed comb that looked like bone. Myra's watery green eyes scrutinized Dell, scowling but not unkind.

"You sure you're not expecting?"

"No. Not possible."

Dell looked up at the flickering light in the ceiling, watched a lone shadow skitter down the wall, disappear at her feet.

Yes, it was possible.

"Oh, Myra." She hunkered down, hung her head over her knees, felt a blank dread filling her senses. "I can't—that can't be. That can't happen."

"I've been wrong before." Myra's voice crackled when she spoke, but she was aiming for comfort. "Just not that often."

The last stall in the row opened and, with a soft click of her heels against the pink tile, Mrs. McCallan appeared. She walked to the sink and washed her hands, her wrists gently tilted downward, and blotted them dry on a paper towel.

"Didn't mean to eavesdrop, ladies." Mrs. McCallan wore the imperturbable smile of a bank teller. "Adella, should I congratulate you?"

The last time Dell had spoken to that woman, she was full of anger. Now, she wilted almost literally under her gaze, leaning forward with an audible moan.

"Have some decency, you bitch," Myra rasped. "Whoever the hell you are. At least this girl's not a self-important old busybody."

Mrs. McCallan raised an eyebrow, smile unfaltering, and walked away as Myra muttered curse words.

"That's the bad kind of woman, girl. There's two kinds of women. The ones that look out for each other and the ones that don't." She slapped Dell's shoulder. "You talk to me. Tell me about your day. Can't freeze up like this. It won't do."

"About how it looks. You're feeling a little unwelcome here, if I had to guess." Sitting on the tiled floor, Dell patted at her neck and upper chest with a damp paper towel. Myra only laughed. She cracked a tiny window near the ceiling and took a crinkled rolled cigarette from her pocket. Dell moved toward the doorway.

"Smoke bother you?"

"I don't care," she scoffed. "But if I walk back out there smelling like weed, Anita will have a field day."

Myra chuckled. In concession, she leaned up on her tiptoes and blew smoke out the window.

"You know what's funny?" Dell said. "Dad wanted to be cremated. He'd be heartbroken, to see all this nonsense. Anita—this was her idea. She's a Scorpio. Moon in Pisces. She's having a great time running this show."

"Well, listen, Dell." Myra reached into a leather shoulder bag and handed her a peppermint. "You never fixed anything by not taking care of yourself."

"Thanks." She unwrapped the candy, stuck it in her mouth. "I'd better get back."

"If you ever wanna talk about your daddy, or you need any kind of help, you come on out to the cabin. We'll be moving in before the month is gone. Gideon wouldn't want his house empty, would he?"

"You think he would have cared?" Dell didn't mind if Myra knew she was angry. "You know what I think? That house has been empty for years now. It's full of ghosts. Take it."

Dell let the door clap shut behind her as she walked into the narrow hallway. She counted weeks and months divided by nights that blurred together. The kind of math most women know how to do, weeks on the calendar running together in her memory. Her shoulder bumped against something and she looked up to see Mrs. McCallan, standing in the hallway looking into a powder compact.

"Oh!" Her voice came out a squeak. The woman was a couple inches taller than her, wearing a navy-blue dress. She had the same incisive blue eyes as her son, but colder. She clicked the compact shut, slipped it into her purse.

"You know, I feel sorry for you, Adella. In a way."

Dell shook her head as though the woman would dissipate before her eyes, an unpleasant vision.

"Here's some advice someone should have given you fifteen years ago." Mrs. McCallan laced her arm under Dell's elbow in a mock-sisterly fashion as they walked. "Find a good man and stand by him, no matter what."

"Huh." Dell saw that she was too deep in whatever lies she'd told herself to see out of them. A life sentence.

"I stayed by my husband despite all kinds of no-good women trying to ruin his name. Your marriage comes first. If you don't have that, you're…" They stood at the entrance to the reception room. She made a sad smile, shook her head. "Well, you know."

She didn't need to say the words that still echoed in Dell's ears. *Little slut.*

"And what makes you think I want to be like you?" A flash of reckless anger snapped her eyes open, stood her up straight. *Stay by your husband while his eyes, his hands slip over the bodies of little girls? Even when he lifts a hand to your own child? No man is worth that.* Dell leaned near her as if they were exchanging confidences. "I'm starting to think I don't want any advice from you. Think maybe your family isn't as perfect as it looks."

"You don't think so?" Mrs. McCallan laughed as they walked. The hallway opened into the reception room and the hum of voices grew closer. "Come and meet them. Have a look."

"No, thank you." Dell tugged at her arm, but Mrs. McCallan didn't let go. She stared down at her free hand, counted the weeks back to her last period on her fingers, folded down one finger at a time, starting over after five: *six, seven, eight, nine… That can't be right.*

"Sweetheart?"

It was a deep voice, a man's voice. Mrs. McCallan's face softened. Dell didn't need to look. Sweetheart—that was what he had called her that night. The same voice that had informed her, kindly, that math didn't come easy to girls. Dell's hands went limp. Dr. McCallan stood in front of them, Mason at his side. Gray jacket over his white shirt. Polished. Dell's arm twitched, but the woman's cool fingers were snug on her wrist.

"Jeremiah," she purred. "Mason. This is—oh, I'm sorry." Her laugh was crystalline. "Ladies first, right? Adella, this is my husband, Dr. McCallan. And this is my son, Mason."

The doctor spoke first. "Pleased to meet you. I'm so sorry for your loss. Kind man, your father."

Dell met Mason's eyes and looked away. Eurymede was turned into a bird. The Heliades, daughters of the sun, became a grove of poplar trees. And here Dell thought she had turned into an adult, and yet the sight of the old doctor set her skin crawling, her feet stumbling in a backward half-step away from him. She was sure she would pass out. Wished she could will it to happen. Mrs. McCallan let go of her wrist, still smiling.

"Son, you don't know Gideon Shaw's daughter. Do you? One of your father's patients."

"Oh, he was?" Dell saw Mason's eyes jump between her and his mother.

"So sad, for someone to die like that. An overdose. I don't know if you heard."

"No," Mason said. "I didn't."

"Oh, there's Mr. and Mrs. Portman. Come on, dear." Mrs. McCallan took her husband's arm. They were a solid, unchanging structure, a machine that ate people like Dell and Dad and threw them away. She would never be anything other than discarded here. Mrs. McCallan would always protect her husband. "Mason, come on."

"Sorry. I'll be right there." He waved them off, stared at Dell for a long second, then turned away. She recognized a younger version of him, one afraid to look away from his mother, to lose her good favor.

"Is that true?" he asked.

"Yes."

"You had no problem prying about my family, did you? But you never told me anything about your father."

"I have to tell you something."

"It's a little late." He crossed his arms, pushed his hair from his eyes, then folded his arms again. That same stress, the way he carried it in his arms, she could always soothe away, but now it felt like he was miles away from her.

"Mason, it's not that." She could see in his every movement that he wanted to walk away from her, but every inch of her body wanted to lean into him, to hold on for reassurance.

"Can it wait?" He glanced after his parents, took a half-step away. "You love me, right? I just need to trust you. Is that it?"

Dell pictured the days and months ahead. She had seen this coming. Not this exactly, but she had known it was a disaster in the making, decided to take the risk anyway. She imagined herself years from now and saw the future in reverse, looking back from there. Poor, single Dell Shaw. Pregnant. Then a mother, alone. How everyone would feel obligated to help her, or how they wouldn't. Which was worse? Maybe she had a gift for this. She saw it clearly. It was a trap. *My baby has no father. Or, my baby has a father, whose family is going to make my life miserable. Either way, my baby.* Maybe her mother had been right on one count; mess with a man like that and you'll get exactly what's coming to you.

"Never mind, Mason. It doesn't matter," Dell answered. "Not to men like you, it doesn't."

She turned and walked quickly away from him, darting through the crowd. Nine weeks, Dell tried counting up again, ten weeks, and she kept losing track and starting over, distracted in turns by her uneasy stomach and a hunch as to its cause. Of all the things that she would not have chosen, this seemed the unkindest. Dell had seen women who could mother, women who were the warm hearts of their families. She had met them and read about them. That wasn't the stock she came from. She made a beeline for the door.

As the glass doors fell closed behind her, she heard her brother's voice.

"The hell's the matter with you?" Scott caught up and stood in front of her, blocking her way. He tugged at his collar in the sun, ill at ease in a suit. "You had to argue with Mom at Dad's funeral? Today, of all days?"

"I'm sorry, Scott."

"Would you stay, for me? Just consider it a favor."

"Not today." She felt tears welling up behind her eyes and, without meaning to, lifted a hand to fan at her face, as if she could dry them away.

When Scott saw her face, his eyes softened. "What is it? You're not telling me something."

Dell shook her head. She threw her arms around his neck, hiding her face in his shoulder like she was a teenager again. "This is something you can't fix."

She squirmed out of her brother's hug and left him standing alone as she headed for her station wagon.

CHAPTER TWENTY-FOUR

Before

July 1990

Dell wasn't sure where she was going when she left, only that she needed to get out. She made a quick stop at a pharmacy, then found herself back at Mason's house. She went to the back door through the screened porch, which was always unlocked. London greeted her in the kitchen; she scratched his ears and hurried past. She tore open the cardboard box holding the pregnancy test, then went into the bathroom. Dell glared at the box, with instructions advertising "results in four minutes" to tell her what she already knew, adding up the nausea, the tired spells, all the little ways her body had told her something was not the same. She didn't have four minutes to wait.

Dell walked up the two creaky flights of stairs, collecting her things: a pair of shoes, a once-worn pair of jeans there, a bra that laid on the floor by the bed. Her father's red baseball cap. She opened the drawer in the dresser that had been designated hers and pulled out its contents in handfuls, stuffing whatever would fit into her shoulder bag with shaking hands. She knew abortions were legal, if not discussed in polite company. She still had an out. But that dread muddled with the rest of the morning, images of Mason's cold eyes, his father's over-polite smile, a picture of her father's body in its coffin. In perplexing straits, the heart wishes for simple solutions. It wanted the stark surgery of the pipeline through the forest, a boundary drawn clean through a tangle of confusion.

Her bag was full to overflowing. Dell saw pieces of clothing that belonged to her, but, without room in the bag, decided she didn't need them. Her old astrology book lay on the bedside table. It could stay there. She knew it by heart, anyway.

There were other things that belonged to her here: the left side of the bed, the tangled garden behind the screened porch, the left-hand chair at the breakfast nook in the kitchen. Those things would have cost her too dearly to keep. But Dell tripped back across the room, took the blue paint chip from where it rested on the floor. She tucked the little square of Juniper Berry Mist into her pocket and gave the loft one final look as she walked out.

Holding the banister to steady her steps, Dell walked back down the stairs. She passed the second floor with its airy bedrooms, the smell of fresh-cut wood and paint in the foyer. Watching the stained-glass panel above the front door, Dell walked right into Mason in the doorway.

"What's all that?" He scanned over her bag, a disorganized bundle of clothes sticking out of the half-zipped top.

"What does it look like?" Dell ducked her shoulder and squeezed past him, walking outside onto the porch.

"Wait a second, Dell." Mason removed his jacket and threw it on the coat rack, then tugged at the top button on his shirt until it pulled loose. "Can you tell me what's going on here?"

"I don't know," she said, considering his question. "I don't think so." The still summer warmth was oppressive even in the shade.

"This has something to do with my family, doesn't it?" Mason followed her onto the porch, pushing the cuffs of his shirt to his elbows in a rumpled hurry.

"Yes." Dell heaved an impatient sigh and sat down on the porch steps. She couldn't remember a time in her life when she had felt so tired from standing in place.

"So, your dad was a patient at my dad's office?" He sat next to her and she turned away, furious at how she wanted to throw her arms around him.

"Your father prescribed my dad painkillers for fifteen years after he got hurt, way past when he clearly didn't need them anymore. He's—he doesn't care how what he does might affect anyone else's life." She felt another shiver of nausea just from talking about the man outright. Hard to say whether Dr. McCallan or being pregnant was making her sicker.

"And what else?"

"What the hell else do you need?" she cried. As if that wouldn't have been bad enough alone. "I thought I could do this, but I can't. I'm sorry, okay?"

"I don't like seeing you like this." He sighed, laced his fingers together, stared out over the yard in thought. Her stomach turned, squeezing a whimper out of her that bent her over her knees. Mason pulled her close against him, his chin resting on the top of her head.

"Don't. Too warm." She leaned away from him. "I have to leave."

"Eat something before you go, then."

"I couldn't if I wanted to," she said with a grimace.

"Okay, how about some water?"

She nodded her head and he headed back into the house. That was good; a glass of water would clear her head, then she could leave. But could she? Dell pictured returning to her apartment, to her job, finding a clinic to end the pregnancy. She looked down at her midsection with a sense of apology. *You came to the wrong place,* she thought, *that's all. It's nothing personal.* London nosed her cheek, whining, as if he knew she didn't feel right. She scratched his head. The thought of returning to her routine filled her with dread. She knew she had enough saved to pay out the lease on her apartment. Maybe there was an alternative. Anything was better than staying here in Blyth.

She heard a muffled exclamation from the kitchen before Mason shouted to her. "Why didn't you tell me we're having a baby?"

"Shit," she moaned, pressing her palms to her eyes as she remembered leaving the pregnancy test sitting on the sink. She heard the door swing open and shut behind her without lifting her head.

"I knew something else was going on." She felt Mason's arms wrap around her and allowed herself a little breath of peace there. "You can stay with me—you can stay here. I know the timing isn't great, but we'll make it work."

"I told you I never wanted kids. Ever." She felt the blood drain from her cheeks as she realized the truth of what she said. "I can't keep it. I can't think of anything worse."

Dell regretted it as she spoke the words, and then even more as she saw shock ripple over Mason's features. But she couldn't find a way to tell him how she had seen this very same dread, that trapped quality, spelled out in every one of Anita's bad moods, how so much of her life had been about what her mother and father had missed out on or done wrong.

"I don't want to lose you," he cried, arms folded over his knees. "What is it gonna take to get you to stay?"

"If I stay, I need you to choose me or your parents. Not both."

"What? No. You can't ask me to do that." His hands opened in shock, a cold laugh of disbelief hanging after his words. "Dell, you only get one family."

She had heard people say that when a woman is pregnant, she becomes a mother before her man becomes a father. And she thought that maybe Mason didn't mean it that way. Maybe he didn't mean to say that to both of them—her, and the growing baby in her belly, like a spark in a well. But she felt it for both of them. This wasn't the family he was choosing. Anita was right. Men don't only hurt you with their muscles.

"I guess. In any case, you've chosen yours." Dell rose to her feet and pulled the strap of her bag over her shoulder. She hurried down the walkway, firethorn bushes reaching out with their spiny arms. One caught in her hair and tangled, but she pushed forward, let it pull a strand right out. London followed her, an anxious whine in his throat. She paused to scratch the dog's big ears. "That's okay, boy," she whispered. "You stay here."

"Dell, wait." As Mason walked after her, a branch from the hedge caught in his sleeve. He spun back and swiped at it, drew his scratched fist away, cursing. "There has to be a different way. I told you how I feel about family."

Dell opened the driver's side door. "Mason, you have no idea what we're talking about here."

"Of course I don't!" His voice raised to a shout. "Not if you don't tell me. I fell in love with you, and you set me up to get this wrong."

"Tell me you never, ever thought your mother or father might be wrong about one thing." She tossed her bag across the seat then moved toward him, focused on his distant stare. He began to shake his head almost imperceptibly. "Look at me and tell me you never saw them do anything wrong with your own eyes."

"No," he said. "I don't know. I—I told you, I don't remember."

"Maybe you don't want to remember," she snapped.

"Maybe I don't! I said I don't know."

"Mason, he—"

"Please," he repeated. "Can you stop this?"

Dell remembered telling Mason that she loved him in spite of whatever had formed him into who he was. Now she didn't believe that she could. Her head spun with iridescent dots crowding her vision, as if someone had thrown glitter into the air. As the air cleared, she drew a long breath, studying the man standing next to her, felt her anger melt into something weak and gentle. What she saw stung, shocked her to her bones to see how ignorant she'd been, as she recognized the dread in his eyes, the wanting to be anywhere but here, realized that she was the reason for it. *He isn't just like his family,* she realized. *I had the bad luck to cross their path two days out of my life. He lived in their house for years.* She loved him in spite of whatever made him who he was, but she could see too that hearing what she had to tell him was going to hurt him more than losing her ever could.

"Mason, you don't know it, but this is the better choice." She crossed the space between them and laid her arms around his shoulders, soft and gentle. "I have to go now."

"I should have known I couldn't trust you." He stepped out of her arms and straightened his shirt collar. "You lied about your father. You probably lied about everything else. I wish you'd had the sense to stay away from me." Somewhere, she knew he was speaking out of hurt, but the words found their mark just the same.

"I know," she said, blinking furiously at her tears. "I know you do. I'm sorry." Again, she reached for his hand, but he shook his head.

She sat down in her car, turned the keys in the ignition.

"Remember what I told you, Mason." She looked up at him through her eyelashes. She wanted to be certain he was listening. "You were never a bad kid, and there's nothing wrong with you." She thought she saw the line of his mouth soften, but registered no change in his eyes.

"Hold on." He approached the car, placed a hand on the open windowsill.

"Yeah?" She placed a hand next to his, inched her fingers as near as she could without touching.

"What about the baby?" He spoke to her like a stranger, as if this were an inconvenient formality.

Her hands dropped into her lap. "I'll handle it."

"Do you need money?"

"Money? No." She wiped her eyes dry, brows narrowing as she sat up straight. "Go to hell, Mason." She swatted his hand away, closed the window, and drove off.

Dell had always been a careful driver, and today was no different. She drove back into Blyth, parked on the curb outside her apartment. She leaned over the steering wheel and closed her eyes, pictured herself carrying her bag inside, unpacking her belongings. Afterward, she would walk up the street to the grocery store and buy a bottle of wine or some beer. Pregnant women weren't supposed to drink, but she wasn't going to be pregnant for long. She would find a clinic or a doctor who would solve her problem, then let her days resume their normal rhythm.

Again, as if she were lingering in sleep and picturing herself waking, Dell rehearsed her steps up the stairs, back into her daily life. Instead, she turned the engine back on, pulled a sloppy U-turn across the quiet street, and drove toward the mountains.

As she drove, dappled sunlight falling on the trees and the asphalt dazzled, disorienting, like glitter as she sped past. The hot light of the summer afternoon glow fell on the hillside by the roadway, as if setting it on fire. She focused on the road and counted: *pavement, oak trees, that hazy cloud over the sun.* In the *Metamorphoses,* Perimele was a pregnant girl thrown off a cliff into the sea. Dell remembered this, though she couldn't recall the date of her last period to save her life. Perimele would have drowned, but Poseidon turned her into an island. All Dell wanted was out. She didn't understand how one person could be so angry and so sad at the same time, and still love someone in spite of it. That was the worst part. Maybe she could just leave all of that right there, at the farmhouse, in the town; just walk away from it.

CHAPTER TWENTY-FIVE

Now

July 1991

"Right there," she said. "You can sit there."

Dell regretted it immediately. The plain fact of being near him left her feeling exposed, like some sort of moss-dwelling animal, something that was all eyes and no bones.

"First, you're back in town, and now you're in my favorite bar?"

Dell's hands twitched. She thought again of how complex times demand simple solutions. "You only like this bar because they let dogs in."

"Got no one else to go with me," Mason answered. "It's an important consideration."

"And I'm not really back in town."

He raised an eyebrow, teasing her. "It looks like you are."

"It only looks that way." She swirled the last inch of whiskey in her glass, watching him with suspicion. "I'm staying with Scott for a day or two. Just here for my mother."

"I see." Mason extended one arm across the bar, hand resting open next to his glass, a barrier between them. Dell felt her dress low-slung on her pale chest, her hair fallen flat with the humidity.

The bartender breezed past, offered him a menu. She refused to look at Dell.

"You hungry?" he asked.

"No." Half-drunk, she was somehow famished and also averse to the idea of food, her appetite distant. Dell remembered the hungry-looking bear who had wandered out from the woods in the spring. While humans spent entire months at a time bored, discovering new worries, other animals spent their whole days working just to eat.

The door opened and swung closed, a warm breeze in the air-conditioned cool. The quiet bar was slowly picking up customers, the afternoon ticking toward happy hour. She was distracted by the electric lights on the jukebox and the smell of cigarette smoke.

Mason was watching a baseball game, glancing toward her every few moments. Every time Dell opened her mouth to speak, she closed it again. Staring without turning her head, she studied the familiar features, which looked as if they would feel exactly the same under her fingertips.

He turned to face her, caught her looking at him. "What?"

"Nothing." She picked up her glass and realized that she had already finished the whiskey.

"So, how did you become a clairvoyant?"

"That's a funny story." Dell slapped a hand against the top of the bar. "It was you."

"Me?"

She rested her hands on the bar and leaned forward, her shoulders heavy with tipsiness. "Do you know what 'disaster' means? It means crossed stars."

"Didn't know that."

"When I first met you, I knew it was a disaster coming. Knew I ought to have walked away."

Mason picked up his glass and gave her a bold half-smile. "But you stayed."

"But I stayed." She felt herself smiling back. Remembering. "It was a mistake, and I knew it. I knew it then."

He turned to face her. "So? How's that make you a psychic?"

Dell knew how to talk without giving anything away. "Because I see things clearly," she said, curling a hand around her glass. "Turns out I'm good at guessing things, and fixing things. I got this one lady who comes to me, every week. She's always got a new hurt, like an animal in a trap. People who go to psychics have… stuff they need to talk over. Puzzles they need solved."

He listened to her, slowly nodded with his chin. "And you're good at solving puzzles?"

"Yeah. Well." Dell corrected herself quickly. She stretched an arm out in front of her, brushed his wrist by accident, then pulled back. "Other people's puzzles."

"And your own puzzles?"

Dell felt the condensation on the glass cooling her hand as she lifted her eyes to his, her expression steady and ungiving. "I find the simple approach is usually best." She tried to laugh, but choked out a syllable that sounded almost mournful. "You already know that, right?"

Dell wasn't in need of reminding how Mason looked when a thought seized him, how the fringe of blond hair fell unnoticed across his forehead when he focused on a thought. Didn't need to remember how she would brush his hair aside, one hand resting on his cheekbone, so she could see his eyes when she kissed him. *Oh, stop.* Holding back this tide of recollection, of memories that rested in her body more than in her mind was demanding more energy than she had to spare.

"To your new calling." Mason picked up his glass. "Blyth misses you, but at least the tourists have someone to tell their fortunes." She clinked her glass against his bottle and remembered that it was empty. They had nothing to drink to, anyway.

"Want me to make it up to you? Look into your future?"

He laughed. "I'll take what I can get. Do you do cards? Palm reading?"

"Oh, it depends on the day. Here—let me see your hands." Dell held out her hands, palms up. Mason angled to face her, reaching across the seat that held her bag. She picked up his left hand in both of hers, then the right, traced a fingertip over the lines in his palm and across the blue veins in his wrist.

The bar was filling up, most of the seats now full, the synthetic-sounding pop music just loud enough to make their conversation private, despite the crowd.

"Which palm do you want?" he asked.

"Both, if you want the whole picture," Dell said. "Your left hand, your non-dominant hand, that's your potential. Your dominant hand, that's what you do with your potential. It's sort of like your left hand is what God's given you, and the right hand is what you've done with it." She turned his hands over, reading his expression along with the lines in his palms. "And, supposing your left and right are different, that would mean your fate has changed. That what you've done doesn't match what you were dealt."

Dell's heart felt loose and too small. She tried to remember what she said to clients when she couldn't think of anything, something meaningless, but the lines in his familiar hands read themselves out loud.

Her fingertips traced over his left palm, across the heart line and back, resting at the line's end, at the base of his index finger. "This is your heart line, there. See how it goes straight across," and again swept her finger across it, "straight across, uninterrupted. But this one..." She picked up Mason's right hand.

"Hang on." He took his hand back, sipped his beer, and returned it. "You don't need to tell me. It's a mess."

"It isn't a mess." She briefly squeezed his hand, then loosened, embarrassed. "But it's different. See the dashes here?" She touched his right palm where several short lines crisscrossed the heart line. "Your fate isn't always set in stone." She traced down the palm.

"You're pretty good," Mason said. "What's all that mean for me?"

She felt a shock of sadness. This was so easy, this energy between them, how he played and how she resisted, until, suddenly, they weren't joking at all. She squeezed his hands tight. "It means you're—you're kind and good and handsome." Her voice dropped to a low, intimate murmur. It was a general rule that, if she didn't think she'd see someone again, she read their fortune as honestly as she pleased. "And you're gonna make some lady very happy."

"I see." Mason pulled away from her and turned back to the television.

The bar was growing louder. Dell looked at the telephone, making sure it was close enough that she would hear it if it were to ring.

"So what brought you back here? Last I heard, I was never going to see you again."

Dell shifted her legs and answered without skipping a beat. "Fate is never set in stone."

"What if I'm asking you, and not the psychic?"

"I should get going." She lifted a cautious hand to the bartender. "How much?"

"Dollar-fifty." The bartender glared at her. Dell opened her bag, planning to leave a good tip as an apology for how rudely she had spoken earlier. She unzipped the inside pocket of the red bag, reaching past the disorganized jumble of checkbook, pens, a pocketknife, scattered papers. She took out a five and laid it on the counter.

"Hey, what's that?" Mason leaned over, looking into her bag.

"Nothing." She pulled the flap closed.

"What was it?" He reached under her hand, opened the bag.

"Stop." Dell swatted at his arm. "Mason, stop it." She pulled the bag onto her lap, saw that she was too slow, that he had already plucked out her worn bundle of photographs, paper-clipped in one corner. "Give it back. Those aren't yours."

Dell watched as Mason studied the Polaroid of her, just shy of halfway through her pregnancy, wearing a perplexed smile. He turned it over, saw the ultrasound photo, breathing out like something had hit him.

"Please," she whispered. "Give those back."

There on the bottom of the stack was her little stolen paint chip, that soft blue called Juniper Berry Mist. The color she'd tried to convince him of, that he'd never really liked. He stacked them carefully, in the right order, and tucked the paper-clip back into place as he handed them over.

"Those aren't yours," she repeated, shrugged away as if she were covering up a bruise she'd rather have kept hidden.

"I guess not." Mason folded his hands on the bar. Maybe those things had once, in some way, been both of theirs. Not anymore.

Behind the bar, the telephone rang. *Anita's awake. No. Anita's dead.* She watched the phone. It rang again. Finally, the bartender answered it.

"This is Bessie's." Leaning against the counter, the woman pulled a pen from behind her ear. "Order for takeout? Sure. What can I get you?"

Dell flopped back into her seat, tipping over her ice water as she reached for her bag. As water spilled across the countertop, she leapt to her feet, knocked the stool over behind her.

"I have to go." She brushed water from her arms with stilted curses. "Shouldn't even have stayed this long."

"Wait." Mason reached for her hand. Dell looked up to find the stillness of his blue eyes, the same steadying glance he had given her the evening prior.

"For what?"

Mason brushed water droplets from her arm, his hand lingering over hers. "I don't know," he said. "Just wait. Before you leave, tell me you're okay."

"Yes." She pulled her hand away. "Sure. Okay."

She realized after she'd spoken; that was two words too many to convince. What had changed, that she could no longer hide her thoughts without any effort?

London lifted Dell's hand with his muzzle, leaned against her thigh, covering her hands with dog kisses.

"Listen, if you need to lie to me, that's fine," Mason said. "You're way past hurting my feelings. But you're not gonna fool London. He always knows when something's wrong."

In the crowded bar, it was hard to hear, or see, or think. A Cyndi Lauper song blared from the jukebox, the blurred light of the television screens and the yellow hanging lights muddled in the haze of smoke.

It was his eyes that made her talk. If the child had taken after her, not him, she could have turned and walked away.

"Mason, it's—it's the baby. She…"

His eyes widened, voice dropped to a whisper. "She?"

"She's missing."

"What?" He took a bill from his wallet and placed it on the counter. Dell could see the strain in his eyes, the way he carried stress in his shoulders and arms. "Why didn't you tell me you needed help? Let's go."

Dell hesitated. London, who seemed to know better than her when she was in deeper water than she realized, took the hem of her dress in his teeth and pulled her toward the door.

CHAPTER TWENTY-SIX
Before
July 1990

Dell drove away from Blyth as the sunset deepened into night. She slept in her car at a campsite, promising herself to go home in the morning. But morning came, and she drove further south, down the road that wound across the Blue Ridge. At a payphone, she placed one call to the farm supply shop to let them know not to expect her back, another to her landlord, promising to send a check for the last two months on the lease.

She passed four more weeks in the mountains, blending in with the summer tourists, wearing her father's baseball cap pulled down low on her forehead. She slept wherever it was easiest—a motel, if she passed one near nightfall. If not, she slept at campsites or in her car. By dark, far from city lights, the stars were so bright she couldn't sleep without pulling a blanket over her eyes.

Absent the people, scenery, and routines that had formed the landscape of her days, Dell found that to be alone with herself was a kind of drug. In her previous life, a few hours of quiet in between work and dinner with Mason were restorative. But days on end of her own company were like falling down an empty well.

She ate at roadside diners, fighting her nausea with the greasy, sense-dulling foods she usually avoided. As July passed into late summer, she found the nausea, the spells of lightheadedness, gave way to a deep sense of well-being. Her fingernails grew in strong and white. Her skin was vibrant, hair lustrous. And her head began to clear. She knew that her savings would deplete in time, that the summer would end. Aunt Myra's gravelly voice followed her everywhere. *Can't freeze up like this. It won't do. You never fixed anything by not taking care of yourself.* The panic of being pregnant had subsided with distance, and each day Dell promised herself that she would find the nearest clinic tomorrow, or the next day. That it was as good as done.

One August evening, the smoked-peach sunlight fading into violet, Dell had just begun to scan for a place to sleep when something caught her eye. In the wide ditch by the roadside, a patch of shrubby, spiny-looking plants with jagged-looking leaves and deep purple stems. In the lowering light, their white-and-violet-streaked whorled blossoms were beginning to open.

She pulled over in the nearly obscured driveway to look more closely, got out of the car and left the engine running. She had seen jimsonweed before, just not this much of it. A nightshade, relative of morning glory, it was also called *Datura stramonium,* or mad-apple, or stinkweed. The night-blooming flowers were long and bell-shaped, the spiny, toxic seed pods clustered beneath. They would turn brown and sharp as the fall turned into winter. True to one of its common names, a faint but unpleasant fragrance rose from the ditch. Dell looked up the drive. Maybe it was a safe place to rest.

Hidden from the road by the jimsonweed and a cluster of locust trees, the parking lot opened to a wide view of the Shenandoah Valley below. She looked down and recognized the shape of Blyth in the distance. In back of the parking lot, she saw a gray concrete building, which, at first glance, looked deserted, until she saw the red neon sign in the second-floor window: THE PSYCHIC IS IN. She parked and walked up the stairs, pausing halfway up to catch her breath, which she had never had to do before. She wore Dad's baseball hat, the green dress from her father's funeral, which was a little more snug than it used to be. To a stranger, she would have only looked five pounds heavier. At the entryway, Dell pushed aside a beaded curtain and stepped through.

"Hello? Is anyone there? I need a reading."

A harried-looking woman rushed up from behind a paneled room divider. She looked close to thirty, with dark blonde hair, a cardboard box precariously balanced on her left hip. "Yes?"

Dell looked over her shoulder at the sign, which, reversed in the window, made a pretty series of loops and curlicues. "Is the psychic in?"

"I'm afraid that's me," the blonde answered. "Look, hon, I'm in the middle of moving out. I can't help you."

"Why?"

"Why, you said?" She sighed sharply and glanced at her watch. "I barely ever made enough here. Enough to cover the bills, most times, but I've got a kid to feed. Rather break the lease than keep bleeding cash."

"I'm sorry to hear that. I could really use a fortune teller right about now." *Someone to tell me where to find a job or a place to live.* Dell took off her baseball cap and wiped sweat from her forehead. She studied the view from the window, glanced back into the small apartment. "Hey, how much is the rent on this place? I have my checkbook with me."

The woman set the box down and eyed Dell as if appraising her.

"It'll save you breaking the lease," Dell added. "I don't have a kid to feed. It's perfect."

"What kind of gift do you have? Psychic? Anything? Tell me you're at least good at making things up."

"Oh, yeah." Dell laughed to cover the shock of sadness that washed over her. It wasn't time to think about that now. "This is something I can do. Astrology. Lying. You name it."

The psychic's eyes looked tired. "Kid, if you want to take over my rent on this place, you go ahead. It'd make my life easier. There's the shop out front. Kitchen. Bedroom in back."

"Great," she said. "I'll take it."

She helped the woman carry a few boxes down the stairs, then wrote her a check for the first month's rent and some furniture left behind that put a good dent in her savings.

Before the woman drove off, Dell handed her one last box. "Any advice?"

"Yeah. First thing, being a psychic isn't just having foresight. You're a therapist. At a fraction of the cost." The psychic fluffed her hair, batted her eyelids in thought. "If you think someone's gonna pay well, or come back again, tell them what they want to hear. Otherwise, you may as well tell them what they need to hear. You gotta balance cultivating your good karma and protecting your interests."

Dell carried in her bag full of clothes, the cleaner items mixed in with the ones that needed washing. She hung Dad's baseball cap on an empty nail in the wall, then stood at the window and looked out at the valley. The summer constellations were bright in the sky. *Scorpius, the scorpion. Cygnus, the swan. Delphinus, dolphin.* She still knew where she was. After several hours spent unpacking, Dell made up the twin bed and pulled the blanket up to her shoulders. She slept heavily, without dreams, and woke with the sunrise. It was her first decent night's rest in weeks—probably since leaving Blyth. Probably, she realized, since she'd slept at Mason's side. Dell threw the bedroom curtain open so the sunlight made her wince and blink. She imagined the bank of jimsonweed outside as a charm, a thorny boundary within which she had no secrets to protect, nobody to worry about but herself—least of all, Mason.

CHAPTER TWENTY-SEVEN

Before

August 1990

It was mid-morning when Dell heard footsteps up the stars, the unfamiliar jingle of the doorbell. A girl of about fifteen walked in: crimped hair, amber-rimmed eyeglasses, toting a faded backpack.

"You the psychic?" The girl sniffed with surprise.

"I guess," Dell answered. "Clairvoyant, if you prefer."

"What's a clairvoyant?"

"Same thing. It means someone who sees things clearly."

The girl cast a skeptical look around. "Doesn't seem like it."

"Yeah, well, I just moved in." Dell slid out a chair and motioned for her to sit. "So why are you here?"

The teen laughed and stretched her legs out in front of her. "Don't know why I came in. I don't believe in psychics."

"Yeah? Then I guess it doesn't matter what I tell you." This would be easy, Dell thought. She reached out her hand, swept her fingers in, until the girl offered her palm. No idea what she was doing. She would have to learn this. Find a book or something. Dell traced over the girl's palm, making up phrases. "Strong lifeline. There's a dash in your—your spirit line."

"Why won't my mother let me go to the spring dance with my boyfriend?"

"Oh, nonsense," Dell answered, waving a reflexive hand at her. "Your mom's worried about you." The same thing she would say to any girl of that age.

"Please," the girl sighed. "I am not spending my allowance on this."

Dell shrugged, let her hand linger on the girl's palm. "Oh." Something like a vision clouded her mind. She saw a picture of a woman slumped over, asleep at a kitchen table. Not her memories. Not her family.

"What?"

"Doesn't matter," she said. "You don't believe in this stuff." Dell saw her father, ten years earlier, hunched over his elbows at the kitchen table, one hand curled lazily around a Mountain Dew. *You sure you gotta go out tonight, Strawberry?*

"You can't do that," the girl answered. "Tell me."

Dell looked her in the eye and released her hand. "She drinks too much when you're not there. You—you don't have to keep an eye on her, but find something for her to do that night. So she's not alone."

"What are you talking about?"

"At least she's asking you to stay with her!"

"Screw you." The girl jumped up and hurried toward the door, dragging her backpack after her with one hand. "How do you know anything?"

"I don't," Dell insisted, her hands raising in a no-offense gesture. "I don't know anything."

As the girl ran out, the door swung shut behind her. Dell glanced after her uncertainly, wondering what had just happened. She wished her father would let her rest, even if he couldn't, not even in death.

Dell turned away from the neon sign in the window and wandered back to her unpacking, hands resting on her belly. She remembered Myra's voice again, telling her *there's two kinds of women.* Maybe she could be the good kind, the helping kind. But as the days went on, she found that was how it happened, sometimes. Dell asked, and got an answer. Sometimes a voice she knew, a face she remembered, sometimes strangers. Sometimes she asked and got none, filled in the gaps with lies and kindly understanding.

She pictured herself in her solitude as if set apart for a purpose, as though she were a nun or an oracle. Her loneliness, then, felt purposeful. It was a gift, mined in solitude, that allowed her to look at a stranger and lay a soothing finger on whatever hurt. Something to hold onto when she felt the rushing current of her loneliness around the edges of her thoughts. In the afternoons she would make long drives to secondhand stores, collecting furniture, clothing for her blossoming figure, and any decor that she found interesting. She had a fond eye for items that once held value to some former keeper: an old Bible, a book of love poems with an inscription from a husband to a wife, a child's handmade ashtray from a pottery class.

And so she began to repopulate her hours. The days assumed a shape: she rose before dawn, took a brisk walk, ate a plain breakfast of oatmeal. She liked to leave her errands, if she had any, for after business hours, warding off the demon of a restless evening alone. Dell flipped on her sign whenever it pleased her, but always by nine o'clock, and generally turned it off by dinner time. Each day, at least a handful of people would come in.

Dell grew practiced at listening, at aiming her advice at the heart of what ailed them, as if setting bones, salving pains. She collected dried plants and made them into wreaths, decked with feathers, pine cones, a fragment of a bird's nest, an empty semicircle of twigs. She filled the little apartment with fragrance and color. And food, because she was hungry, snacking every couple of hours.

Every year, the waning of summer had brought her a deep sense of relief. To feel the pinch of a cool breeze returning to the mornings and evenings relaxed her. With all its blossoms and harvests, summer carried a kind of imperative with its bounty. Autumn was always welcome. But this year, she felt only anxiety. Who could say the seasons would pass as they had before? She slept uneasily in the twin bed, waking too cold, then too warm. Dell dreamed that she had woken with blood slick between her legs, that she was no longer pregnant. When the sun rose and she found her state unaltered, she felt a prick of guilty dismay. To rise from her bed was a physical challenge: she swung out one leg, and then the other, and then heaved her pendulous weight to standing. Remembering that she still had months to go, she whimpered a tired breath. But how many months? Dell knew that the baby hadn't moved. She knew she couldn't be more than four months gone. She tried, again, to count back to her last period, and couldn't remember. It wouldn't do not to know, not to have someone helping her who knew about stuff like this.

So Dell made an appointment for herself at a women's clinic two counties over. The morning of the appointment was golden but also chilly—a delicate balance between climates. The equinox was only a few weeks away. As she started the engine, Dell realized she had not driven her station wagon for nearly two weeks. Her gently rounded belly was visibly nearer to the steering wheel than before.

The waiting room was small but clean. A nurse weighed her and checked her blood pressure and pricked her finger to draw her blood. She was measured with what felt like an endless series of numbers: weight, one hundred and forty pounds; height, five feet, eight inches; blood pressure, one hundred and twenty over eighty; weeks and days along, eighteen and three.

The nurse proclaimed, "Healthy mom and healthy baby."

Dell answered, "I know." She had a sense that she was in better health than ever.

Dell unbuttoned her shirtdress to her hips and laid back on the table, the chipped yellow vinyl covered with a sheet of waxed paper, a gesture at sanitation that echoed the sharp scent of disinfectant, crinkling with her every breath. Finally, the nurse spread some clear, cold stuff on her exposed belly. Dell did not care for the smell of disinfectant and the hum of the machinery. Their presence put too much weight on the faith she felt in her little sprout. After all, by every sign she'd seen her body was well, deeply and intensely so, all her senses sharp and all her features bright. When the nurse pressed a little wand to her belly and Dell heard a quiet heartbeat, warm and steady, the room around her seemed to shake. She receded into herself, and she felt that she and the new creature were passengers in the same vessel.

Dell flinched when she saw the staticky, black-and-white image that pulsated on the screen. Heard her intuition whispering to her again. *Someone else is in the room.* It was never the shadows in the corners. The baby's head was large, and it stretched one arm behind its shoulders. Little legs, bent at little knees.

"How big is it?" she whispered. The nurse smiled and cupped her hands. Dell hadn't expected it to look so much like a baby, so soon.

"Congratulations," the nurse said. "At almost four months along, you're both perfectly healthy."

"I know," Dell repeated, and she felt proud, if perhaps a bit rude.

While the nurse did the ultrasound, she pointed out the perfectly forming body.

"These are the baby's hands," she said, "and these are the baby's feet."

Dell rested a hand on the side of her rounded, warm belly. Pregnancy was a state of being, but a baby had two parents.

Finally, the nurse asked, "Do you want to know the sex?"

Dell shook her head. It was easier to think of her current form as a liminal state, a transient state. She was with child. That was all.

"This your first?"

"Yes."

"It's normal to be nervous."

"I don't know if I'm nervous, so much." Dell caught the nurse's eye as she filled in numbers on a chart. "So much as I just wish I weren't pregnant."

The nurse's eyebrows raised, although she quickly recovered her reaction. She frowned as if she had been told she was serving an inferior product. "It's way too late to do anything about that now."

"I wasn't asking you to." Hands resting on her belly, Dell intended her words to scold, but they echoed pleading. The nurse printed an image from the screen and handed it to her. Less than halfway gone and she could see its little hands, a face, a belly and folded legs. She tucked it carefully away in her bag, folded in half over the blue paint chip, and whispered the words quietly, "Juniper Berry Mist."

She remembered her father's funeral. That little thing inside her, with its gentle heartbeat, had thrown a grenade into the fragile balance of her life. Pushed her away from Mason, away from home. *I found one good thing, one safe place, and you showed up to ruin it.* Dell didn't know how it was possible to be so angry at something so small, something that was only there because of her own stupid mistakes, in any case.

Outside, she glared at the clinic building, at the general direction of the unfriendly nurse, and thought out loud. "There's two kinds of women. The ones that look out for each other and the ones that don't."

Of course. Myra.

With a heavy foot on the gas, Dell drove north, toward Blyth, away from her psychic shop, until she saw the naked strip of land that surrounded the pipeline, and she knew she was close to home. Or, at least, where home had been. Route 7 intersected the parkway where it met the pipeline. To the left, it headed back toward Blyth. To the right, it twisted down into a steep decline, wandering into the mountainside, toward the house that had been Dad's. She turned right.

By twilight, the familiar driveway looked cast in black and white, less than real. Twilight, Dell recalled, referred to that time of day when the world was lit by two lights, the crossing of the sun and moon. The monochromatic cast of the familiar yard seemed to wash it clean of old, and newer, memory.

Dell walked up the hill to the sound of children's voices, and as she drew closer, she saw small bodies whizzing around the yard in the near dark. The three children—no, four—of varying, indistinct sizes, chased and jumped after fireflies. A boy leapt and caught one in cupped palms, shouted, and ran several yards to deposit it in a big glass jar at the foot of the juniper tree.

When they heard her footsteps, they responded like a flock of birds. Weird little chirps and cleared throats alerted the rest of the gang to an intruder. The children clustered together as she approached them.

"I'm here to see your grandmother," she said. "Can you tell her Gideon's daughter is here?"

The boy, the tallest one, nodded his head. "Grandma!" he shouted. The others shortly joined in, their little voices thin and harsh, shouting *Grandma!* over and over as they led her to the front steps. Two little girls took her hands, and a third took her duffel bag, tugging at the zipper as she trailed behind her. In the familiar rocker near the front door was one of Myra's daughters, green-eyed and plump, who had the comely, soft-limbed complacence of a house cat. Dell hoped she might stand up and greet her; instead she, too, turned her chin toward the front door and called, "Momma!"

In a red flannel bathrobe and her long, salt-and-pepper hair hanging down her back, Myra was waiting behind the screen door.

Myra's voice was metallic, almost a rasp, but not unmelodic. "I figured we'd be seeing you, Dell." She opened the door and stepped aside to let her in. "Come on in. I see the kids got your bag."

The children deposited her duffel bag like a carcass just inside the doorstep and circled it like vultures. One of the littlest ones picked up the strap and chewed on it; the others began to unzip the various pockets. Dell didn't have the energy to stop them.

She cleared her throat. "You said I could come if I needed help. Well, I need help. Myra, I don't want to be pregnant anymore."

CHAPTER TWENTY-EIGHT

Now

July 1991

Outside the bar, the afternoon sun was bright. Dell squinted, held a hand over her brow.

"Come on," she said, pointing to her station wagon. "My mother's having surgery right now. I'd like to wait at the hospital. We can talk on the way."

"I'd rather you didn't drive."

"I only had—"

"You said yourself you hadn't eaten," Mason said, cutting her off. "And you never drink."

"Like you would know." *Classic Taurus. Always had to be right.* Yet, he was right. This time.

Mason unlocked his Jeep, took out a thermos and a dog bowl, poured cold water for London. They stood in the shade on the sidewalk.

"Well?" He looked up at her from where he was crouched next to the dog, ruffling his fur. "Why don't you pick up from last summer, and just tell me what happened."

Dell sank down beside him, leaned her back against the brick wall. "We can skip to last winter. She was born in February. I had the church send a social worker. Closed adoption." She shrugged her shoulders and let her head droop over her knees. The hot sun felt like it was turning the whiskey to vapor in her stomach. "Skip to yesterday. Anita visited me at work. Keep in mind, I've spent the last year trying not to let her or anyone know where I am."

Mason's answer was a cough, a breathy syllable of laughter. "I'm aware."

"Anita said that she's missing. Well—what she said exactly was that she's as good as homeless."

"And?"

"And then she stormed out and drove her car right in front of a truck. Been in the hospital ever since."

Mason had always been even-tempered, almost to a fault. But he turned away from her so suddenly, his eyes so cold and hard to read, that it frightened her. He picked up London's water bowl, climbed into his Jeep and turned the engine. At the growl of the motor, London whined and followed him, leaping into the back of the cab over his lap.

"You're angry at me." Dell climbed in, perched on the edge of the passenger seat, half expecting him to push her out.

"Adella…" Mason swiveled in his seat to face her, expression incredulous. "Angry doesn't begin to cover it. You walked out on me, had our baby, gave it away, and now it's missing?"

"It?" she snapped. "Her. Not it."

"You have no idea how much I've worried about you." Mason narrowed his eyes, looked at her as if he wanted to say more. He was right again. She hadn't considered it. Figured he would have stopped worrying as soon as she was out of his sight. It didn't matter.

"I'm not here to fix things with us, okay?" She held his gaze, waited for him to nod, then continued. "I waited for Anita to wake up at the hospital. I looked through their records there. Asked some people my mother knows from church. They had an idea, but it didn't go anywhere. Mason, I don't know what to do now."

His nervous gesture was familiar to her, the square, suntanned hand tugging a crease into his blond hair. "Why'd you get your mother involved? You don't even like her."

"Yeah? Well, you sure as hell weren't there." Dell was shocked, then, at the sudden shout that she couldn't hold back.

"Are you kidding? I begged you not to go." His voice rose along with hers, eyes bright.

Dell leaned forward on one hand, index finger pointed as if she wanted to put a curse on him. Her fingertip brushed the fabric of his t-shirt. "That is not how I remember it."

"Why don't you tell me how you remember it?"

Dell sighed, reeling in her anger. "I came back for one reason, okay? I just need to know she's okay, then I'm gone."

"Fine." He crossed his arms and stared out the windshield.

Dell clicked the door open, swung one leg out. "Now, unless there's anything else, I need to get back to the hospital."

"Wait. Sit down." Mason's tone softened. "There is something."

"What?"

He faced away from her, turned into the back seat to pet the dog, as if he were talking to London instead. "I have an old friend who works for the city. Social Services. She's a receptionist. You know—file cabinets everywhere. Office closes at five, though."

"What time is it?"

"How would I know?"

Dell looked at the dials on the dashboard. "If that clock is right, it's quarter till. I'll follow you there."

"Buckle your seatbelt, please." Mason braced one arm around her headrest and looked back over his bicep, backing out of the parking lot. "It hasn't even been five minutes. I'll bring you back to get your car later."

Dell crossed one knee over the other, started to protest but held her tongue. She wasn't used to letting someone else drive.

Mason took a turn and headed down a hill, past a tree-lined park, and down Blyth's old Main Street, lined with brick shop-fronts and streetlights hung with baskets of flowers, coleus and sweet potato vines, dusty and wilting. They slowed to a near stop in front of the block that held the municipal buildings, then he parked in a courtyard that opened off the road in front of a tall gray stone building. Dell waited, soaking in the yellow sunlight, the haze it cast over the sleepy street. This was her favorite time of day: the golden hour. Mason opened the door and held his hand out. "You coming?"

Dell took his hand and stepped down. For a moment, it could have been any day; they could have been any two people, and she almost wished that they were. London glanced up at Dell as if he were glad to see her.

She followed Mason through the parking lot and to the front door, a glass door next to a green-striped awning. A sign over the door read DEPARTMENT OF SOCIAL SERVICES. Mason rang the doorbell. He leaned down and whispered to his dog.

"Be polite now, boy."

The woman who came to the door was about forty, with highlighted blonde hair, frosted with gray. She wore it youthfully, pulled back gently, a few loose strands framing her face, which had high, broad cheekbones.

"Mason McCallan! I haven't seen you in years." She had straight teeth and a manufactured smile, and she wore a red dress with a row of buttons at its wide collar. Her eyes landed on Dell. "We're just closing."

"Adella, this is Caroline. She lived next door to my folks growing up."

"Your first babysitter." She gave his elbow a gentle, playful squeeze.

"So you were," Mason said.

"Who's your friend?"

Dell didn't wait for him to speak. She reached out, took Caroline's right hand, picturing Anita as she smiled. "I'm Adella. It's really nice to meet you." A gentle squeeze, then she let go. "And this is London. After Jack London. He's really Mason's dog, but he likes me better." She almost winked, beamed a sweet smile.

"Jack London. You would." Caroline laughed, smiling at Mason. "What brings you here?"

"I need to ask you a favor. Can we come in?"

"Oh." Caroline's smile faltered, her gaze jumping between Dell and Mason. "Come in. London has to stay outside, though."

Mason tied the dog's leash to the mailbox, patted his head, asked him to wait. "You don't like her better, do you?" he murmured, looking sideways at her. "She's just jealous, isn't she?"

"Shut up," Dell whispered. "Inside. Now."

Dell saw that the office was darkened. Caroline flipped on a light. She led them past the cherry wood reception desk and behind a row of tall file cabinets. A clock on the wall read five minutes until five. There was a quiet confidence in how Mason observed before he spoke, the ease of someone more accustomed to the company of trees than people. He leaned with one arm on top of the metal cabinet.

"Caroline, what kind of files does this department keep on adoptions? And foster children?"

"We have a file on each case," Caroline said. "It's sensitive, as you can imagine. Closed adoptions are not public record."

"Of course. And if I asked you to let me take a look through them?" As he spoke, Dell hovered uneasily near the door. She started to angle her weight from one hip to the other, then, worried she would appear impatient, stood up straight and awkwardly. She clasped and unclasped her hands, afraid she would look nervous.

"Adella, why don't you take a seat?" Mason pulled out a wooden chair from a small round conference table. Dell sat down, then looked coolly up at Caroline.

Caroline spoke only to Mason, throwing occasional, annoyed glances in Dell's direction.

"Is it for work, or something?"

"No," he said. "Not for work. We wouldn't be here if we had the time to go about it a different way."

"And if I were somehow getting the impression you don't want anyone to know…"

"You'd be correct."

Caroline sighed. "Let me think." She filled a teapot with tap water from a sink in the corner, then walked through the office watering each of several plants.

"Come on, Carrie. For old times' sake?" Mason asked.

Dell could have shielded her eyes from his knowing smile. When he decided to charm, he did not miss his mark. She winced at the resemblance between him and his father, the source of so much worry, like a scratch she picked at, refused to allow to heal. But then she realized, and wondered how it had escaped her before—Mason didn't smile like his father. His smile drew you in because he was kind and honest enough that you could see it on his face. Dell shook her head as if it would clear her thoughts, then found herself dizzy again. The whiskey was a mistake.

Caroline took a ring of keys from her desk drawer. "The files you want are in boxes twenty-eight through thirty. Right here." She unlocked a closet and tapped the top shelf with the heel of her hand.

"Caroline, thank you."

She glanced at Dell again, whose presence, and silence, announced she had some implicating role. "Hope you find whatever you're looking for."

"Thank you," Dell murmured.

"I'll leave you to it, then," Caroline said. "Lock the door on your way out, and don't use the phone. Remember, you're not here."

Mason called after her. "It was good to see you."

As Caroline walked out, she flashed a smile, and Dell saw that she was shockingly pretty when she wanted to be.

"Well, don't you just charm your way through town?" She sat her bag on the table and picked up the keys.

"And you don't."

She walked toward the closet, looking up at the boxes, which were just out of reach. "Yeah, if ruining some poor bartender's day counts as charming."

"Everybody has bad days." She didn't see him coming until he was right next to her, lifting one box down, placing it on the table, returning for the next one. "Sit down. I've got it."

Dell sat at the table and pulled the lid up from the first box. Her hands came away gray with dust. The first box held files marked with the letters A through F.

"It looks like these are in alphabetical order," he said, checking the next box. "This one has G to M."

"I was hoping they would be chronological." She wiped her palms on her black dress, leaving two dusty handprints on her sides. "We only need to see anything from the last six months." She moved her chair so that it was in front of the third box. "I'll start at this end. You take the A through F box and start there. Just pull anything that has my name, or Anita's. Anything," she said. "Anything with a baby born about five months ago."

"Did she—did the baby have a name?" he asked.

"Just look at the dates."

Dell felt she was balancing something unwieldy, heavy. For several minutes, only their occasional baffled sighs broke the silence. The files were in disarray: social workers' cases, occasional photos, handwritten notes, only the odd photocopied certificate or official letter. Dell got from Z to T before she found any record from the last year, which was an adoption file for a little boy, four years of age.

Mason sat down with a yellow file folder and brushed the dust from his fingers on his blue jeans. "So, you're really not gonna talk to me? You don't think I've wondered—even once?"

She focused on the papers she was holding. "Wondered what?"

"Where you were. If you were okay, healthy. I figured if you had the baby, that you would keep it. Kind of liked thinking of it that way."

"Yeah, well. Sorry to shatter your illusion." Dell shuffled papers into a stack, felt a paper cut on her left thumb. She hissed a quiet swear word, held her hand out to look at it.

"You okay?"

"Yeah." Left thumb. As if she needed a reminder. An injury to the left thumb meant family, community ties out of sync. "Nothing I didn't know."

"Huh?"

"It's a palm reading thing." She pressed her thumb to her forefinger to stop the bleeding. "And to answer your question? I like picturing it that way, too, sometimes. Truth is, I have nothing to offer a baby. Or anyone else. I hope you don't think I didn't love her." Suddenly, she was on the edge of crying. Pulled it back in. "I'm just—drunk. Hungry. Stupid, I don't know."

"That's okay, Dell." From the opposite side of the table, Mason studied her, his face unreadable.

Dell bit back a useless apology. She remembered that the key to escaping apology, as she used to tell herself, was making mistakes on a scale that defied repair. Was that not what she had achieved here? She remembered that day in the woods, last spring, when she and Mason talked about the forest, nature's limited availability to replenish itself, and heard her voice echoing from that day. *They use different poisons now.* Not everything healed with time.

"Talk about something else," she said. "Now, please."

"Okay, one thing I've always wondered." He sat a folder on the tabletop, fingertips drumming a tense, muted rhythm. "Why do you call your mother Anita?"

Dell laughed without smiling. "Well, it was her idea. Whenever I was younger and she inconveniently had to watch me when she had a date, the guy would always ask if I was her little sister." She stared hard at the paper in her hands without focusing on the words. "The first and last thing you need to know about Anita? She's so beautiful. Even right now, in her hospital bed with half her head shaved. But back then, you wouldn't believe it if you saw her. Probably didn't look old enough to have a teenaged daughter."

"She couldn't just make the time for you instead?"

"I was fine," she shot back. "I was old enough to look after myself. But calling her Anita instead of Mom started to stick after a while."

Mason nodded and pursed his lips. He looked as though he would speak, then shook his head, filing the thought away.

"Why are you looking at me like that?" Between a day of humidity and all the dust, Dell felt sticky and messy, her hair out of control. She smoothed it into place with her palms.

"Nothing."

"Well, would you stop it? I need to focus on this." Dell sighed and turned her mind from the familiar topic. It was such a fragile peace between them—as fragile as it was shallow, a coating of ice, a surface she did not intend to break.

"I'm never having children," she said. "There's just too much room to do wrong."

"Yeah, you said that before." He began to smile. "And now here we are."

Dell smacked a file down on the table. "A birth mother is not a mother. That's not the same thing. Maybe it's better if we don't talk."

She opened another file, browsing the details of another stranger's life. She remembered reclining on the sofa after she had the baby, letting Anita braid her sweaty hair, mumbling to herself. *Maybe the measure of love is how badly we want to do right.*

Mason stood up suddenly, knocking a stack of papers to the ground. "Here. Look."

Jumping to her feet, Dell drew close to him, looking over his shoulder. The certificate was filled in with loopy handwritten print. Age: three months. Year, birth mother: unknown. Town: Blyth. Dell's finger trailed to the month. "January. Too early."

"Oh," he said. "What was the date?"

She answered instantly. "February nineteen."

"Pisces, huh?"

"Yeah. Pisces." She smiled, daydreaming. "Wait. How'd you—"

"You left your big astrology book at my place."

"You didn't read it," Dell laughed. Stopped laughing. "Did you?"

Mason turned back to the papers in his hand, shrugged one shoulder. "Skimmed it."

Working backward from Z, Dell was already at the M files. Although they were disorganized, and not what she sought, each one was a small comfort. Each one meant a child in a home, a child in a family.

"I never called her Mom again. Not until—oh." She had, that day Anita came after the baby was born. She had called her Mom and cried.

"What?"

"Nothing." Dell continued to ramble, continued distracting herself. "My dad wasn't like Anita. He was sweet, easygoing. He just couldn't get anything to go the way he wanted. Not even when he was dead. You remember the funeral? He was supposed to be cremated. That was in his will." She felt herself smiling, surprised at the absence of anger when she mentioned Dad. "He would've done whatever Anita wanted, so I know he wouldn't mind, not really. Just isn't quite fair, though."

"You miss him?"

"No," she answered. "Not like you miss your grandfather. He'd been halfway out the door since I was a kid. I used to stand there while he slept and pinch his arms so he didn't sleep too deep and quit breathing."

"See, I never knew that." He looked at her unhappily. "Sorry. That's…"

"Don't be. It's done. I just wish his funeral could have been the way he wanted it, that's all."

Dell looked up at Mason over a lapful of papers. They had reached the edge of the things they could still talk about. The funeral was where it ended.

Dell studied a small photograph that was paper-clipped to a file folder. Adoptive father Haney, Alvin. "This one goes in your stack," she said. "These are so out of order."

"I've already looked through those."

"So that's it? That can't be."

Mason sighed and pushed his chair back with his feet. "This was my only idea. Can you read your palms or something?"

"It doesn't work like that." She opened her hands, then closed them. "Besides, don't you think I tried?"

"You wanna tell me how it does work?"

Dell shook her head no. "Anita knows something." She propped her elbow on the table and leaned her chin in her palm. "Even in her exaggerations, there's always a truth somewhere."

"You said she was at the hospital."

"She's been out cold since yesterday. She was in surgery this afternoon. I need to call and check, see if they're still keeping her sedated."

"Don't. Remember," Mason said, "Caroline doesn't want us using the phone. No one's supposed to be here."

Dell sorted the files, in a neat stack, back into their box. "These are probably in better order than when we found them," she said, tucking everything in. She lifted the box with both arms, maneuvered it to rest on one hip, and hauled it back toward the cabinet with tottering, uneven steps.

"Let me."

"No," she stepped firmly out of his way. "I've got it."

She lifted the drawer up onto the shelf. It took all her muscle to raise it above her head. The file box teetered on the edge of the shelf, and she pushed it back with one hand.

"Let me help," Mason repeated. He lifted the files as if they were a box of matches, pushed it back into place, then locked the cabinet. "It's heavier than it looks."

Those arms, she thought. Still. Always. The swell of his biceps cast a momentary stupidity over her. Dell turned and walked away, waiting by the door as he turned off the lights. She couldn't tell if she was trying to fight back crying or sneezing from all the dust.

"There has to be something else. I can talk to someone at the church," she said.

Mason held the door open and she walked out ahead of him, untied the dog's leash, handed him the lead. The sun crept near the mountains, and the street was deserted except for an ice cream shop two blocks up, where a line of teenagers and families with children extended out onto the sidewalk.

"Maybe I could ask around nearby towns," Dell continued. "Maybe it's a mistake to only look here."

"It's past six." Mason stopped outside the Jeep and turned to face her as London waited impatiently, pulling toward the door. "Offices will open tomorrow, but nothing else is going to happen tonight."

"What offices? Tomorrow's Saturday!" she cried. "I'm not ready to be out of options."

"We're not out of options," he said, squinting against the sunset light. "But we are for today."

"I don't know what to do. I feel like you don't understand this." She grabbed his hand, squeezed tight. "She's my baby, and I don't know where she is, or if she's okay."

None of the tools in her arsenal was ready. Yell, walk out, hide? None of those options was going to help her here. Dell was so hungry and so tired that her thoughts eddied and pooled uselessly. She hadn't felt so faint since she was pregnant. Mason rested an elbow on the hood of the car and met her dread with his patient stare.

"Look, come home with me. I'll make you something to eat. You can use my phone, call and check on your mother. If she's awake, I'll take you there right away. Or to your car. Whatever you want."

"I don't know, Mason." She'd promised herself not to return to Blyth because of him; how was she supposed to stomach not just being here, but going home with him?

"Mind, this is not a date." He held a hand out to emphasize his point. "If the mother of my child needs a hot meal and a place to sit down, I owe her that."

"I'm not hungry. Would you take me back to my car now?"

"I never had a chance to do one decent thing for you." Mason leaned back against the Jeep with an exaggerated sigh. "Not when your dad died. Not when you were pregnant. I would have done anything for you, and you couldn't even tell me the truth."

"Mason, it isn't that simple. You know it's not."

"Oh, I do? Maybe I'm just supposed to take it on faith." He clapped a hand over his eyes and tossed his chin back. "And now you want me to leave you half-drunk at a dive bar. You are intolerable, you know that?"

"Yeah? So are you," Dell grumbled, flushed with shame. "You've always got to be right."

She walked to the passenger side door, climbed into the familiar seat, let the dog clamber up over her knees, into the back. "Come on," she said. "Let's go."

CHAPTER TWENTY-NINE

Before

August 1990

"You said I could come if I needed help. Well, I need help. Myra, I don't want to be pregnant anymore."

As Dell spoke, the children, Myra's grown daughters, and even the room around her fell silent. She realized, standing there in the doorway, that the cabin barely looked any different. Only two months had passed since she had been here last. It was adorned with Myra's accessories, her earthy smell, a litter of brightly colored plastic children's toys, but the shape of things was the same. There, under her hand, was the coarse, heavy kitchen table Dad had built. Memory washed over Dell, tugging like a riptide: the door left ajar, her father's body, flashing lights in the driveway. She suddenly, desperately wanted Scott to show up looking for her, wrap her in a hug. In the silence, Dell heard a baby's cry from another room.

Myra cleared her throat with a rumble. "Introductions first. Everyone, this is your cousin, Adella. Dell, these are my daughters, Rosie and Alma, and the little ones are my grandchildren: Everett, Sadie, Beryl, and Marigold. And that crying babe you hear is Rosie's youngest one, Hope."

"Hello," Dell stammered. The baby's cry grew louder.

Myra waved her wide, fleshy hands to dispel the small crowd.

"Children, back outside. Rosie, go feed your baby. Alma, why don't you get your cousin a glass of iced tea?" Myra wrapped Dell in a hug, her arms fleshy and soft but strong with muscle underneath.

Dell wriggled in her arms. "Come on, Myra."

"You need a hug," she answered, squeezing. "You just don't know it."

"Will you help me? I asked you if…"

"I'll help you," Myra said, a knowing reassurance in her green eyes. "But let's talk first."

Myra opened the cabinet over the stove, took out a glass bottle with a black label, and unscrewed the lid. She poured a splash of whiskey into a coffee mug and took a sip.

"The last I heard, you had a job in Blyth, the same job for years." Myra spoke in her rolling, gravelly drawl, watching Dell as though she already knew what she wanted to hear.

"I quit."

Myra cleared her throat and continued. "Your brother lives there. Policeman, right? Everybody knows the Shaws."

"Everywhere I go, there's someone who thinks they know me better than I do," Dell said. For all she had learned to talk at length to her clients, she hadn't spoken about her own thoughts in months. She felt her voice grow thin and sharp in her throat and tried to hold it even. "I'm done with that town. You were at Dad's funeral. You saw."

Sniffling, she felt a rustle of movement around her, pausing to wipe at her eyes. When she opened them, there were Myra's daughters, the thin one with a glass of iced tea, the rounder one cradling an infant. Their green eyes were avian in the low light, and she wished she were their sister. If Myra had the eyes of a hawk, Rosie and Alma's were swan's eyes, softer and less mean but every bit as penetrating.

"What about the father?" Rosie asked, patting the baby's back. She smelled like milk and the sour-sweet smell of a baby.

"What about him?" Dell snapped. She set her jaw and felt her resolve start to wither. Her breath stung in her throat and she felt her chest prickle, holding in her fear.

"He didn't make you happy?" Myra asked.

"He did make me happy."

"It's okay if you don't know who he is," Alma said, handing Dell a glass of iced tea. The cold glass felt good under her fingers.

Myra and her daughters waited for her to explain. Dell opened her mouth to say something about her baby's father, but felt her eyes begin to water again and shook her head.

"I wanted to get away," she said. "I wanted to get away from my whole life. Now I'm finding I'm reminded, all the time. How am I supposed to forget, with…" Her hands rested on the gentle curve of her belly.

"Come out to the porch and sit with us," Myra said. The three women seemed to move as if they all had one mind. She followed them outside. Alma offered her a rocking chair. Myra sat in another rocker and Rosie sat on the porch swing with the baby in her arms, while Alma leaned against the railing.

"I'll tell you what I think," Myra said. "I've been helping women birth babies for forty years, and both my girls have grown up helping me. I'll give you what you need if you want to get rid of it. But I'd rather you stopped to think a minute here."

"You said you'd help me," Dell cried. Her empty hands clapped against her knees. "What, is there a password or something? You said there were two kinds of women." She picked up her glass of tea to take a drink, then changed her mind, angrily set it down.

Myra laughed, an exasperating, assured rumble, and spit tobacco into a cup at her feet. "I know the sound of a woman who wants a pregnancy to end, and I know the sound of someone who's heartbroken and wants to talk."

"I can just as easily be both," Dell said. "Did I come all the way here for nothing?"

"Very well," Myra said, as if she were calling a bluff. She leaned back in her chair and stretched out her legs. "How many weeks?"

"Eighteen."

"Alma, would you get that little brown bottle from the top cabinet in the kitchen? You know the one."

Alma walked inside. There was a shuffling sound. Dell drew a sharp breath. Soon, Alma returned and sat the bottle on the porch railing in front of her. "This is it. Plan to stay with us for a couple days if that's what you want."

Dell eyed the bottle. The liquid in it looked dark and thick. "Then what?"

"It depends," Myra said. "Could be, it'll pass on its own. If not, there's a number of steps. About one in four chances say we take you to the hospital if it doesn't work. It's later than it should be for this, but if it's what you want, it's what you want." Myra spoke slowly, her tone even and gentle and rasping. "Pour it into your tea. Way I figure," she muttered, "woman who wants out of a pregnancy will do it one way or another. Rather you do it safely."

"Go on," Alma said. Tall and sharp-limbed, she looked ghostlike in the low light of the late summer evening.

"You poor thing." Rosie's whisper was a singsong, as if she were talking to both Dell and her baby. Cradling the child at her breast, Rosie, her dress unbuttoned, leaned back on the porch swing. Though she offered no answer, her eyes were soft.

Dell looked from Myra, to Alma, to Rosie. She reached for the tiny brown bottle and nobody moved to stop her. She was alone. She had chosen to be alone. Her thoughts turned to Anita, beautiful and inscrutable, and Gideon, who, with all his pillheaded Christian goodwill, still had no power to help the world around her make any sense. *I'm sorry,* Dell thought, one hand resting on her belly. There was a deep and inherent fault line in her, something she didn't know how to fix.

CHAPTER THIRTY

Before

August 1990

Without any warning, Dell felt a twinge in her belly, just under her hand. Something kicked and wriggled, soft but with a strength that she felt resonating down to her fingertips. She was not alone.

"What's wrong?" Myra asked. "Second thoughts?"

She prodded at her belly and felt it again: a slippery nudge just under her navel, echoing in her heart. A childlike smile broke across her face. "Myra, it's moving."

Myra took a box from her pocket, opened it, and began to roll a small cigarette, her eyes glancing up at Dell as she worked.

"I can't do it. Goddamn it, Myra, you were right," she said, smiling as her eyes watered. "Listen. I'm not the maternal type. Will you help me keep this thing healthy until I get it born?" Myra and Rosie turned to each other with their knowing, birdlike eyes.

"You're in good hands, Dell." Myra drank from her coffee cup full of whiskey and wiped her mouth with her hand. "Being with child is a funny turn of phrase. It's a difference in your being. Not just a belly that tags along with you."

When she grew tired, Rosie showed her to an extra bedroom upstairs. Dell turned Myra's phrase over in her mind as she fell asleep that night. *A difference in your being.* She held the ultrasound photo, clipped to her paint chip, in her right hand, and slept heavily, without dreams or waking, for the first time in weeks. In the morning, she woke early, wandered downstairs to chilly air, all the windows open in the autumn morning, and the smell of strong coffee. She packed her red bag with the few pieces of clothing and toiletries she'd brought along with her and sat it by the door. The house was quiet, so she walked outside into the yard.

"Up here," Myra waved, standing underneath an apple tree near the edge of the clearing. As Dell approached her, two small children sprinted past with barely a wave, engrossed in their business, as if they were officials of some sort and she were too lowly to be acknowledged.

"I'm just about finished here." Myra stood next to a bucket full of apples. "Sit down, help yourself."

Dell sat on the soil, though it was damp, pulling her thrift store jacket close. She bit into one of the yellow apples and looked at Myra expectantly.

"I'm collecting juniper berries today," Myra said. "This is the time of year to do it."

"The little blue ones?"

"Yes."

Dell looked across the yard at the juniper trees, then back at Myra. "I lived here until I was eighteen. We never picked those berries."

Myra laughed her big, raspy laugh. "Come on down. I'll show you how."

Dell pushed herself up with both hands, holding the apple in her mouth, and followed Myra to the juniper trees. Standing up was becoming a balancing act. The fanning evergreen branches were clustered with tiny dark blue berries that were coated in powdery white wax.

Dell bit into the apple, then wiped her mouth with her sleeve. "I'm worried."

Myra clucked then leaned over and spit tobacco juice into the grass. Dell watched her for an answer but she continued at her work. She unfolded a couple of wide, white sheets that were tucked into the lowest pocket of her apron. She grasped one of the low, larger branches and shook it, littering the sheet with a shower of fragrant berries.

"Take that end," she said.

Dell picked up one side of the sheet and they folded it together until all the berries ran into the center. Myra emptied them into the bucket with the apples. She moved the sheet over and spread it in another spot on the ground.

"They're not really berries, you know," Myra said.

"No?"

"They're little pine cones."

Dell picked one out of her hair and crunched it between her fingers. It smelled like a pine cone.

"We dry them and use them in seasonings. Dry rub for meat, good on game." Myra shook another branch; the tiny berries rustled and bounced off her arms as they fell. "Dried and made into a tea, they'll help bring on your labor, when the time's right."

"Really? Won't it just…" Dell trailed off.

"Oh, it will," Myra laughed. "Babies pick their own birthdays. But sometimes your body wants a hand. Just the right amount of help. Come on inside."

They each took one handle of the bucket and walked back toward the cabin.

"How will I know what to do? When should I go to the hospital?"

"You've got some time still," Myra said. "You come back and see us every few weeks, we'll take care of you. And you don't have to go to a hospital. Of all the women whose babies I've birthed, I've only sent fifteen of them to the hospital."

"What should I do?"

"Well, don't ask me. There's no wrong way to have your baby, as long as you're happy with what you choose." Myra heaved the bucket of apples onto the counter with her big arms. "All I'm saying is, I think you may be less likely to be able to choose freely once you're in a hospital." She handed Dell a knife and a bowl. "Would you take a seat and start on peeling some of those?"

Dell took the apples from the bucket, two at a time, and washed them in the sink. It was harder than before to bend over. Myra began to take the juniper berries in handfuls from the bottom of the bucket and spread on wide metal trays. At the kitchen table, Dell pulled out a chair, filled one crooked arm with apples, and sat down.

"I don't know enough to decide."

"Let me tell you what I think." Myra pointed one finger at Dell. "You don't like people telling you what to do. More than anything, you can't stand people telling you what's good for you."

"Hm." Dell chose an apple and took a sheepish bite.

Myra cackled again. "See? You don't even like for me to look at you and know that much. Now, a hospital's going to do what they think is the most safe for the most people. But that's gonna include some precautions that aren't necessary for all women. And if you do want to birth your baby your own way, you're not going to appreciate any distractions."

The windows were cracked, letting a cool breeze blow through. Bundles of dried plants lined the walls. The sound of small feet and children's voices bounced from room to room. Beryl, eleven years old, in jeans and a too-big shirt, ran in at the door. Sadie, six years, but almost as tall, followed shortly behind her.

"You get," she laughed. "Grandma, she's chasing me around with the camera."

"That Polaroid? Shit," Myra cursed quietly. "Tell her put that thing down. The film costs more than her shoes. Sadie!"

The six-year-old laughed and Dell heard the camera shutter click.

Myra recovered the camera, scowling, and set it on top of the fridge. She handed Dell a still-dark, developing print. "Looks like she got one of you. Beryl, Sadie, you two either help or get on out of here and go plague your mother instead."

The two girls scampered from view, the screen door swinging shut as their voices trailed off across the yard. Dell set the print down without interest.

Dell nodded her head. Where she was awash with unknowns, Myra had answers, even opinions. Next to Myra's certainty, she was cast adrift, some alien buoyancy holding her afloat in a tide of silent chaos.

"I don't know." Dell began to wonder if she only tolerated her own indecisiveness because it counted as one of her Libra traits.

"You don't have to decide now," Myra answered, focused on her work. "You've got some choices. Bring the rest of that bucket over here, and pour the berries on this tray," Myra said. "We'll let them dry a few weeks, then we can use them for cooking."

"And the tea?"

She shook her head. "Not yet, no. That's the type of brew you'll take when you want that baby to come out."

Dell closed her eyes against the fear of being alone, of bearing a child alone. The sharp, sweet fragrance of the juniper berries mingled with the apples' sticky fragrance. Something rested in her core that was solid and certain, something deeper than her fear. Dell breathed in deep to fill her lungs with their perfume and pictured the soft blue of the wax-coated berries. Juniper Berry Mist. It was that same blue. She remembered holding Mason's hand, that last night. *Promise me you love me. Promise me this room will be blue.*

It was a bright, warm day, just a hint of a chill on the breeze. The parkway would be crowded with tourists and she knew she would lose business if she stayed away too long.

"I should get back," she said. "Thanks, Aunt Myra."

"Sure, you should," Myra answered, squeezing her again in a tobacco-juice-scented hug.

"You didn't even ask where I've been."

"Makes no difference," Myra answered. "There's two kinds of women, you know."

When Dell left, Myra gave her a jar of homemade soup, some extra blankets, and the Polaroid photo Sadie had snapped. It was a white-framed square around a bright-faced woman, her hair sunlit, one hand on her belly, which was just round enough that she looked obviously pregnant. Dell put it in her bag between her ultrasound photo and the paint chip.

That autumn turned as coppery-brown as her eyes, with hints of gold and amber, before the leaves darkened and fell to the ground. Soon, morning saw the leaves and branches edged in frost. Business at the psychic shop waned, but Dell still had some of her savings from the time she referred to simply as *Before*, and some from the busy season.

Dell felt a deference to her pregnancy. It was a certainty among vagueness. In the way she enjoyed the weather, a sprout unfurling, she felt a deep respect for its lull. She kept appointments at the women's clinic, but also visited Aunt Myra, who always sent Dell home laden with fresh flowers, dried herbs, tinctures for any ailment. Dell allowed herself to feel that the pregnancy was Myra's project, tended by her gardener's hand, Dell's ripening body just another patch of malleable ground.

To be with child, to carry Mason's baby, was an odd, singular, beautiful state of possession. Dell was alone and also not alone. Later that night, watching the far-off lights of the highway from the window, Dell held a hand over her middle, smiled when she felt it move again, and remembered the little heartbeat, steady and strong, qualities the small creature must have inherited from its father, for she felt cold and strange and unpredictable. She ebbed like a blue tide into herself, just a passenger, along with the growing baby, who was safe and loved, with mother, with child.

So then, that was what rested beneath her snap impulse to flee, to jettison anything she looked at long enough to name. A deep, still ocean of love. From the mountains outside, she heard a thin, rolling howl. A coyote, probably. Wolves were so rare, now, although once, the gray wolf had been widespread through these mountains. But she listened to the pitch of its howl, the music it cast through the air, the same bewitching, hypnotic mood that she had heard before, on a different night in the woods, barely half a year earlier but now so far gone.

A mist clung over the mountains in the distance, but high overhead the stars were clear, pinpricks of light on wine-black sky. Her eye fell on the Pleiades, seven bright little stars. In Ovid, they were seven gods' daughters, pursued by—her eyes scanned the sky again—she forgot. Did it matter? Now that they were stars in the night, not women?

She thought that to live in the shadow of the Blue Ridge was to color your measure of normal with an ever-present fear of loss, and actual loss. The shape of the land was a measure of change, of stone plates under the earth breaking, and their story forward from there was of eviction and fragile balance. The howl pealed with the crest and snap of a wave, a diphthong of regret. The mountains were home to a whole host of unquiet spirits, the sighs of creatures of all sizes rooted out by what called itself progress. One day, people would say that there had been white-tailed deer here, once. That day was coming, but she hoped to never see it, though her hand pressed with sadness against her rounded belly. The howl sounded again. Its baying lull was tender, and Dell felt feral and warm in her loneliness. It was a love deep enough to drown in, and wide enough to be set adrift on, never to be found.

CHAPTER THIRTY-ONE

Now

July 1991

As she watched Blyth go by from the passenger seat, Dell remembered how calm she felt when Mason was driving. He was the type of driver who would take a curve just a touch too fast, but only on a road he knew well. Calculated risks on a familiar path. He always knew where he was.

London's lean nose was tucked contentedly over the shoulder rest, looking out the open window. Dell opened the passenger window and leaned her head back, let her eyes fall closed. She had always liked Jeep rides in the summer, even on hot days like this. With the canvas top on, the warm breeze, the smell of outside. She opened her eyes to the sound of gravel under the tires and saw the familiar driveway, the chipped concrete lions standing guard. She looked for Mason right away, saw that he was still real, caught his far-off stare as he watched her wake. For a moment, she wondered if any time had passed, if she had dreamed the last twelve months.

But the farmhouse was different. Where last year had seen the paint chipping, the hedge that lined the walkway unruly with thorns, Dell saw that the hedge was carefully trimmed, the house painted a crisp, fresh white. As Dell followed Mason and London up the walkway, she saw lilac-hued storm clouds rolling over the horizon, darkening the sky. It was difficult to say where the mountains and the clouds broke; the violet and shadow tones were near the same.

All the gingerbread woodwork around the front porch was repaired, under a fresh coat of white. She sucked in her breath as he held open the front door. All the old hardwood floors were refinished, and every cracked windowpane replaced. She peered through the doorway that opened from the foyer into the living room and saw checked curtains over the windows, a knotted rug, even a pair of armchairs accompanying the sofa that had been alone there last year.

"Take your bag for you?"

"Thanks." Stunned, she let him take the bag from her hand, hang it over the coat rack by the doorway.

"Here's the phone." He tapped a round table by the entryway. "I'm going to start cooking. Hope you're okay with pancakes and eggs."

Dell nodded her head as he walked away, picked up the receiver and dialed for the hospital. The phone rang three times before a woman's voice answered.

"Commonwealth Memorial. Can I help you?"

"I'm calling for a status update on Anita Barden," Dell said. "I'm her daughter. Is she still in surgery?"

"Hold, please."

As she waited, Dell faced the window, admiring the meadow, the hyacinth-blue mountains beyond.

"Hello? This is Dr. Beaton." A man's voice answered on the line.

"I was calling to ask about Anita Barden."

"Ms. Barden is recovering just fine. Are you her daughter?"

"Yes, I am."

"The surgery went as expected. We are keeping her sedated throughout the night so that the swelling and inflammation can go down."

"Will she wake up?"

"We'll begin reducing the paralytic medications early tomorrow morning. I wouldn't expect her to wake up before, say, nine, at the earliest."

"Does my brother know?"

"The police officer? Yes, he was just here."

"Thank you, doctor."

"Yes, ma'am."

Dell hung up the phone and sighed.

"Good news?" Mason called from the kitchen.

"No news." She joined him in the kitchen. "At least, not for now. They're expecting her to come to tomorrow morning."

"Well, then." As Mason answered, he seemed to intuit her fear, to answer what she had yet to voice. "You'll just have to find a way to get through until morning."

Muscle memory steered her to the same stool at the counter, the same seat where she always watched him cooking. He broke eggs into the same glass bowl, warmed the butter in a frying pan. He flipped a pancake, turned away to scoop a bowl of dog food, shook it with a whistle and set it down.

"The house looks nice." She stood up, opened the top of the Dutch door to let the air in. To see the herb garden still overgrown, still fragrant, gave her an odd sense of relief. "Really nice."

"Yeah. I've had some free time." Mason filled two plates, set them on the counter. "Guess it almost looks like someone lives here now."

Dell sat next to him, took a fork and gladly ate. "No tour this time?"

"No." A stern-looking distance crept over his face. "No tour this time."

Right, she thought. *Of course.* It didn't matter, anyway, what he had done with the bedrooms on the second floor, the sunroom with all its windows, the loft bedroom on the top floor. She had packed her things from this place and left it behind. They ate quietly, silverware tapping against their plates. The pancakes were soft, crisped with butter on the edges, pillowy in the middle, and the scrambled eggs creased and flecked with pepper.

"Just like I remembered," she said, eating with all the appetite of the last twenty-four hours.

Dell was so engrossed in her food that she didn't notice the rain beginning to fall, until it was blowing in through the half-open door, the lavender-spearmint fragrance flooding the kitchen. That sudden, furious first downpour of a thunderstorm. Mason stood up and closed it, pushed the latch across.

"Hey, don't you have the canvas top on the Jeep?"

"Shit. Yeah."

"Come on," she said. "I'll help you get the cover on."

They ran outside, back down the walkway, into the cool static of the downpour, the kind of rainfall that soaks clothing instantly. Mason took the cover out of the trunk, threw her one side of it. It was awkward, an oversized, weatherproof cover, like a fitted sheet, the edges difficult to line up. Dell pushed rainwater off her brow, pulled one corner down by the front left tire, another mismatch. Mason's arms brushed against hers as he tugged it the other way, back into place.

"Is that right?"

"Close enough."

She let her footsteps slow as they walked back to the front porch. The cold rainwater was a relief, waking her up.

"Good catch. Thanks for the help."

"Sure," she answered, laughing. "I needed a shower, anyway."

Mason reached forward, traced away a lock of her hair that the rain had glued to her forehead, his thumb lingering on her cheek. It was a reflexive gesture, one that came as easily as her smile, the tilt of her head as she looked up at him, until she saw the crisp, freshly painted white house behind them and remembered.

"Mason, don't. I…" Her hands opened and closed, wanting to reach for him, wanting to push him away. All the muscles in her arms remembered holding him.

"Right." He turned away from her, walking back inside, crossed his arms and pulled off the drenched t-shirt. "I'm gonna change. Be right back."

Dell didn't mean to watch, didn't mean to see the muscles in his back moving as he walked up the stairs. She turned away with a gasp. Rainwater pooled around her feet, no doubt trailing rivulets of sweat, dirt, dust. Eyeing the newly refinished wood floors, she decided to stay outside. She sat on the porch swing, gave a little push with her feet, kicked off the soaking black shoes.

The storm meant that Dell was stuck here, at least until the rain calmed. With food in her stomach, sobered by the rain shower, and that soft shock of his touch, she felt awake. She leaned back, pushing against the ground with her bare feet, saw that the porch ceiling was still blue.

Dressed in dry clothes, Mason let the door swing shut behind him, rubbing his hair dry with a towel. He dropped into the swing next to her, throwing it off balance, the seat waving on a diagonal.

"Where's your dog?" she asked.

"He's upstairs, hiding under the bed. Doesn't like storms. Here." He handed her the towel. Dell wrapped it around her arms like a shawl, blotted at her hair and forehead. "Sorry about that, just now. I guess I forgot for a second." He rested his chin on his fist, looked up at her uncertainly. "You know, when I saw you walk in at your brother's house last night, it was all I could do not to jump up and hold you. Just to see if you were real."

"I don't think we should talk about this." Dell clasped and then opened her hands, her nervous fingers fluttering, drawing a tangle of threads she didn't know how to explain.

"Why not?" The storm clapped and hissed, hail hitting the roof over the porch.

"Because nothing's changed." She raised her voice over the noise of the weather. "And I don't need to hear you say all those things again. I remember just fine."

"I guess I don't blame you."

Too late, though, she thought. She could hear it all again, that familiar afternoon, distilled into a few choice moments: *You only get one family, Dell. You probably lied about everything else, too. I wish you'd had the sense to stay away from me.* She tossed her chin back with a hopeless sigh, focused her glare on the pale blue of the porch ceiling.

"So much for keeping ghosts out," she whispered.

"There is something else, though." Mason rested his elbows on his knees, sat with hands clasped. "I know why you left, Dell. I talked to my father."

The stray raindrops that had misted her arms turned cold, freezing her in place. Dell felt her lungs grab for air, suck in a quick breath, then caught hold of it, letting out a silent, controlled exhale. "How did that work out?"

He looked down at his feet as he spoke, nervous eyes flickering toward her every few words. "You know how families talk about things that go wrong?"

"In theory."

"Well, mine never did. If you opened your mouth to point out a problem, you were the problem." Dell saw the tension in his arm, the elbow crooked, chin resting on his hand, fingers across his mouth as if deciding which words to keep back. "It took a few tries, but I kept asking him why you knew him, why you didn't like him."

She began to tap her fingers on her knees, looking out over the field. She could still walk away from this conversation, and anything else she pleased. But something pinned her to her seat, some reflex that should have made her run but trapped her instead. Counted the first three things she saw: *a car passing by on the road, a flutter of distant lightning, a cobweb under the railing edged with raindrops.*

"Well?" she hummed, her voice sounding far away and strange. "What'd he tell you?"

"That he had an affair with your mother."

"Anita," Dell whispered sharply.

"I'd hate him, too, if I were you," he said. "Every so often I think I do anyway."

She turned to study him, a sense of disbelief settling over her. He still didn't know. Suddenly, she remembered him telling her: *There's a lot I don't remember. Maybe some broken pieces in here.*

"That wasn't easy for you," she said. "It couldn't have been. Talking to him about that."

"You know what wasn't easy? Losing you without knowing why. Watching you leave, knowing there was something you couldn't say to me. Spending a year in this house alone. Even once I did know, that was the hardest part."

"That's not what I wanted," she said. "That's the opposite of what I wanted."

"No?" He laughed, but his smile faded. She rose to her feet, feeling the cool, solid boards under her toes, let herself draw a few breaths as she put a few steps between them. "Somehow, you did want this. See? Part of you always wants to disappear."

He wasn't wrong. Dell would have run off that minute. Off into the meadow, in the thunderstorm, on foot. *Count three things,* she thought, *count three things and calm down.* But all she could see was him, head hung down, shoulders tense, like they could snap. His knuckles white, hands squeezing together. The flop of damp blond hair that fell low over his eyes when he was distracted. He never cut it short, not after spending his teenage years with a haircut he hadn't chosen, didn't like. They had that in common. She remembered the psychic lady's advice, the day she'd given her the lease. *If you think they'll come back, tell them what they want to*

*hear. If not, tell them what they need to hear. Balance karma with
protecting your interests.*

"Well, your dad told you part of the truth."

"What do you mean?"

"Do you remember being about eighteen, going out for ice
cream with your folks on a Saturday? It was 1979. March."

Mason raised his chin to let her know he was listening, his
eyebrows knitted together.

"You remember that girl with a little boy haircut? Walked up
to your mom and told her where your dad had been the night
before?" Dell dared to look at Mason and found a bleak familiarity
in his half-frown, a face of disappointed removal, hands crossed,
his mouth a thin, quiet line.

"What are you telling me, Dell?"

"Your dad had visited my mother's house the night before. I
guess they—whatever." She leaned back against the porch rail, hips
angled, trying to convey carelessness, or removal, or anything but
what she really felt. "I was alone outside when he was leaving. He
said he was going to help me with my homework. Didn't know
the first thing about geometry."

"What?" Mason bolted to his feet, approached her. It was too
close. Dell stepped backward, inching along the railing.

"You know. Kissed me. Touched me." Dell reached up to fuss with
her hair, crossed her arms tight, fingertips tapping on the opposite
elbow. More than ten years later, she still hugged her arms over her
ribs, remembered that feeling of wanting to disappear out of her own
skin, naming off women changed into streams, reeds, stones, doves.

Mason was only an arm's length away, but as her words sank in
she saw him eighteen again, the boy watching while all the grown-
ups assessed her, put her in her place. His eyes were downcast,
unreadable, one hand at his brow. She wondered how fast she
could clear the porch railing and run for it. Run anywhere, till
her heart beat so fast it finally flew out of her chest and escaped.

Dell felt Mason's hand close around hers, a light touch, a question. She squeezed back. Then, it was his arm around her back, her stiff shoulder blades. She leaned in, let his arms fold around her, felt the tremble in her ribs as she breathed in.

"Baby, I'm sorry." His cheek pressed against hers, lips moving against her temple. He always saw the whole thing, not its pieces. "I'm so sorry. I wish I'd known."

Dell felt the mad pace of her heartbeat as he held her near, once again that frightened bird, trying to beat its way right through the cage of her chest and crawl into his. "You really don't remember?"

"That day, I remember it was spring break, but it was cold. Knowing everyone was upset, not knowing why. I hated holidays—wished I could have stayed at school the whole time."

"What was it like after?" she wondered. "Did they talk about what happened?"

"Definitely not." Mason stretched his arms out in front of him, let his knuckles crack. "If you asked the wrong question, my mom would act like she hadn't heard it. If Dad was in the room, you'd be just as likely to get a black eye." He picked up the wet t-shirt he'd discarded outside and wrung the water out of it, twisting it between his hands. She could see the shadows in his eyes, reflections of something she couldn't see. "Things like that, though? No questions were right. I wasn't good at pretending nothing was wrong. I guess I just tried not to think about it—over time, it turned into a habit." Mason shook the t-shirt loose, then wrung it again; Dell began to wonder if it would tear between his hands. "I wish you'd said something, Dell."

"How could I have told you?" she asked. "I knew how much your family means to you. The way it seemed last year, what happened to me was only a problem for you if I was here."

"That's what I wanted, though." Mason's stony features softened into a helpless smile. "I wanted you here with me."

Mason waited what felt like a long time before he spoke again. To the west, Dell saw a glow of yellow in the sky, the sunset peeking through a gap in the storm cover.

"When people like my dad get old, they seem softer. They're less in control of you. But they don't change. When I came back, after my grandfather died, I forgave my parents for a lot of things. All things I figured they'd done wrong to me, or to each other. Not you." Chin raised slightly, he shook his head, a hopeless stare cast at the haint blue of the porch ceiling. "Not you. This is different."

Dell saw Mason's hand squeezed tight against the railing, the muscles in his arms strained, his mouth a tense seam of a frown. A soft instinct seized her and she stepped close to him, placed a gentle hand on his arm, whispering some wordless syllable of comfort. Mason wrapped her in a fierce, close hug, tight enough to squeeze her breath a little, his cheek pressed against her hair.

"God himself could walk up those steps right now," he whispered, lips close and warm near her ear. "And I wouldn't forgive him if he made you want to leave me." He released her and stood back, a careful arm's length away.

"It's alright now." Dell formed a smile and held her hands up in a cheerful gesture. "See? All in one piece." Dell replayed those words, saw herself at twenty-seven, looking for her lost child, a stranger to the man she had loved, and wondered if that was the truth.

Dell blinked her eyes and saw again that March afternoon, only last year, when he was a bright-eyed stranger in the woods. How their conversation had flowed right away. How he'd flashed that smile and said to her, *If you spend enough years listening to people yell at you, believe me. Nothing sounds better than walking off into the woods alone.* He didn't know how right he was.

"You ever think we're not really that different?"

"You're just realizing this now?" There was that pensive laugh, his eyes teasing. "I thought you were a psychic."

"Hey, I told you." Dell wagged a finger at his chest again, this time a playful gesture. "I'm good with other people's problems, remember? Not mine." Her hair had begun to dry, the rainwater settling into a new layer of dried grime on her arms, her bare feet. "Mind if I take a shower?"

"No—um." Mason stretched an arm behind his neck, looked at her with hesitation. "Of course not. Upstairs. You know where everything is. Thing is, I'm rewiring the lights upstairs. Bathroom light still works, but don't touch the light switch in the bedroom." His eyes flashed, beamed a nervous smile. "Or else."

"Thanks." Dell left her wet shoes by the door, stepped inside and took her bag from the hook.

"You need clothes?"

"No. I brought a change. Back in five minutes."

CHAPTER THIRTY-TWO

Before

February 1991

Summer's crowds of tourists, who were drawn to the Blue Ridge for its colors and charm, dissipated as the leaves browned in autumn. By the time winter settled in, the scenic roadways were almost deserted. No one would have come there for day trips, and besides, the psychic shop was hardly the sort of place anyone found on purpose.

The cold wind seemed to blow perpetually. The mountainside beyond Dell's bedroom window was the soft gray-violet of bark, dotted with an occasional evergreen. Business was slow, which suited her fine, as she had money put aside and no stomach for visitors anyway. By February, she was bigger around than she'd imagined possible, and the baby's kicks were an hourly occurrence, waking her through the night. When it came to birth, she put off deciding between the hospital and Myra's cabin. She told herself she would make the right choice when the time came. That she was a Libra, and this was where she excelled—making careful choices.

In the end, she did not leave herself time to decide, and that may have been because she was afraid of the hospital with its bright, clean lights, the way they seemed to shine on anything anonymous about a person, and not least because that was where Abby worked, and doubtless other people she didn't want to run into.

On one night, a night that seemed especially cold, Dell woke late with a squeezing pain in the bottom of her belly. She swung one leg onto the floor and then the other, then stood up, holding her metal bed frame for balance. As she did so, she felt her waters break, damp between her thighs and trickling onto her feet and the floorboards. *This is the time to go,* she thought. *If you're going to the hospital, this is the time.* She paced until the throbbing pain subsided, then returned to bed.

By sunrise Dell was unable to sleep. The squeezing waves came over her at random, but gripped her strongly, forbidding any meaningful rest. Dell wrapped her thrift store jacket over her long nightgown and, figuring she might be stuck there by herself if she waited much longer, walked through the dark apartment, down the stairs. As she commended herself for remembering to lock the door, she felt the ice-cold pavement under her bare feet, having forgotten her shoes. She walked to her station wagon, then gasped, doubled over. It felt like a bad menstrual cramp, but spread through to grip her thighs and lower back.

Hands braced on her knees, Dell felt her nightgown sweeping the asphalt. She pulled open the door of the car and some loose change fell out to clink against the ground. Her breath caught in her throat. She began to count slowly and reached fifteen when the vice loosened again. Where was that musical-sounding wolf's howl now, when she so badly needed anything other than the raw facts of the world in front of her? Were they still out there, she wondered, way out in the woods, beyond? She tried to remember what that magic had felt like, how it had charmed her fear right out of the air, but could not.

"Goddamn it, Mason," she murmured, hearing her voice high-pitched with fear, trying not to cry, "goddamn you." She tried to imagine his voice, steady but kind, telling her to be calm.

All she could see was him shaking his head, the blue of his eyes cold and empty as a warehouse. *You only get one family.* Out of blunt necessity, Dell coaxed herself to stand up, get into the car and start the engine.

As Dell drove to Myra's house, she was more careful than usual, the roads narrow and eerie in the early morning's winter light. She winced through one contraction behind the wheel, wished she could stretch out and walk through it. It was only good luck that meant the roads weren't icy, snowy, that she wasn't stuck with a half-tank of gas and some spare change to her name before she made it there.

"Myra?" She rapped at the door in the cold, her breath crystallizing in front of her face. "Aunt Myra? Rosie?"

When nobody answered, Dell opened a window and climbed in. She started the kettle to boil and sat at the kitchen table, rocking back and forth when it got bad.

In a red bathrobe, her wild gray hair pulled into a rough braid, Myra walked downstairs and took a seat next to her.

"So, it's time?"

"Like I would know," Dell said, snapping through her pain, talking so fast she tripped over her words. "It hurts, that's all I know. I have no idea what's happening to me here. I…" She felt another one start, take the words right out of her mouth, as she leaned over the kitchen chair, tightening her fists around its frame.

Myra left the room. Dell heard her wake Rosie and Alma, and she returned with an armful of blankets. Alma appeared shortly after and set to work lighting a fire.

Rosie walked downstairs, plump and beautiful in a flowered nightgown. She approached Dell gently, as she was breathing her way through a contraction. "I've had three," she said. "You'll be fine. I'm going to get the kids out of the house for the day."

Dell closed her eyes. "Okay. Thank you."

Rosie kissed her forehead and went back upstairs to collect the young ones.

By the time the sun rose high overhead, Dell was somewhere deep within herself. When she was able to, she walked across the porch, in circles around the house. She was aware of Myra hovering nearby, sometimes with water or a damp cloth.

Dell thought that she had only to get out of the way of labor, as she had throughout her pregnancy. That if she stood out of the way of her body and its knowledge, it would do its work without her oversight. But the mind is never truly supposed to work separately from the body. Throughout the last several, lonely months Dell had stayed in the back seat, leaving all the work to her physicality. Then, it came in waves, squeezing and releasing, coming on worse than she could stand, and then more than that; then stayed unbearable.

CHAPTER THIRTY-THREE
Before
February 1991

When the surges were at their worst, Dell could not bear to be touched. She slapped Myra's hands away. In the *Metamorphoses*, Ctesylla was a woman who died in childbirth, who was turned into a dove. But the volume of Dell's pain let her know she was all too alive. She only wanted Mason. Wanted the sound of his voice, deep and calm. Wanted to feel his arms holding her. She had wondered, now and then, if she still loved him, or whether those currents that still pulled at her were just hormones, just habit. But now there was no doubt. Her eyes smarted, not from pain, but love. Dell had never loved him more than she did right there, where she had never been more alone.

"It won't be much longer," Myra promised. "You're doing fine."

"This is worse than you said it would be," she yelled.

"This is exactly how I told you it would be," Myra answered, offering Dell her hand to squeeze. "You're having a baby. Are you ready? One more push."

"No," she insisted. "I'm not ready. Not by myself." *Not without him.*

Suddenly, the pain was gone. There was quiet. She sank back into the pillows, drained.

"It's a girl," Myra said. "A healthy, perfect little girl." Myra laid the warm bundle on her chest and covered them with a blanket.

The baby was in her arms, cradled against Dell's tired body. She was ordinary, quite small, soft, all her connections tenuous, with her father's wise eyes. She was a tiny face, a flailing arm. Dell cradled her with one arm and touched the tiny hand with her other. The little fist closed on her finger. To say that a baby is ordinary is to say that it commands a great deal of love, right away, with all the force of an iceberg breaking through water to the air above. Dell's body was dismantled and then, just as quickly, her heart.

Dell was not alone, with Alma and Aunt Myra tending to her, bringing water and salves and cool cloths. They tied the cord with a clean piece of twine and cut it, instructing her through the afterbirth, holding her wrist and counting her pulse.

And yet Dell felt that she was among strangers, that everyone in the world was a stranger to her and her baby, except for one. And as badly as the baby needed guarding, needed holding and warmth, so did Dell, who had never felt more like an animal alone, who had never been more certain, in Mason's absence, that she had a counterpart. She hugged the baby to her chest, silently cursing him again. What mattered was that he wasn't here. Seemed like the people she loved had a way of being gone exactly when she needed them the most.

Awake through the night, long after the fire had gone out and the house was quiet, Dell lay nestled with the baby between her breasts. Though physical, Dell's love for the baby was not romantic, but seated within her body nonetheless. She loved the tiny girl with every facet of her being, a love that rendered other sorts of love frivolous, unnecessary. If love for a lover was an evolutionary favor, love for a baby was a command.

The baby was calm and awake, her expression resentful that she was out in the cold, that she had a world full of things to worry over, the little eyes asking Dell, *Why have you brought me here?* And Dell thought, *Sorry. I'm sorry. I don't know.*

Dell wondered if one way to measure love was by fear—fear that you would fail to do right by the object of your love. She looked at the little face and thought that she should be crying, and for some reason found that she could not. *There's some deep, irreparable fault line in me. Something you'll be safe from.*

Alma came downstairs in the early dark of morning, crouched by the fire, and poked at the smoking embers until the sparks danced around little growing flames.

"Alma, I need your help."

She jumped. "I didn't know you were awake. What is it?"

"You've got to help me find someone to take her. Call the church. One of their officers is a social worker. They'll send somebody."

Alma hesitated, a strange look on her face, her thin cheekbones sharp and uneven in their uncertainty.

"Are you sure?"

"Yes. Do it."

The next morning, Dell left the baby in Rosie's arms to take a shower. She washed with Myra's fragrant homemade soap and put on a borrowed skirt and t-shirt that belonged to Rosie, over three pairs of cotton underwear. Her feet felt steady on the ground, already returning to their normal size. She felt sad, suddenly, in spells, and forgetful, although she generally knew when she was not herself.

"Aunt Myra?" she called through the closed door. "Has anyone come from the church?"

When there was no answer, she turned to walk into the kitchen, rubbing her head with a towel. There were Rosie and Myra, and the teacup Dell had left half-finished on the counter, and there, seated next to Rosie, the baby in her arms, was Anita.

"You said to call the church," Alma muttered.

"My beautiful daughter." Anita looked up at Dell and nudged tears from her eyes. "Why didn't you tell me?"

"Oh," Dell whispered. "I didn't expect you to come."

"Of course, the church office told me first. Gideon's old address, they said they couldn't not tell me."

Anita settled in as if the house belonged to her, and Dell was reminded that she had never looked in place here. "Sometimes a woman needs her mother," Anita preened. "Sometimes she always will."

"Mom, you can't tell anyone. Nobody. No matter what," Dell said.

Rosie stood up and offered Dell her chair, all the while holding her suspicious stare on Anita. "Come on, baby, sit."

Dell was painfully aware of her ill-fitting clothing, mismatched, her body still puffy and tender. Anita was trim and neatly dressed in a black wool coat and suede pants, boots with a high heel that somehow bore not a speck of dirt. She made a beatific, perfect picture, like a mother in a magazine. The baby, sleeping, leaned her head back over Anita's forearm and Dell moved close, her hand supporting the little limp peach. "Hold her head up."

"You forget I've had two of these." Anita smiled and leaned away from her. "You never forget what to do with a baby."

When the baby girl began to cry, the small, squeaking sound of a newborn, Dell looked to Rosie.

"She's hungry." Dell's eyes stung.

"See if you can feed her," Alma said. She cleared her throat, watching as Anita absentmindedly stroked the soft little head. When Anita did not move, Alma lifted the baby and settled her into Dell's arms.

Dell clumsily took the child, once again offering her breast, shrugging away from her mother. The baby latched onto her nipple hungrily, although only a little butter-yellow milk came out.

"This little girl knows what she's doing." Dell held the baby close as if it would quell her appetite. "I'm the one who's got no idea."

"Here." Rosie leaned over, took the baby from Dell and without ceremony opened her shirt and held the baby to her own breast. Anita raised her eyebrows and then looked away with a forced half-smile.

Myra stood behind Dell's chair. She refilled her teacup with hot water when it was low. "Rosie, Alma, why don't we give Dell and her mother some space to talk?"

They walked from the room and, as Dell heard their steps go up the stairs, she moved into the den, curled onto her side on the sofa. "Let's sit by the fire. I'm cold."

"Cold? You're sweating. Is that normal?" Anita sat on the couch without taking her coat off. She picked a piece of lint from the cushion and dropped it onto the floor. "Oh, dear. You had your baby here? Was it safe?"

Dell nodded her head.

"Myra tells me you want to give her up."

"I guess." She shuffled her legs, trying to find any position that wasn't painful.

"Well. Your mom helped you out. There's a social worker on the way from the church."

"Already?" Dell watched the firelight skipping, felt her throat thick with tears, not knowing why or why not.

"Not everybody is cut out to be a mother." Anita swept a cool, dry hand across Dell's forehead, braided and unbraided her hair. Dell began to feel convinced that she could not move, though she feverishly pictured Anita wielding a pair of scissors. "What a feeling that is, holding your brand-new baby."

"I know, Mom," Dell answered. Anita went into the kitchen and opened Myra's whiskey, poured some into a clear glass.

"This will help, baby." She sat at the end of the couch so that Dell's head was almost in her lap.

Dell drank absentmindedly. "Maybe the measure of love, sometimes, is…" Her head swam. "Is how bad you want to do right. How afraid you are you're not going to." If that were true, she had a lot of love to give, a lot of not messing up to do. The whiskey settled heavily in her stomach. "I'm scared, Mom. What if I don't do a good job?"

"Dell, you're incoherent." Anita's cool hand pressed against her forehead. "More people who feel this way about having children ought to listen to their guts instead of doing a bad job. I know I haven't done a perfect job with you." She smoothed beads of sweat from Dell's forehead with a fingertip, resumed braiding her damp hair. "You were my difficult child. You hurt being born and you always seemed to know if I was lying. Even little things, like why the sky was blue."

"Mom, what if I…" Dell rolled over and felt perspiration on her forehead. "You really don't think I could—"

"Poor girl," Anita murmured, as if she had not heard her. "Every lady needs her mother sometimes, no matter how old you get."

"Mom, listen." Dell drank from the glass again, let her voice raise. "I want to keep her. You could help me."

"Oh, Dell." Anita smoothed her sweaty hair down with her perfectly cool hands. "I should not have been a mother. I rushed right in, with no self-doubt. I should have kept my freedom and left town. This is your chance to do the same." She grimaced and her face wrinkled in a way Dell had not seen before. "If you keep her, in time she'll just make you angry when you look at her." She sniffed and wiped at her eye hastily.

"I don't think so." Dell shook her head tearfully. "That can't be true."

Anita looked back at her coolly, sadly. "It is true. You don't know it now, but I'm trying to help you."

"Help me?" She pressed her hands to her eyes. "Where were you, Mom? That night the doctor came over to your house?"

"What are you talking about?" Anita's hands stopped moving, her fingers tangled in Dell's half-finished braid.

"Why did you let that happen to me?" She lifted herself up on one elbow. "The next day, that woman slapped my face and you just let it happen."

"If that did happen, it wasn't as bad as you're remembering it." Anita's fingers picked up, working at the braid again.

"You don't remember? How she called me a little slut? You don't remember how you cut my hair off and told me I'd end up pregnant and single?"

"If any of that's true, you know it wasn't my fault." Anita gave a long sigh, stroked her clammy forehead again. "And besides, I wasn't wrong, was I? Hush," she whispered, a long, crooning noise. "You're not feeling well. Try to calm yourself."

Dell sighed and tipped the glass back as she downed the last of the whiskey. She already knew Anita considered her a mistake. She didn't know why it hurt her now, more than it had before. She was pliable, wounded. She wanted someone to speak for her, someone to stand guard and let her rest.

"Fine," she whispered. "If you say so, Mom."

Alma knocked on the doorframe to announce her presence as she walked into the room. "Anita, it was nice of you to come," she said. "But I think it's time Dell got some rest."

Anita sat up straight and smiled politely. "Well, like I said, every girl needs…"

"Thank you for visiting," Alma interrupted. In the firelight, her eyes turned sharp as her mother's, leaving no doubt that she was not thankful to Anita for visiting at all.

"Dell, where can I find you?" Again, Anita made the sad, ugly-crying face, which made Dell feel nervous and more upset. She fanned at her eyes fast and then faster, squeezed her eyes shut so that Dell saw the wrinkles at the corners of her eyelids.

"You won't. Stop crying," Dell answered, her voice flat as she felt. She couldn't find a reason to lift her head from the sofa. "Promise you will not look for me."

But Anita did not promise. "There's a social worker on her way. She'll come later this afternoon." Rosie cleared her throat and glared, and Anita moved nearer to the door. "You're making the right choice. Now, you might want to have your friends clean up a little bit. The Baptists are coming, after all."

Anita left, still picking bits of lint from her black coat. Drunk and overtired, Dell continued to weep weakly. Rosie arranged a clean blanket over her, while Myra stomped through the kitchen as she brewed more tea.

"I'm sorry, girl," she said, "but I don't know how else you thought that was going to go."

Still crumpled on the couch, Dell felt blood trickling between her legs, involuntary tears trailing down her face just the same. All her muscles ached. "I'm leaving," she muttered.

"I'll believe that when I see it," Myra scoffed. But she watched over her with an apprehensive gleam in her eyes.

That afternoon, when a strange car parked outside the cabin, Alma leaned out the doorway and repeated Anita's phrase. "The Baptists are coming."

The woman from the church was old and kind, dressed in warm and shabby clothing. "I don't usually come out right away," she said, "but Anita's an old friend."

The woman knew of families that wanted a baby, with plenty of money and stable houses. The kind who would never do anything by accident. Closed adoption meant the records would be sealed. But she was surprised that Dell was anxious to have the affair finished that day.

"If you feel strange about it, you should know that's normal. You're making a huge self-sacrifice," she said. "It's only biological that it feels wrong to walk away."

"Thank you."

"There's paperwork I didn't bring with me," she added. "I can't possibly have it all squared away this afternoon."

"Well, I can't stay." Dell got to her feet, felt herself moving still with the waddle of a pregnant body, though the solid weight in her belly was no longer there. "I'm leaving. For real, this time."

Myra and Rosie studied her as she spoke, their green eyes sorry.

"This is too much," Dell continued, talking to herself more than anyone else around her. "I tried everything I could. With Mason. With Anita. With Dad. Everything I touch—a mess…"

"Miss, please wait." The church lady had that type of personality that, though gentler than Myra's, was similarly shocked by nothing. "Before you go, please tell me, do you have a name for her?"

"Why does that matter?"

"Birth names mean a lot to many adoptees," the woman said. "And it makes for easier paperwork than just 'Baby Girl.'"

Through the fog of weariness and discomfort, Dell gave a moment's thought to things that made her feel happy and whole, remembering, from the far side of a schism, an afternoon forgotten.

"Yes," she said. "I do." She took the pen from the woman's hand, then quickly scratched a word on her form.

Dell took one fleeting look at the tiny baby in Rosie's arms. Her eyes had fallen closed. Just as well; another look at those eyes and she'd be stuck where she stood. Dell traced a hand over the baby's soft cheek, down her little arm, felt the hand curl around her fingertip. *This is where I leave you.*

Aunt Myra followed her onto the porch, her round arms impervious to the cold. "One day you're gonna have to quit doing this."

"Don't let me go then," Dell shouted, pleading. "Do something to make me stay."

"It has to be you," Myra answered. "If that little girl in there can't make you stay, nobody but you can do it."

Shaking her head, Myra watched as Dell turned and walked down the steps. The air was sharp and cold around her ankles, and it hurt to walk. Dell drove away as fast as she could stand to, returned to her apartment where she could see the whole valley on either side, and locked the door.

Two days later, her breasts filled with milk, so tight and tender she thought they would burst. She knew Myra would have a remedy, but instead just waited, held frozen washcloths to her breasts, her eyes smarting with the pain. She looked at the mountain range, bleak and iced, with the bare patch of the pipeline splitting it in half, and wondered if the milk would freeze in the cold off of her heart, or if it would curdle inside her breasts.

The *Metamorphoses* were only stories. How many times had Dell waited for someone to intervene, to magic her body into a safe place to live? Nobody was coming. She remembered that wolf in the woods, her tender howl. *Were you a woman once? Who took mercy, who transformed you? Are you safe out here?* She already had her answer. If nobody would reach down and turn her into a tree, a wolf, a stream, she would do it herself. Line her little nest with sticks and stones and wreaths and knick-knacks, and become just as whittled, as hard, as quiet, as untouchable. With cold washcloths tucked under her arms, folded over her chest, Dell walked to the stove and set a kettle to warm for tea. *You can't freeze up like this. It won't do.* She hummed as she walked. *Of bodies chang'd to various forms I sing.* While she waited for the water to boil, Dell walked to the door, flipped on the light in the window: THE PSYCHIC IS IN.

As days passed and the winter cold eased, Dell would sit on the stool at the counter by the beaded curtain, near her space heater, and watch the weather change over the layered blue mountains that spread into the distance. Before long, business picked up pace again.

She never went back to Myra's cabin, and when she looked out over her skyline, she turned a blind eye on Blyth, happy to pretend it was a blank spot on the map. Happy to see the familiar trail of the pipeline through the woods in the distance, to stay on her side of the line. Except for a weekly grocery trip, she almost never left. Her red bag stayed on the same hook by the door for days on end. But once or twice a day, she would open it and reach into the zippered inside pocket to touch the little blue paint chip, paper-clipped to her ultrasound photograph, the Polaroid of her halfway through the pregnancy. If Anita had thrown the world off balance, she had restored it by finding the baby a home and keeping well away.

One day in April, Dell had seen a brown Jeep pull up in the parking lot. She skipped down the stairs so fast her feet barely touched, holding the banisters with each hand. She'd thrown open the door to see a startled stranger unloading a basket of clothes to the door of the laundromat. She went out, treated herself to a bottle of wine, which she regretted the morning after. Some memories weren't worth the headache.

Dell would stretch out at night in the twin bed, her toes peeking out of the quilt, face turned toward the window with its view of the mountains. It was lonely, but she had nobody to keep secrets from. It wasn't bad, for a change. Something she'd never had before in her life: the perfect freedom of being a stranger. As long as she knew the little girl was safe, everything that came before was all worth it. The time passed, the busy season rolled around again. Some of her customers liked her so much they came back regularly. Business was good. The first time lonely Rhonda came in, Dell was soft on her. She was a sweet-eyed woman, close to fifty, a Cancer with her moon in Capricorn. It was an infelicitous combination. Rhonda was a crab without a shell. At first, Dell told her what she wanted to hear. But as she kept coming back, she began dropping in hints of the harder truths, and even to talk with her a little.

"My mother would say you're asking for trouble," Dell mused during one of Rhonda's afternoon visits. "That if you get your feelings hurt or worse with any of these men, it's your own fault. She's wrong, of course," Dell added swiftly. "But I can think of a couple times I wish I'd been more careful with my own heart. Well, maybe just one." Rhonda had given her a smile that was knowing and yet kind. Dell wondered if it was a motherly look.

Yet, if Anita came up short on motherly smiles, Dell held onto a cold gratitude for her help calling the social worker. This certainty, her faith that Anita had done her one final favor, was all her peace, the salt on her meals. Until Anita turned up in Dell's psychic shop on a summer afternoon, announced that the baby was lost, and then crashed her way into a coma.

CHAPTER THIRTY-FOUR

Now

July 1991

"No. I brought a change. Back in five minutes."

Up the two flights of stairs, each step creaking just the same, Dell smelled fresh paint and sawdust, felt the hardwood floors smooth and polished under her feet. The loft bedroom was dark, though she saw the familiar shapes of the bed frame and fireplace, hard to make out in the low light. Following his request, she didn't touch the light switch, found her way to the bathroom in the dark.

The high-ceilinged bathroom, with the closet that led to the attic, was the same, clean and sparse. She washed with a bar of soap from her bag, homemade, Myra's own, fragrant with lavender and chicory root. She scrubbed her scalp and ears and under her nails. Wrapped in a towel, she brushed her teeth, neatly laid all her things to dry. She slipped into a clean bra and underwear. The only remaining clean dress was a white, threadbare Gunne Sax dress, with long, ruffled eyelet sleeves and an empire waistline. Dell hadn't packed her escape bag very practically, but then, she'd never planned for this.

As she stood in the dark, the loft was dim and quiet. Dell let herself linger, breathing in the familiar air, remembering all the spirits in this big, airy room she had loved. She ought to have thought this could have been some other lady's favorite room in Mason's house, that it was his and not hers and had never been. But she felt an uncanny ease, a comfort that rooted her to the floor. She poked her head around the corner of the door, looking in the dim light toward the familiar window with a sigh. The sunlight was just waning, its peachy warmth settling over the meadow. The pond in the distance wore a little cloud of mist, a reminder of the recent storm.

I don't belong here, she told herself. *This isn't mine anymore. Maybe it never was.*

She resolved to go downstairs. The bathroom light clicked off under her hand. *Hold on, hold on,* she thought. The bathroom and the bedroom light were on the same fuse. Mason had told her so himself, last summer, the day she'd seen her father's face in the mirror. What didn't he want her to see in there? Some girlfriend's clothes, thrown across the bed?

She could still find the bedroom light switch in the dark.

The light flickered on and the walls lit up blue. Pale blue, with a gentle, tidal gravity. The room had the same sparseness as a campsite, the familiar bed frame in the corner, the old children's toys scattered about the edges of the wall. *Promise me this room is gonna be blue. Promise you love me. Never leave me.* It was a blue deep enough to drown in.

London's nose inched out from under the bed, then he crept out and circled around her ankles. Dell sank to her knees, covering her face in her hands. *This was the one thing worth getting right.*

She didn't hear Mason's footsteps on the stairs, didn't realize he was there until he was standing in the doorway behind her.

"I guess you decided to go ahead and give yourself a tour."

Startled, Dell turned her chin over her shoulder to look at him, one hand clasped across her mouth. Arms crossed, he stared out the window, right over her head, though he seemed to be staring into an even further distance.

She shuffled to her feet, wiping hurriedly at her eyes. "I'm sorry. I was just—" She trailed off, shrugging one shoulder.

"The same as you always do, right?"

"The rain's stopped." She brushed her dress off. "I think I should leave." She felt a soft shock at seeing how he had guarded this, to see the pain on his features when he finally met her eyes.

"You *think*?" He spoke softly, without fight. "Why don't you just tell me what you want and do that, for once?" He crossed the room and dropped into the sofa by the fireplace, London at his heels. "I bought the paint the day you picked out that color. Turns out it looks half decent." He waved to indicate the walls around them. "That's not why I did it, of course. None of this was for me. Dell, when you left, I thought you were going to stay at your apartment for a couple days. I didn't think you were going to disappear." She took a step forward and he held up a hand. "Wait. I'll say it one more time. Figure out what you want and…"

But her footsteps continued. She sat on the sofa next to him, speaking in a creaky whisper as she tried not to cry. "I know what I want." Dell leaned her head to the side and blotted at her eyes with the sleeve of her dress. "But I shouldn't be here."

"Yes, you should." Mason pulled her hands from her face, held her chin in his hand, his thumb brushing at the tears on her eyelashes. "This is exactly where you should be."

His arms were already around her, as if they had always been there. She let her lips brush his, let the familiar gravity of his warmth pull her deeper in. Dell's arms strayed from her lap, circled around his back, a fingertip slipping just below the collar of his t-shirt. She felt a shock at how his body still enticed her, so immediately, regardless of context. In his hands, under his touch, she had always felt more whole, less in pieces. But this kiss was different. There was a space in between them she couldn't close. Dell leaned away from him, holding his hands in hers, her chest flushed. Their conversation waned, both of them apprehensive in the presence of what felt so sure, but also unknown. Dell leaned on Mason's shoulder and watched the sky from the window, every so often pointing out a meteor, as she felt her limbs become heavy, her thoughts slowing.

"Do you miss her?"

She nodded her head. "She had eyes just like yours."

Dell needed to move away from him, needed to distract her hands. She walked into the bathroom and retrieved her bag. Sitting on the floor by Mason's feet, she took a hairbrush from the jumble in the bag and began to brush out the tangles in her hair. Over her shoulder, he reached down and took the photographs out of her bag again. This time, she didn't stop him.

"You're so pretty." Mason was holding the Polaroid. His hand reached over, brushed her shoulder, grazed her waistline, small again, but softer than it had been before. "What was it like? Being pregnant?"

Dell's eyes brightened. "It was incredible. I mean, I was sick as hell, the first few weeks. But I was okay after that."

"I remember."

"It felt like every part of me had a reason to be there." Dell swept her hair over one shoulder and began to braid it. She pulled his hand to her midsection, held it there over her navel. "I felt her kick, right here."

Mason's hand curled around hers. "What was it like when she was born?"

Holding Mason's hand between hers, Dell remembered the strange, and yet not strange, sensation of swelling and ripening, the heaviness of her breasts and her belly, how she believed she might break apart as the baby left her body.

"It was winter. Early morning, probably two. I drove to my Aunt Myra's house once I couldn't stand it anymore."

"All by yourself?"

"Well, obviously. No one else was there." She laughed a little, but her hand tightened around his. "I moved through the pain, as long as I could. I remember walking around the cabin in circles and seeing the sun come up, realizing I was barefoot. I hadn't even noticed the cold." Her fortune teller's instinct knew that this was a good story, but the drumbeat of her heart, the muscle memory that awakened as she spoke, pulled her closer to him, thankful not to be alone this time. Something in her chest felt warm and tender, to look up and see him waiting for her to speak. He knew how much it mattered. *Maybe this is the opposite of being alone.*

"It went on like that through the morning. I think she was born in the afternoon. I would say it felt like it took forever, but honestly it was more like time just stopped."

Mason fixed an intent stare on Dell's hands. "What was she like?"

"So sweet. She was so little. That's what people always say about a baby, but it's different when it's yours." She hesitated, pulled her lip into her teeth. "And hungry. I didn't know how to feed her."

In images, rather than in words, she recalled the first night with the baby, how her tiny softness lit up the dark. The days afterward, still bleeding, sore and tired, and wondering how any life could be left in her, having created a creature so flawless and new. Her arms involuntarily crossed as she remembered when the milk came, waiting empty-armed for it to be gone.

Dell felt a tear roll down her cheek to fall on her chest and realized distantly that she was crying. She wondered if Mason could tell that he was not only sitting next to her body, but the site of a metamorphosis. She wished she could tell him how safe it felt to be alone, how she had scraped her shipwrecked fragments back into human form and built a sound structure from nothing. Her own metamorphosis. *These gleaming shards I have braced around the wreckage.* All her days were the same: the same simple thread

held each day to the next, like beads on a necklace. Until Anita
had to go and shake things up.

"I still can't believe I wasn't there with you." Mason spoke in a
soft, low voice. He held one of her hands, palm down, his fingertips
tracing over the back of her knuckles.

"Well, that isn't your fault." She couldn't take her eyes from
him, marveling to see him there in front of her finally, even as her
eyes began to water again. "But I'm not gonna pretend I didn't
miss you. That was probably the worst part."

"What do you mean?"

"Not having you there," she wept. "That was the only part of
it all I couldn't stand." Finally collapsing under the strain and fear
of the last twenty-four hours, or, more accurately, of the last year,
Dell dissolved into sobs, soft at first and then racking. Mason
held her softly and let her lean onto his arm. He comforted her
as he always had: tentative, out of the way of her grief, only there
if needed. But she felt herself break like water over his shoulders,
reached up and clutched herself against him. She spoke between
shuddering gasps: "As long as she had a home, it was worth it.
Even being without you. Being pregnant, alone. All of that, as
long as she was safe, happy. And now what?"

"Slow down," he said. "It's alright. You're getting ahead of
yourself."

"No, it isn't alright. I've never been scared like this." She clung
tight to him, drawing big, heaving gasps, arms shaking.

Dell was in the middle of it now, of the deep apprehension
she'd stuffed down for the last two days. There was no point trying
to count three things. So this was where her fear took her, right
back to that day. She let the memories pull her down and felt, for
a moment, that squeezing pain, wished it could once again conjure
her baby into her arms. Short of breath, at the outer reaches of her
consciousness, more alone than she had ever been.

"Baby, I know." Both of his hands pressed against her shoulder blades, holding her tight against him. She listened as he whispered to her: "Breathe out. That's good. In, out. Hold onto me, okay? You're not alone."

"I can't do this."

"Yeah, you can." As his hands traced over her arms, across her back, rested on her shoulders, she felt the tension lighten. "I know you, Dell. Once your mind's made up, you're a force of nature."

She sniffled, pressed her face against his neck. "Making my mind up is the hard part."

"And you've already done that," he murmured, stroking her back. "See?"

Finally, she felt the storm ease, her sobs loosen, drew an even breath. "I have to find her," she whispered. She lifted her head, saw that her tears had left a damp spot across his collar.

"We'll find her." Mason's hand rested on her shoulder, trailed the slope of her neck, compelling her to look at him. And she wasn't alone, because she could see that he was scared, too.

Dell closed her eyes and felt his nearness, the warmth of his skin through his shirt, her heart beating, like the wings of a scared bird that wanted out, wanted to get closer to him. She leaned forward to kiss him, felt the familiar current beckoning. Again, she wanted to fall all the way down, drown in it. That time, it was Dell that reached for him, her hands sweeping over his arms, one resting to tangle in his hair, the other tracing over his chest, wrapping around his waist. "Promise we'll find her," she whispered.

He kissed her forehead. "I promise, Dell."

"No." Her voice curled and scratched, her hands resting around his waist. She stood up, tugging at his arms, pulled him toward the bed. "Promise me again."

*

After, she curled into the warmth of his arm, habit finding her on the left side of his bed, as always. It wasn't the same, wasn't the idle contentment she remembered. Again, there was an empty space between them. Mason yawned, nestled his chin over her shoulder, his nose in her hair. "You still sleep on the left."

"I sleep in a twin bed now," Dell answered. "All by myself, in the middle." She looked out the window in the dark, saw the stars over the meadow, the same stars she could see from her window at home.

Dell let him pull the blankets over her shoulder, let the heaviness of her tired limbs pull her into the bed. Soon, his breaths were level, steady. Asleep. Resting with her head in the crook of his shoulder, her knee crossed over his legs, she wanted to tell him how she still loved him, even now. Tell him that a year lost between them meant nothing. That she would love him just the same even when a century had passed.

"Mason, this was so good," she whispered. "This could have been so good."

Half sleeping, he pulled her closer, until she could hear his heart beating under her cheek. He whispered to her in a voice almost as soft, "It still is."

Dell woke to the dim gray light of early morning, before the dawn. She heard birds singing outside, and from the window saw a heavy blanket of mist on the meadow and over the pond. Mason was warm, asleep. She got to her feet as quietly as she could. In the early morning light, her white dress was the same shade as the shadowed blue walls. Walking barefoot across the floor into the bathroom, Dell felt a chill, and wondered how the attic was anything but warm this time of year. She dismissed it, bending over the sink to wash her face.

She had never revisited her father's face appearing in the mirror. She had blamed it on an eerie stray thought, a trick of the light. But when she looked in the mirror and saw her mother's features behind her, she knew. This time, she didn't scream or even startle, but looked straight at it as it withered into shadow. "Don't you dare, Anita," she whispered. "Don't you goddamn dare leave me."

She kneeled at the side of the bed and touched his forehead.

"Mason, wake up."

He inhaled suddenly and opened his eyes. "What time is it?" He stretched again. "You okay?"

"It's Anita. I—I have a feeling. I need to go to the hospital right away."

CHAPTER THIRTY-FIVE

Now

July 1991

Inside of five minutes, Dell was waiting on the porch. She took in the misty dawn light, her duffel bag hanging from her shoulder. The air was fragrant and peaceful, humming with the gentle, anticipatory sounds of early morning. Her heart beat steadily and determined.

Mason pulled the door shut behind him without stopping as he walked down the steps, whistled for the dog to follow him.

"Ready?"

"I'm ready."

With the dog at his heels, he opened the door of the Jeep and held her hand as she climbed up and took her seat, then got in and turned the engine, brushing condensation from the inside of the windshield with his arm.

"I could have slept next to you for hours," she said. He turned to her smiling and pushed a strand of hair behind her ear. Again, Dell thought, in this moment, they could have been any two people, in any circumstance, and she wished again that they were.

"What happened? Bad dream?"

She leaned back against the seat, her limbs stiff with sleep. "Do you remember last year, when I saw a face in the mirror?"

Mason nodded and turned onto the main road.

"Right before I left to visit my father."

"I remember."

"Would you believe me if I told you it was his face I saw?"

Mason glanced at her, then turned back to the road. "Are you telling me that you actually are some kind of psychic?"

"I certainly hope not." Dell opened the window and held her arm out, feeling the cool rush of the breeze. "But I know I saw Anita's face in the mirror this morning, and I don't want to turn down some kind of warning, if that's what it is."

Mason's hand found hers, squeezed her chilly fingers as he drove. She had always found him handsome right after sleep, his body warm and his hair tousled. From the passenger seat, she could smell his sweat and the soft, cottony smell of his bedsheets.

As the road led into town, he pulled his hand back, shifting gears. Dell felt the strange tension of the moment as he came to a stop outside the hospital. The dog whined, nosed at the window.

"Do you want me to go with you?"

"No." She didn't have any time. She might already be too late. Dell's mind began to race. Perhaps Anita was already dead. Maybe she would walk in and find her lifeless.

"Really?" He laughed without smiling, turned away as if she had slapped him. "You still don't want me to meet your folks."

"Not now," she said. "When I saw my dad in the mirror last year and I got there, he was already dead. Don't—I can't think about this right now."

If there was no baby, if she couldn't find her, she knew she could never look at him again. *When I find you, then I'll know.*

"How will you get back to your car?"

"I'll get there. It's close. Mason, I have to go. Now."

"When am I gonna see you again?"

"I wish I could answer you," Dell said, pulling her hand free. "I can't think about that right now. I just have to find her."

She wasn't sure what she expected. Not for him to sigh, wave at the door. "Fine. Go."

"But…"

"You want me to beg for you to stay again? That it?" She shook her head, took a breath to speak. Mason stopped her with a wave of his hand. "I need you to tell me yes or no."

Dell couldn't answer him. Her hands clenched on the white gauze of her dress with damp palms. *When I find you, then I'll know. You're all that matters.*

"I have to do this on my own," she repeated. "Please, just wait." She looked at London in the back seat. *Make him listen,* she pleaded.

"Again? Wait, what, another year?" Mason turned to face her, his back leaning against the driver's side window. His voice was low and calm, the voice she knew, but something in his eyes was cooler. "Dell, I'm here for you. I've been here. This should be the easy part."

"This was a mistake." She squeezed her hands to the side of her head, covering her ears. "I should have come straight here last night. I should have been here with my mother all along."

Mason reached across Dell and pushed her door open. "If you leave like this, I want you to promise you're not coming back."

"Fine. That what you want?" She threw her bag over her shoulder and climbed out of the Jeep, gave him one last look. "I promise."

She breathed in softly, the morning air and gentle birdsong reflecting nothing of the shock she felt. Stupid white dress, stupid black slippers, her stupid hair, still wavy and bent from sleep. It was better to be alone than to be compromised by things like hurt, soft bruised spots in your psyche where things could sting you, where the winter wind could find you.

Beneath her impulse to flee, she remembered, she had once discovered an expanse of love so deep and still, she had spent quiet months floating in its soft blue depth, as otherworldly and warm as the tender howl of a lonely wolf. Dell closed her eyes and searched for it but found only ice. Without knowing that her baby was safe, there could be nothing else.

At the front desk, Dell recognized Bonnie, the nurse who had welcomed her in two nights ago.

"Welcome back," she said.

"How's Anita?" Dell leaned over, curling her clammy fingertips around the countertop. "Is she okay?"

"She's sleeping," Bonnie answered. "We tapered off her sedatives this morning, but she's still quite heavily medicated, so…"

"She was supposed to wake up today, right?" Dell turned to walk down the hall.

"Honey, wait." Bonnie caught up with her. "Stuff like this, head injuries? There's a fine line between coming back and not coming back. I don't want you to get your expectations up. You want to go in there and keep her company, you're more than welcome."

Dell walked away without waiting. Anita could already be dead in her bed, Bonnie none the wiser. No doubt she already was. This was the same way it had worked when she'd seen Dad's reflection in the mirror: just a maddening heads-up that you were too late to make a difference. As she rushed down the hall, she looked out a window, looked for the Jeep, hoping for a second that he would have waited for her. But she knew she wouldn't find it. Complicated times call for simple answers, and some choices you only get once.

Dell's eyes watered, spilled over as she pushed open the door. It was as she had feared. Anita was so disheveled, her face so pale and blotched without makeup, that Dell knew with only a glance that she was beyond recovery. Maybe her body was alive, but she wasn't coming back. She sank into a folding chair at the bedside and leaned over her mother's torso, let her face rest on her ribcage as she wept. She had only needed Mason to wait. For what—and for how long—she admitted that he was right: she didn't know. She recognized the repetitive beep of Anita's monitors, and felt her ribs rising beneath her damp cheek.

Anita wasn't supposed to be breakable. She was too pretty for that: it was supposed to be the only thing about her you could rely on. Some part of Dell had not been prepared to allow her mother to be permeable flesh and blood. "I'm sorry," she sniffed. "I should have been here sooner."

Dell heard a weak, rattling cough, then tensed and held her breath.

"Mom?"

Anita's response was another low, scratching cough, her lips moving helplessly. She was awake, regarding her with an almost regal air from the hospital bed.

"Don't try to talk. You've had a breathing tube down your throat." She wiped her eyes on her sleeve and tried to brush her hair neatly behind her ears. "You were in a car accident. You've been here for two days."

Her mother groaned softly in answer, her lips moving again. Dell took a paper cup from a dispenser on the wall and filled it with tap water. Anita took the tiniest of sips, pursing her mouth as though accepting any form of help tasted bad. Dell felt her eyes water again and fanned at her face.

Suddenly, in the screen of one of the monitors, Dell saw her reflection. It was a slim, dark-haired woman, waving a pale hand at the tears she didn't want to cry. Dell remembered herself at fourteen, with her hair freshly hacked off, studying her mother as she fanned her pretty face, consumed with her own sadness, and heard an echo of her younger self, tough-mouthed and angry, whispering, *It's not about you, Mom.*

Anita bent over in a yawn that turned into a grimacing sigh. Tethered to the monitors by an IV, her right hand raised to her head. Dell saw the pride in her expression collapse, the fear in her eyes as her fingers traced the bandage and the baldness of her scalp on its borders. Anita looked up at her daughter with tears in her eyes.

"I tried to stop them." Dell sat lightly on the edge of the hospital bed and smiled at her mother. "The doctor needed to be able to see your scalp so he knew where to cut. They told me the operation saved your life. You hit your head pretty good."

"My hair." Again, she traced her scalp, sniffling. This shock seemed to have hastened the return of her vocal function; though her words came out hoarse, there was no keeping them in.

Dell wondered if there were some deficit in her, something missing or broken, that made her unable to comfort Anita more warmly. But she offered her the best thing she could, which was to tell her the truth.

"Well, I'm sorry about your hair, but I'm glad that you're alive," she said. "I'll, uh. I'll help you brush your hair when I come back tomorrow. And your friend Judy, she brought you a change of clothes. Seems like a nice lady." There are two kinds of women. Dell wanted to be the kind that helped others.

Bonnie knocked and leaned her head in the door. "Miss Anita! We didn't expect you to be awake yet. Let me go get my things. We need to check how you're doing."

Dell stopped her. "Please, if we could just have ten minutes. It's important."

She turned back to her mother, who opened her lips and rasped. Dell held her hand out to quiet her. "Don't try to talk, Anita, please. Just—I don't know. Blink once for yes, twice for no. Do you remember when you came to visit me?"

Anita blinked once.

"And what we talked about?"

Again, Anita blinked once, slow and deliberate. Yes.

"Mom, do you know where she is?"

One blink. Anita opened her mouth to speak, coughing until her body shook.

"You do? And you couldn't have told me two days ago?" Dell leaned in close over her mother, her voice rising of its own accord. She stifled an impulse to grab Anita by the wrist, demand that she stop coughing and talk. Biting down on her lip, she let a couple of breaths in and out until she felt calmer. "Why am I still surprised?" she murmured.

Anita attempted again to speak, issuing only a half-formed, unintelligible syllable. Dell picked up a ballpoint pen from the tray by the bed, looked in vain for anything to write on.

"Here." Dell handed Anita the pen, then held out her palm. As Anita gripped her hand, touching the pen to her skin, she turned away wincing as if she were about to get a shot. Dell squeezed her eyes shut against her fear. She was grateful she'd come in alone. When she felt her mother push her hand away, she opened her eyes, stretched out her fingertips, and looked.

Across her palm was written one word: Myra.

"Myra?"

One blink.

"At Dad's old house?" Her voice began to tremble. "Are you sure? I can't go there. Tell me anywhere else."

Anita didn't need to blink. Eyes narrowed, she lifted one shoulder in a shrug. She didn't care what Dell did or didn't do.

"You could have saved me a lot of trouble, you know," Dell said. "I had to come back here, talk to people I never wanted to see again."

Anita's stare needed no translation. It was the long-suffering rolled eyes, the scorn she turned on anyone who insisted her behavior had a consequence. The way Anita liked to say *Dell has never downplayed her aches and pains.*

"I know you feel that way," Dell said. "I've always known you felt that way."

Anita gave her a satisfied, knowing gaze, one that would normally have infuriated her, but which Dell found comforting now in its familiarity. Anita cleared her throat with a grating wince. "You were a difficult child."

Dell pushed the chair back with a screech and stood up to leave. "I grew up difficult, too, Anita. You know, if you wanted to help, you could have just walked in and told me where she was, instead of..." Something wasn't right. Startled, she paused, repeating her words aloud: "If you wanted to help..." Shock bubbled in her throat, a blossom of bewildered laughter. "You were helping me," she said. "In your screwed-up, backward way, you came up to find me because you knew I wanted to find her."

She pressed the call bell. Bonnie returned with a tray full of instruments and charts. "Your ten minutes isn't up, honey. Everything okay?"

Dell imagined pleading for ten minutes more, imagined loving someone so much that you could beg just to hear their voice for a few brief moments. It was not Anita that she pictured then. "Everything's okay," she answered, taking her bag and walking to the doorway. "I've got somewhere to be."

Anita called after her. "When are you coming back?"

"Don't worry, Mother," Dell responded, her smile pleasant and unyielding. "I'll see you around."

The hallway was half-lit. It was not yet eight o'clock. Dell could barely form a thought, save that she needed to get to the cabin. It could not be more than a mile to the bar where her station wagon was parked. She tried not to imagine returning to the cabin, those four familiar walls and all the versions of herself she preferred to forget. Dell bumped into someone as she walked down the hallway and apologized without looking up.

"Whoa. What's the rush?"

Dell looked up to see her brother. "Oh—Scott!" She gave him a quick hug, breathing in the familiar, comforting smell of smoke and coffee. "Um. Good morning. Anita's awake."

Scott looked tired, older than his years. He was dressed neatly in a buttoned shirt and jeans, but his eyes were bleary, the shadow on his cheeks darker than usual.

"So, where are you off to?" Scott asked. "Haven't you been waiting these last two days to speak to her?"

"I already did." Dell shifted her bag from the crook of her arm to her hand, the strap biting into her shoulder. "You don't mind if I just squeeze past you here, I—"

But Scott lingered in her way. "I was worried about you last night. Figured you'd need to sleep somewhere."

Dell could tell Scott knew something, but she didn't want to guess what. "I stayed at my apartment."

Scott shook his head, scratching his chin. "Try again."

"What?"

"Let me catch you up on a couple things. After I finished my shift last night, I came by here hoping to check up on Mom, and you. When you weren't here, I thought you were probably already in the guest room. So I'm driving home, and I see your car outside Bessie's."

"Oh, I…"

He interrupted her again. "Just hold on, Dell. So, back at Bessie's, it's midnight, and they're closing, and your car's been there for eight hours, so they're calling a tow truck."

"They didn't!" Dell swore. "Scott, you didn't let them, did you?"

"Dell, I tried to convince them otherwise. I figured you'd either been kidnapped, or gone home with some stranger, and I figured kidnapping was the more likely of the two, but here you are," he said, "so what do I know?"

His jabs reminded her that she was good at not caring, at absorbing disdain. She waited for him to finish.

"So, finally," Scott said, "it's half past midnight. I go home. Been at work since 6 a.m. And picture this." He held one hand up as if painting a picture in the air. "Abby's moving out. She's got all those damn paintings out on the porch, says she's taking her things and she's leaving."

"Oh no, Scott."

"You're involved." Dell guessed that Scott was using the same tone he did at work to let someone know they had really messed up. His mouth made a mean half-frown and he pointed one finger at her chest. "I don't know how, but I know you've got something to do with it. You were talking about those paintings yesterday."

Once he had made up his mind, it was useless to try to talk Scott out of being angry. He tilted his chin and rubbed the sleep from his eyes.

"Scott, listen," she said quickly, "if you can trust me, I promise I'll tell you everything."

"If I can trust you? Rest assured," Scott said, "as Mom says, this is classic Dell."

"Well, at least I'm nothing like my mother."

"That's right," he said, with a sad smile. "You're nothing like our mother. You're on the outside of everything. Nobody can help being fascinated by you."

"People gossip," Dell said. "It's not a compliment."

"People offer you their help and their lives and you take what you want and then walk away."

Dell felt her cheeks grow hot and stood still to listen to him.

"And any time you drop in, you leave total chaos in your wake. But by all means," Scott continued, "you're nothing like our mother. When you get wherever you're going, you won't have anyone by your side. Not even me."

"Maybe that's what I want." Dell would have said anything to get him to drop the subject, but regretted this almost right away.

"Yeah? Well, I don't think it is. Please." Scott's voice lowered, softened. "Dell, surprise me. For once. Stay here with me and Mom. Haven't I always said she loves you? In her own way?"

Dell glared up at him. After all this time, it should have been obvious. "Whatever she wants to call it, it wasn't good enough."

"If that does you any good, then so be it." Scott yawned and leaned against the doorway. "All I know is, she's not going to change. You always said you were too little to remember when she and Dad were happy."

"I think I was."

"Do you remember when Dad started to really lose touch? Missing work and everything? I was nine, so you were little. Anita spent weeks going through phone books from nearby towns. Trying to call anyone she knew, anybody we could go and stay with instead."

A picture flashed across Dell's mind, Anita hunched over the kitchen table, her manicured fingernails chipped. She flipped through the white pages with one hand, cradled the rotary phone between her ear and shoulder, dialing numbers with the other hand. "She would have been…"

"Your age," Scott answered. "Funny to think about that, isn't it?" He waited for her answer with a look that suggested he didn't find it funny one bit. Dell wondered if Anita had ever felt, as she had, this desperate, empty-handed need for a solution. If she had ever leaned over the steering wheel and asked herself *how am I going to fix this?* If there was a time she really had tried her best to fix things. Dell's mind began to cloud with images, with memories that might not have been what they seemed. But maybe Anita never had the chance that she had now. There wasn't time for this: no time to stand in place, let the mosquitoes bite.

"I can't stay," she said, her feet nervously shuffling, ready to walk. "I have to go now. This is important."

"What is more important than your family?"

Mason and the baby were always going to be her family. No matter where she ended up, no matter how alone.

"Nothing, Scott." She squeezed his hand and finally pushed around him. "You'll see."

As she hurried to the door, she re-examined the last two days, as if thumbing through pictures, wondering what kind of trail she had left.

CHAPTER THIRTY-SIX

Now

July 1991

Dell moved quickly to the sliding glass doors and outside. It was still morning, and it was already too warm for comfort. She tried to imagine who could help her, what she might do. Myra's house was too far to walk, though she would get there by evening. Dell began to walk to the edge of the parking lot. If she had to hitchhike, which she was not above doing, she preferred not to waste any time.

She saw Abby's blue sedan, saw her walking toward the hospital, dressed for work, and felt her focus waver as she remembered.

"Hey, Abby," she waved.

"Hey." Abby slowed cautiously and approached her, carrying a Styrofoam coffee cup.

"What—what happened? You're leaving Scott? Why?"

"Oh, Lord. Is he in there? I can't go in. I'll call out sick or something." Abby walked back to her car and Dell followed her as if she were lost. She saw that the back seat was full of paintings, clothes.

"Is it because of me?" Dell clasped her hands together, felt sadness rushing in her chest. "I didn't mean to—when we talked yesterday…"

"No. I figured you'd be upset." Abby took a cigarette from the pack in her purse and lit it, exhaled. "Excuse me for chain-smoking today. I'm not having the best morning."

"Oh, I didn't want you two to break up." She shook her head miserably.

"But you were right when you said those things. I never felt like it was my home. Any time I even hinted at us getting married, or even—I didn't even care that much if we got married or not, but I want to be a mom. He'd say *not now, Abby. I'm tired, Abby*," she continued. She kicked at a loose rock in the pavement with a quiet, girlish sigh. Her eyes narrowed and she waved at Dell with the cigarette. "And where the hell were you last night? Your brother's lost his mind worrying about you. He's always got time for his fragile little sister and all her feelings."

"Hey, watch it." Dell expected to feel angry, but found herself laughing. "I am not fragile."

"No," Abby agreed, beginning to smile. "But whenever you think you're gonna crumble, you just make some kind of scene, then run off to hide. You're not that hard to read." Abby held out her coffee cup. "You look tired. Have some?"

"Thanks." Dell sipped the coffee, looking in the car windows at the stacked canvases.

"So?" Abby eyed her, taking the coffee back. "Where were you? I wanna know."

Dell had an idea. She wondered how badly Abby wanted to know.

"I'll tell you," she said. "If you give me a ride somewhere."

"Deal." Abby threw down her cigarette and unlocked the car. "Get in. Sorry about the mess."

Dell sat down on top of a pile of scrunchies, laundry, an assortment of tossed-away accessories that smelled feminine and too sweet, like drugstore perfume. She buckled her seatbelt and sat up straight in her seat, watching Abby to study her reaction.

"Where are we going?"

"Remember where my dad used to live?"

"That's a hike. This had better be good." Abby was only halfway joking. She turned left out of the hospital.

Dell drew a quick breath and spoke, her hands open as if to show she wasn't hiding anything. "I was with Mason last night."

Abby laughed, and then abruptly stopped. "Scott's Mason?"

"Yeah. My Mason. No, no." He was not hers. She had promised.

"But you just met him!"

"Not really," Dell said. "We go way back."

"How long have you two…"

"It's not that simple. God knows, I wish it were." Dell took her hairbrush from her bag and nervously swept it through her hair. "I'm sorry. You don't need to hear me ramble."

Abby laughed her pretty, sparkly laugh. She took another Marlboro from an open pack that rested by the gearshift and lit it, rolling the window down a hand's width. "To be honest, you're a welcome distraction."

"I won't bore you with the details," Dell said. "I messed it up. It's over."

The evenly spaced buildings that lined the outskirts of Blyth grew sparse as the road twisted uphill and out of town. In the shade of the trees, the morning was cooler, almost pleasant.

"Scott just wasn't sure," Abby said. "I don't want to wait on someone who isn't sure about me." She took a long drag on her cigarette. Dell cracked her window to let more of the smoke out. They passed a produce stand by the side of the road that sat at the edge of an overlook.

"You'll turn right in about a half mile, here."

"I remember." Abby braked hard and took the abrupt right turn. The gravelly road bent sharply back from the highway, downhill for a quarter mile before it wound its way back up. "No insights from the psychic realm for me today?"

"None. Nothing." Dell frowned at herself in the rearview mirror. "If there's a shadow of a doubt, you're wasting their time. That's usually my move."

"Oh, yeah?" Abby's expression of curiosity, which Dell had so often read as catty, fishing for gossip, suddenly looked kind and interested instead.

"Yeah," Dell said. "Equivocating. It's what Libras do. Like Geminis are nosy."

"Ugh." Abby exhaled smoke, wrinkling her nose. "Know-it-all."

"How did you know you were so sure, with Scott? How do you know if you love someone enough?"

"It's simple." Abby flicked her cigarette out the window, rolled it back up. "Love isn't how much. It's yes or no. If you're wondering how much, it's no. With Scott, I never wondered, ever." Her expression grew distant. "You remember when I moved in with him? How long ago was that?"

"It must have been about three years."

"He asked me to move in because I was pregnant," Abby said. "It was an accident, but we decided to make the best of it." She picked up a smudged, oversized pair of dark sunglasses from the center console, set them over her eyes without looking away from the road. "I lost it, three months in. He didn't want to try again. Said, maybe we should take it as a sign."

"Oh no, Scott!" Dell groaned.

"In every way you could think of, he wanted to pretend it hadn't happened. But I guess he was too decent to ask me to move back out." She laughed, bitter.

Dell threw herself across the seat, wrapped her arms around Abby as she drove. "I'm so sorry," she said. "Of course—you should leave. Find someone who won't play around with your time," she said, leaning away, patting Abby's shoulder. "Scott grew up too fast. He's got a real problem with anything he can't control."

"You think I don't know that?" Abby let out a long sigh. "I know Scott. You know why he's such a square? It's because he cares too much. He got a call at work once from a little boy whose dog had got hit by a car. The poor kid was at home by himself."

Dell could imagine Scott's reaction: no-nonsense. Probably pulled the dog out of the road and kept driving.

"He was out there for hours," Abby went on. "Came home in tears. Dell, I know who he is. But maybe he just can't be that for me."

"Abby, you'd make such a sweet mother."

"Oh, shut up." Abby smiled. "You're ruining my makeup. Anyway, answering your question, Dell. If you love someone enough, you won't be wondering."

Dell wondered if the depth of her doubt reflected the gravity of how much she cared for Mason, how far she knew she could fall. She yawned and pressed her hands over her eyes. "Everything is such a mess."

"You and Mason? Try me."

"When I left last year, I had just found out I was pregnant."

Abby's eyes trailed over her body and she raised her eyebrows. "Oh, no. What happened?"

"Watch the road," she hissed, clutching the armrest as the car swerved and gravel rattled around the tires. "I had a baby, and I gave her up for adoption, and just a couple days ago I heard from someone that she was missing. And I think—I mean, I hope…"

"For whatever reason, you think she's at your dad's old place. Your aunt lives there now, right?"

Dell nodded her head. "I'm hoping that's where she is."

"She," Abby echoed, wistful. Then she grinned. "You and Mason had a baby girl."

"I had her by myself, really. I was alone." She eyed Abby, something like regret on her face. "I was never meant to have a baby. Maybe Scott and I have that in common. If I can just see her and know she has a home, I'll pack up, you know, get on my way again." She shrugged her shoulder to indicate her bag. "I never unpacked."

Abby slowed the car as the road neared Myra's cabin. "You're really going to leave?"

"I don't think I've left myself any other choice."

"With Mason? What happened?"

"This morning, he asked me—yes or no. Couldn't wait." Dell laughed, angry with herself, her hands patting her knees rapidly, impatient. "I have to know that I can sort this out. Just me, without any help. That has to happen before I can love anyone else."

"So it was a yes," Abby said. "Loving someone enough doesn't mean you give up your own needs."

"Maybe you're right."

"But he needed you to let him in, Dell." Abby managed a smile, but she looked defeated. "Man, you and your brother both. You know something? All the love in the world isn't gonna do the work for you."

"Well. Stuff like this, you only get one shot."

Abby lit another cigarette and laughed softly. "Except for you. You had two shots, and you missed them both."

CHAPTER THIRTY-SEVEN

Now

July 1991

Finally, Abby's little car slowed at the foot of Myra's familiar driveway.

"I'll get out here."

"I think you should tell him," Abby said. "Just tell him what you told me."

"Uh-uh. No." Dell unbuckled her seatbelt. "When I left, he made me promise I wasn't coming back."

"If he didn't care about you, he wouldn't be trying to protect himself." Abby rolled her eyes, pretended to clutch at her heart. "Didn't you learn about boys in high school?"

"No, I didn't." She slung her bag over her shoulder, prepared to get out. "What I need to do is see that my baby's safe and get back to where I belong. Wherever that is." She leaned in and gave Abby a quick, warm hug. "Thanks for the ride."

"Thanks for talking."

Dell studied Abby's pert features, pretty and sharp, with a sudden affection. "Look, if you ever need to talk, you know where to find me."

She stood up and shut the car door behind her, waving as Abby drove away. Her smile faded as she turned to look up the well-worn gravel drive that led to the house. The sprawling cabin rose over the familiar swell of the land, framed by juniper trees. She felt the fear in her chest, cold as ever, her body a haunted house of spirits and failed starts. But it wasn't the same as she remembered. This old house was the site of so many memories she'd never wanted—a childhood better forgotten, her father's death, the loneliness that had overwhelmed her when she had the baby. These things did not frighten her; they had already passed. What frightened her was back in Anita's hospital room, buried within her chest, the self-preservation impulse of women who grew bark over their fear, turned into trees, to whom vulnerability was anathema. That future frightened her more than anything else.

Walking uphill, Dell began to count reflexively, something to keep her feet on the ground. *Gravel, echinacea blossoms, the herb garden by the front porch.* But she passed three and continued. Here was where she had paced a circle around the house to walk through the contractions, her bare feet on the ground, her breath leaving a trail in the air behind her. The door that had hung open the day she found her father here. And there, under her feet, the walkway to the front porch steps. Here was where she had retreated to her station wagon and left, promising herself and her tiny baby that she would never come back. *Here is where I left you.*

And right in front of her, as the familiar steps creaked under her feet and she stood on the porch, right in front of her was Aunt Myra, a mountain of a woman in a faded dress, parked in her favorite rocker, her coffee cup half-full of whiskey at her side. There was no child in sight. There was no sound of a child. Dell's heart raced in her chest.

"Sit down, Dell." Myra waved kindly at the empty rocker to her left. "How you been?"

"Where is everybody? It's—" She sat uneasily on the edge of the seat. "It's so quiet."

"Let's talk a minute." Myra sipped from her coffee cup and wiped her mouth with her wrist.

"Oh, Myra, I want to talk." Her hands clasped and wrung together. "But I didn't come here just to talk."

"And why's that?" Myra's omniscient laugh was almost more than Dell could bear to hear. She knew exactly why she was there. "You left in a hurry, seems like you're still in a hurry. Made up your mind to run off again?"

Dell opened her mouth to speak, starting and abandoning several half-formed thoughts: apologies, excuses, explanations, retorts. In the expectant silence, she heard an infant's wail from inside the house.

She rose to her feet. Myra, gazing out over the yard into the forest, tilted her head and smiled. "I'll never tire of that noise. I'm a mean old woman, but I love a baby. It sounds like nap time's over. Go on in," she said, her hand making a sweeping gesture as if pushing Dell into the current that already pulled her toward the door.

"Myra, is she really here?"

"I knew you'd be back," Myra rasped. "You think I was ever gonna give her away to that adoption lady?"

Dell walked in through the kitchen, the curtains ruffling in the warm breeze. Following the sound of the cry, she walked up the stairs, one trembling hand on the wall to steady herself, and followed it further, right into her own childhood bedroom, which appeared to have been turned into a nursery, with pillows and toys lining the floor, a crib in each corner of the room.

Rosie stood with her back to the door, leaning over the crib. She was round-limbed and fair, with her thick hair in a long braid. She turned with surprise when she heard Dell's footsteps, then broke into a grin, cradling the squeaking bundle over her shoulder.

"Dell, it's you!"

"It's me."

"For all the fuss people like to make about crying babies," Rosie said, "isn't it a sweet sound?" She drew close to Dell, close enough to kiss her cheek, close enough Dell could smell the faint, powdery fragrance of baby hair from the child she cradled. She saw wisps of blonde curls and a round, soft cheek, a small hand that curled around Rosie's collar. As Dell studied the tiny face, she saw Rosie's daughter Hope, now more toddler than baby, stand up in the other crib.

"Here," Rosie said, leaning toward her. "Take her."

Suddenly, the baby was in her arms. She was sweaty and warm from sleep, dressed in a cotton onesie with a strawberry print. Softly crying, the baby girl's hand closed around Dell's finger, clinging to her body with the innate trust in being held that is solely the gift of babies. She began to quiet as Dell rocked her, whispered wordlessly in her ear.

"It's you," she thought, then realized she was speaking out loud. With round, rosy cheeks that quivered with emotion, with her father's blue eyes and golden hair, and little creases of chubbiness where her hands met her wrists. "It's really you."

"She's a sweet baby. Easygoing, gentle," Rosie murmured as she let Hope down to the floor.

"She didn't get that from me," Dell answered without taking her eyes from the child.

"And I can see looking at her that whoever her daddy is, he must be very nice-looking himself."

As the baby studied her, Dell remembered that, to the child, she was a stranger, patting her back and swaying gently. Already, a swarm of worries hovered in her mind. But the baby was a more certain fact, her sweet, healthy features a greater relief, than any worry was able to compete against.

"Let's have a seat outside," Rosie said. "Before it gets too warm. I know my mom's pleased to see you."

She followed Rosie to the porch, where she resumed her seat in the rocker next to Myra, while Rosie sat in the porch swing. Half-awake, the blonde-headed baby settled on Dell's lap.

"Thank you," she said to Myra, rocking softly in her chair.

"We were waiting for you," Myra answered. "I knew you'd come back."

"But I…"

These last three days, Dell had promised and promised herself that she would leave as soon as she had seen the baby alive and safe and well. That that knowledge would make her quiet little life whole again, that it would make it all worth it. She felt the soft weight of the child on her lap, against her chest, and suddenly remembered Abby telling her, *Love isn't how much, it's yes or no.* Her love for the baby was less an invitation than a compulsion, and she was reduced to a terrified, wholehearted acceptance.

The baby turned in her arms, and the little creaking and hiccupping noises a baby makes as they protest the wake from sleep pulled her back to the first time she'd held her against her bare chest. *What did you bring me here for?*

And, suddenly, Dell remembered. *Because I love you, from your tiny heart right down to your fingertips. That's where you came from, why you're here with me.* She felt tears slipping down her cheeks, dropping over the baby's forehead. Love like a wild animal, a tender wolf howling in the evening air.

When Myra had laid the child on her chest, she was numb with relief: that the baby breathed, that her pain had eased, that the spinning of the world had slowed for a moment. That gladness had been overshadowed by the fear that followed. *What the hell next?* Now, the newborn's eyes looked up at her with their soft, hungry stare that said, *Why have you brought me here, and what are you going to do about it?* Nothing had changed. Wasn't she still the same, all in scattered pieces of a woman, paralyzed by her doubts, sitting at the bottom of whatever abyss it was that separated her past from her future?

"Dell, you're crying."

She looked down at the tears slipping over the baby's arm and saw that it was true. She smiled helplessly at Myra and Rosie. "I'm scared. I can't possibly leave her."

"That's perfectly ordinary," Rosie answered.

"I don't want to take her away from everyone she knows." Dell saw how the child looked at Rosie for comfort. "I'm not gonna do this wrong. She's been here her whole life."

"Spend time with her here," Myra said. "With us. She'll come to know you. Then, one day soon, when she goes to live with you, she'll take it easier than you expect."

The child shifted on her lap, began to toy with the eyelet lace at the hems of her sleeves. The late morning light warmed the air, diffused through the plants that lined the porch, casting hazy yellow over everything she could see beyond their shaded seats. Deep in reverie, alone with her baby, Dell thought she heard her father's voice saying, *Okay, Strawberry.* Again, she repeated, *May God rest your soul,* although she felt clumsy and inadequate to even try to think of something that was infinite, to speak its name.

"Do I even have what you need to take care of a baby?" Dell asked.

Myra spit tobacco juice into her cup and laughed kindly. "It doesn't take stuff to care for a baby," she said. "Just lots of time. Don't listen to anyone telling you you need special furniture or special this or that. Keep her warm and clean and fed. Loved."

"Come on, Mom, you're such a purist," Rosie scoffed. "Dell, you should get yourself a swing. They're lifesavers. And you'll obviously need a car seat. And you won't be alone. We're here."

"Yes," Dell agreed. That had been true for some time now. "I'll sort it all out. Somehow, I will."

It occurred to Dell that she had not once, in the last three days, asked for help and been turned away. That had to be worth something.

"You need anything, you know we'll be here," Myra agreed.

For a town like a sleeping dog, blind in one eye, populated with more than its fair share of gossips, Dell thought Blyth had treated her better than she deserved.

"Myra, there is one thing. I need to talk to my brother. You remember Scott?"

"I haven't seen little Scott in ages," Myra said.

"Big Scott now," Dell answered. "He always had to duck to walk in the doorframe here. I guess you saw him at Dad's funeral, but not for long."

"After that, too," Rosie said. "He came here once hoping we'd heard from you. Last summer, right after you left town."

Dell walked into the kitchen, the baby on her hip, and dialed. As she stood in Myra's kitchen, listening to the phone ring, she reflected that the old house was now no longer her father's home. Though it bore the same shape, it smelled like Myra, and her tools and herbs filled every surface. Finally, he answered.

"Hello?"

"Hey, Scott, it's me." In the pause after he answered, she held her breath.

"What do you want?"

"I was thinking we're overdue for a catch-up. I'm at Aunt Myra's."

"Okay." He drawled the word, confused. "Are you alright?"

"Yes." She leaned close to the baby's blonde head and breathed in her fragrance. "I've got someone I want you to meet."

Dell held the child and walked up and down the porch, letting her reach out to touch leaves, railings, a twinkling spider's web, with perfect curiosity. Myra and Rosie talked in low voices, their laughs and murmurs blending in with the sounds of the forest at the edge of the yard.

She barely noticed the sound of Scott's truck approaching until she heard his feet on the steps.

Scott had cleaned up since Dell had seen him that morning. Clean-shaven and freshly showered, Dell thought that he still looked tired, but perhaps it was just that he was a year older.

"Aunt Myra, hello." Scott shook her hand, stood straight up, polite and direct.

Rosie approached and shook his hand, holding her toddler in one arm. "Scott, I'm Rosie. You probably don't remember me, right?"

"I remember when you were little, and all the cousins getting together," he said. "These your babies? They sure are cute."

Rosie only smiled, and again, Dell was reminded of a pretty, complacent house cat.

"Come on, Mom." Rosie took Myra's arm. "Let's take Hope and go play in the garden." She picked up little Hope on one hip, in one practiced arm, and helped Myra up. They quietly filed down the porch steps, out of view in the yard beyond.

"Can you sit?" Dell nodded at Myra's empty rocker.

"I'm fine." Scott crossed his arms, leaned against the porch rail. He stared past them, eyes fixed on the wall behind her.

"How's Mom?"

"Mom?" His eyes flickered to meet hers, back away into the distance. "Okay. The nurse is pleased—her memory seems okay."

In the uncomfortable silence, Scott cleared his throat. He looked at Dell, still holding the little one, and she could see the worry on his face, the hardened set of his mouth. "You wanna tell me why I'm here, Dell?"

"Scott, this is my child." Dell stood up, drew closer to him so that he could see the baby's face. The infant looked up at Scott with a combination of suspicion and curiosity. Dell cradled her shoulders, caressed the soft curls at the back of her head. "This is Juniper."

CHAPTER THIRTY-EIGHT

Now

July 1991

It felt like another year passing as she stood there, waiting for Scott to speak. He tilted his head, gave the baby a bemused smile, glanced nervously at Dell, hesitated again. Maybe he'd yell, she thought. They wouldn't be here if she hadn't disregarded his overprotective advice once or twice. Maybe he'd at least scold her, ask her why she couldn't have told him. Most of all, she feared he'd turn around and walk away.

"Come on, Scott," she whispered. "Please, don't be disappointed. I need you to say something."

But he didn't. She saw him pinch the corners of his eyes, tilt his head back. Then, finally, he stepped closer and wrapped them both in a gentle hug.

"I had no idea," he said. He sat heavily in the rocking chair, jumped up again, pulled the chair close to her. "Take a seat, Dell."

"I'm okay," she laughed. "I had her five months ago, not yesterday."

"She's—beautiful." He caught the baby's eye, smiled and raised an eyebrow at her, winning a shy, one-toothed smile from the baby. "I knew something was different about you."

"I wanted to tell you," Dell said. "I'm sorry for disappearing. For these last few days, too."

"I guess you did what you needed to do." Scott waved her concerns off. "You're an adult. I'm the one who can't always see that." He sighed, looked up at her dolefully. "I'm proud of you, Dell."

She did sit down then, felt her chin droop down. "For what? I've done just about everything wrong. I don't even know where to begin, here, except now I have her. That's something."

"You can tell me if you want to."

"I'm going to tell you." Dell let a few moments pass as she let the baby rest against her, the sweet-smelling head growing heavy, resting her fingertips against the spiderweb-soft curls. "That's why I called you."

"She's five months, you said. So—last March?"

"Near the end of February."

"This is why you left," he realized.

"I left her here with Myra and a social worker. Filled out some paperwork for a closed adoption. Scott—when Anita came to see me the other day, she told me she was missing." As Juniper nodded into sleep, Dell lifted her into her arms, cradling her head against her chest. Their voices lowered to near whispers. "And then, before I got to drag the details out of her…"

"The car accident."

"Yes." Dell's breath caught in her throat as she remembered.

Scott laughed. "Classic Mom embellishment."

"Well, I couldn't take that chance."

"Of course you couldn't." He looked at the baby. "So you were at Mom's bedside, inexplicably agitated, until you found out. You know what I'm going to say." He sighed heavily and rubbed his eyes.

"Go on," she said, grinning. "It's been almost two hours since I got an earful from my cop brother."

"Haven't I always helped you?" Scott asked. "I could have helped you find her. Why were you so keen to keep it secret?" He chuckled and rolled his eyes, slapping his knee as he spoke. "Ask for help when you need it."

Her eyes lowered. There were reasons she hadn't told him. The sun was high overhead, the sky the unbroken blue of midday without a cloud. Suddenly, when Dell meant to tell Scott everything, the hum of the summer air dropped to a perfect silence. She heard an echo of herself saying, *Fine. That what you want? I promise.*

"Who is he?" Scott's hand rested on her shoulder, his voice edged with anger. "Dell, if someone hurt you, I am going to walk into the woods and dig a grave for him right this minute. Whoever he is, he's about to need it."

"It's not like that," she said. Dell held Juniper's sleeping face to hers and touched her nose. She stroked the back of her neck, where the gossamer-soft curls sprang up and caught the light like dandelions. She looked so much like him.

"Does he know?"

"He knows." She looked at her brother cautiously.

"What worthless son of a bitch—"

"Scott, he is anything but." The edge in Dell's protest surprised her. "If anything, I'm the son of a bitch. He asked me to stay. He helped me look for her."

"So, what's the problem? Where is he?"

"That's the thing. I thought you would understand." Dell looked over her shoulder, studying the crooked apple tree, the junipers that edged the yard. She studied the sleeping child in her lap, wishing for Juniper to inherit all of Mason's goodness and none of her disquiet. Her breath caught up in her chest and felt tangled.

"Understand what?"

"He asked me, yes or no. And I guess I froze up. Just let it go by me." She looked to Scott, hoping to see some kind of understanding. "I love him. I don't know what's wrong with me."

"Well, listen," Scott said. "You listening?"

"Yes."

"You can do this, raise your baby. You'll have all the help you need. And about – are you really not going to tell me who he is?"

Juniper's ears were as soft and perfect as tiny pink seashells. Dell let the baby hold her fingers and pretended she hadn't heard her brother. Scott leaned over, smiling in amazement at her sleeping face.

"I realized something," he said, "when I saw Abby's stuff all across the porch."

"What's that?"

"That I'm gonna feel doubt every day of my life." He scratched his jaw, cast his eyes down. "I think when you grow up watching people make huge mistakes out of their whole lives, being overcautious is in your bones. But Dell, let me tell you this. That kind of fear will tell you lies."

Dell considered his words as she watched the baby resting in her arms, the little mouth suckling in sleep. Beyond the yard, she heard the passing sound of a car on the dirt road, footsteps and voices.

Scott leaned back in the chair, tilted his head back. "Abby and I could have been happy, if I weren't such a jackass. When you make choices out of fear, you're only going to get further from where you want to be."

"Right."

Scott looked at the baby again and she saw his expression change, pull away from her. "We almost. Once. Me and Abby—"

"Scott, she mentioned it." Dell reached over to squeeze his hand. "I'm sorry. I can promise you, you'll make a great dad."

"Does that help?" he asked, changing the subject. "Do as I say, not as I do, whatever?"

"It's over, with him," she said. "But I'll keep all that in mind for the future."

Dell thought she heard the sound of footsteps on the gravel. Everett, she thought, or Sadie, but the steps were too loud and heavy for a child – and besides, the children went everywhere at a sprint.

She heard Aunt Myra's gritty shout ring across the yard. "We're not interested, whatever it is."

And then she heard his voice.

"I'm not selling anything, ma'am."

"We don't need Jesus, sir," Rosie added, her voice a kinder echo of her mother's. "We've already got him."

"I'm looking for Adella. Is she here?"

"Might be," Myra answered. "Might not. I guess that depends on whether she wants to see you or not."

Scott looked at Dell, then glanced out toward Myra, then back at Dell, who, despite all circumstance, could not contain her smile at the sound of Mason's voice.

"I'm not here to bother anyone," he said. "If she doesn't want to see me, I'll go."

"I'm here." Dell raised her voice, found that she was already walking down the steps, crossing the yard to meet him. "Myra, Rosie?" she asked. "Give us a minute."

Her aunt and cousin walked back inside, Myra all knowing smiles, Rosie leading Hope by one hand as they walked back inside. Dell stood facing him, her white dress blotted with tear stains on either shoulder, the baby asleep in her arms. His eyes were the same shifting blue as the juniper berries on the trees at the edge of the clearing, the same blue as the eyes of baby in her arms, as the bedroom he had painted for them. She had no idea what to say, and no words came, so instead she stepped close and placed the baby in his arms.

"This is her," she said. "This is Juniper."

She saw his eyes widen, saw his whole person transformed, just as she had been, as his arms circled around the baby to cradle her against his shoulder. One of Mason's hands spanned the width of the baby's back. Her eyes fluttered open, narrowed as she studied him. A little fist closed on a lock of his hair, pulled tight.

"I don't know how to do this," he whispered, his breath catching in his throat.

Dell knew that look, that pulse of absolute terror as he realized he was somewhere new. She put her hands on his arms, squeezing the tense muscles, and looked up at him. "I know," she said. "It's okay. We can do it. If—" She let her hands drop, looked at him with a question in her eyes. Fair was fair. She had gotten two shots, and missed them both.

Then Scott was standing at her side. "Dell, you could have told me."

"Hey, Scott." Mason's eyes were calm, unwavering blue. "Go ahead."

"McCallan, I see you every month. You couldn't find a second to tell me that the reason my baby sister left town was because you weren't there for her?"

Dell took a firm step away from her brother, planted her feet on the ground next to Mason. "I told you, Scott, that isn't what happened."

"Yeah." Scott frowned, his eyes copper-dark and angry. "But I want to hear it from him."

"Listen, Shaw…"

"No, you listen. How many years have I known you?" Scott glanced with concern at the baby, kept his voice low. "Maybe I shouldn't be surprised. Maybe no one in your family's ever given a thought to the consequences of how they act." Juniper whimpered and Mason curled away from Scott with a protective gesture, bending close to Dell as he bounced the child softly.

"Stop that," Dell scolded. "He isn't like them."

"It's alright." As Mason spoke, he patted the baby's shoulders, turned her so she could see his face. "Scott, I'm sorry. No more surprises, I promise. It was her secret to keep."

"You're damn right it was." Scott nodded his chin, gruff, using his angry voice, but Dell saw that he was satisfied. He looked to his sister. "Do you need anything? Are you okay?"

"When you asked me what was more important than my family, what did I tell you?"

"Nothing," he remembered. "Okay. I'm glad you're back." He brushed his hands on his jeans, then gave Dell a hug. "I'm proud of you, Dell. And you? I'll wait and see." He smiled at Mason, halfway serious.

"Thanks."

"I'll leave you two alone. Thanks to you and Abby, I'm due for a drink. Hell, maybe you two can catch up and join me later."

She watched Scott's truck as he drove away, let the midday lull settle around them. Mason curled his shoulder in, shading Juniper's face from the sun. She stood back from herself, back a year before, saw where she had covered and hidden pieces of herself, left behind what didn't fit, or what was too fragile to carry forward. Saw how she had bargained too many times with what scared her.

"What do we do now?" Mason's eyes widened as the baby's little hand wrapped around his thumb.

"Mason—about this morning." She traced a circle in the dirt with her toe. "You think I could try to answer you again?"

"Okay." The baby fussed quietly; he leaned close, handed her gingerly back into Dell's arm.

"Because if I could, I would say yes. I had my reasons for leaving. But for whatever it's worth, I never stopped loving you for a minute. I don't think I ever will." As she spoke, she felt a weightlessness in her chest. There was nothing left to say, no fear for anything left unspoken.

"Oh, and if you do?" His eyes lit up as a knowing grin spread across his face.

Dell stepped in closer, her toes touching his, and stood up tall to kiss him, the baby cradled against her chest. "You know I can see these things. I'm always going to love you."

She felt his arms close around her and the child, let her forehead rest under his chin.

"But what do we do now?" he asked. "Can we keep her?"

"Yes," Dell said. "But we need to make it easy on her, as much as we can. Let her get to know us before—"

"Before she comes home with us for good."

"Yes, if…"

"Stop saying if." Mason placed both hands on her cheeks, kissed her again. "Come home with me, baby."

Home was the three of them, together. Some choices you can only make once. Certain other choices find a way back to you, find a way to let you choose again.

"Mason, your family."

"You're my family," he said. "And anyone who's anything less than good to you isn't. Trust me."

Dell's gaze flickered up and met his blue eyes. "Okay," she said. "I will. Hey, why don't we go inside so you can meet Myra?"

"Sure."

With his arm resting around her waist, they walked up the path to the cabin. Dell lifted one hand to shield the baby's face in the bright light. "I do have one question, though."

He followed her up the path that led to the cabin. "What is it?"

"How did you know to come here?"

Mason laughed. "I'll let you guess. I bet you don't even need a crystal ball for this one."

Dell closed her eyes and smiled. "I'm seeing a pretty little busybody, blonde hair, and she's driving a blue car." She opened her eyes and smiled again, because he was still real.

"Drove right to my front door and told me. 'Mason McCallan, I know something you don't know.'"

Dell laughed out loud. "Sweet Abby."

"She waved her cigarette in my face and said, 'Didn't you ever learn, all girls want is for you to listen?'" Mason pushed his hair off his forehead, touched her shoulder as she walked. "You asked me to wait. I should have listened."

"What'd you tell her?"

"I told her thank you, of course," he said.

As Mason took her arm, she saw old Ruth hovering several yards off on the other side of the fence. Dell pulled her hand free, lifted it high, waving. "Hello, Ruth," she called. "This is Mason. And this is our baby."

Ruth waved. "You're looking well," she yelled back.

Dell slipped her arm back into his, leaning over to kiss him as they walked. She stayed close, cradling Juniper, her shoulder brushing his. "My mother once told me," she murmured, "that if people are gonna talk about you anyway, you may as well stand up straight."

A LETTER FROM KELLY

Dear Reader,

Thank you for taking the time to read my book. If you'd like to stay informed of my future releases, please sign up for my email list below:

www.bookouture.com/kelly-heard

Your email address will never be shared and you can unsubscribe at any time.

Although this story is entirely fictional, it was born out of a very real recalibration of my understanding of myself upon becoming a mom. In a society that doesn't want us to own our own bodies, embracing women and ourselves as both whole people and mothers is an act of revolution, but it can also be daunting. As I wrote this story, even when it meant writing in the dark on my iPhone while nursing a cranky baby, my heart has grown close to the "women who help other women"—midwives, doulas, moms, and friends, in my own community and everywhere.

I loved writing this story and would be happy to talk with readers about it further, so do feel free to get in touch via my Twitter or website.

Kelly

kellyheard.wixsite.com/mysite

@heardkj1

BOOK CLUB QUESTIONS

1. What does the title *The Fortune Teller's Promise* mean to you?
2. The Blue Ridge Mountains are as prominent in the novel as many of the main characters. How far does the setting influence the characters?
3. There are several complex mother figures in the novel. Which of these characters did you relate to most, and why?
4. This story was set in the early nineties, how do you think the characters' lives might have been different if the story took place today?
5. How do you interpret Aunt Myra's statement to Dell that "there are two kinds of women: the ones that look out for each other and the ones that don't"?
6. Why do you think Anita discourages Dell from keeping the baby? In Dell's position, what choice would you have made?
7. How are Dell and Scott different, and how are they alike? What are the reasons behind their similarities and differences?
8. How did your feelings toward Anita change over the course of the novel? How would you explain her behavior?
9. Which traits do Dell and Mason possess that cause their breakup after her father's funeral? How do you think they have changed when they meet again a year later?
10. After the events of the story, do you think that Dell and Anita's relationship will change? If so, how?
11. How did the structure of the book, alternating between present and past, affect the story for you?

ACKNOWLEDGEMENTS

Massive thanks to my amazing editor, Leodora Darlington, for believing in my work. I also want to thank the entire team at Bookouture for all the ways they have supported me, particularly the wonderful Kim Nash.

I'm forever grateful to my beta readers, and give special thanks to Monica Poole, Laura DeNoyelles, and Bekky Cunningham.

Thanks to my family, Campbells and Heards, who always encourage me to write.

CPSIA information can be obtained
at www.ICGtesting.com
Printed in the USA
LVHW091738251019
635356LV00002B/367/P

9 781838 880064